SOMETHING WORTH DOING

Center Point
Large Print

Also by Jane Kirkpatrick and available from
Center Point Large Print:

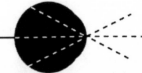

**This Large Print Book carries the
Seal of Approval of N.A.V.H.**

SOMETHING WORTH DOING

A Novel of an Early Suffragist

JANE KIRKPATRICK

CENTER POINT LARGE PRINT
THORNDIKE, MAINE

Dedicated to the ever hopeful,
especially Jerry

A storm was coming
But that's not what she felt.
It was adventure on the wind
And it shivered down her spine.

ATTICUS, THE POET

Character List

Abigail Jane (Jenny) Scott Duniway—daughter, wife, mother, farmer, teacher, milliner, novelist, owner/editor of *The New Northwest*, nationally known suffragist

Benjamin Duniway—husband of Abigail, horse trainer, farmer

ABIGAIL'S SIBLINGS
Mary Francis—Fanny
Margaret—Maggie
Harvey
Catherine—Kate
Harriet
John Henry—Little Toot, Jerry
Sarah Maria—Maria

Mary Gibson—Ben's sister

*Shirley Ellis—friend of Abigail, wife, mother, divorcee, suffragist

John Tucker Scott—Patriarch of the Scott family

Susan B. Anthony—friend of Abigail, president of National American Woman Suffrage Association (NAWSA)

CHILDREN OF ABIGAIL AND BEN DUNIWAY

Clara Belle
Willis
Hubert
Wilkie
Clyde
Ralph

*****Harold Bunter**—suitor and nemesis of Abigail
*****Eloi Vasquez**—second husband of Shirley Ellis, California attorney
Sarah Wallace—member of Stephens-Murphy-Townsend wagon train and president of California suffragist association

*fully imagined characters

Prologue

Her dreams of late had been of books with maps of unknown places. Jenny Scott wished she were dreaming now instead of sitting here beside the family wagon, a gushing stream to serenade them. They'd left Illinois two months previous—2 April 1852. She had written the date in the family journal she'd been assigned to keep as they crossed the continent. Since that first roll-out of wagons toward the west, Jenny traveled without maps. She needed them to help her reduce the fear and anxiety of the unknown; but she did not have them. Though only seventeen, she'd already learned that living required coming to terms with uncertainty—not that she did that well. She had lost another kind of map as well—the map of her mother.

A different kind of pain awaited this June afternoon.

"The agony will be worth it." Jenny spoke with conviction as she eyed the fat needle her new friend blackened in the flame. Then, "Won't it?"

"It does have a sting," Shirley Ellis said. "Fair warning."

Jenny lifted the dark curls to hold them behind

her ears. She thought of her hair as unruly with its thickness and natural twists that made morning brushing a chore. She envied her brothers who kept their hair short, curls under control.

Kate, Jenny's twelve-year-old sister, patted Jenny's shoulder while Shirley continued. "Shakespeare had this done and even biblical Jacob gave a pair to Rachel way back when. The pain has to come before the glory."

"Ha," Jenny said.

"I'm here to comfort you," Kate said, "but I don't understand why you want to hurt yourself for fashion."

Ignoring her sister, Jenny took a deep breath. She sat on a three-legged stool they used to milk the cow. The stool did double duty as a seat for medical ministrations. Jenny squeezed her eyes shut. "Go ahead. Do it."

Kate pinched her sister's earlobe as hard as she could, then said to Shirley, "Now."

The pain of the needle seared. Her sister's pinching simply wasn't enough to dull the agony. But at least Jenny felt misery for something physical instead of the heartache she'd carried since the deaths. *Did I know that physical pain could distract from emotional hurting?*

She felt the blood trickle down her neck as Shirley pulled the needle out. "It's a good thing I have a strong stomach," Jenny said. Kate dabbed at Jenny's bleeding earlobe. They'd have to soak the handkerchief to rid it of the red. "Are you certain that Jacob gave Rachel a pair of earrings? What chapter and verse?"

"I don't really remember," Shirley said. She had thick, naturally arched eyebrows that framed her blue eyes. "It's too late for second thoughts, though if you don't put the pin through, it'll grow new flesh right over the hole." Shirley dabbed at Jenny's ear with a clean handkerchief, then wiped the needle, and now rolled it in the flame again until blackened.

"Ready," Jenny said.

She straightened her back. Kate pinched the other ear and Jenny closed her eyes. The second piercing commenced. Her older sister Fanny, standing to the side, winced. It took a team.

"Finished. And you didn't even faint," Shirley said.

Kate dabbed at the blood on Jenny's cheek, then held out the tourmaline-studded gold rings. "I'll put them in for you."

Jenny felt the metal push into her ears, surprised again at the sting and pain.

"You'll have to twirl them a few times a day until they heal," Shirley warned. "You don't want the skin to attach itself to the rings." She eyed the earrings now adorning Jenny's ears. "They're really pretty with that one gold gem in the middle of the disc. A good size too. Won't draw too much attraction."

"Isn't attraction the point though?" Kate said.

"The point," Jenny corrected, "is not adornment but memorializing. Momma loved these. She got them from Grandma who received them from her mother, and she left them to me."

"I thought one of the stones like those we covered Momma's grave with was your memorial keepsake. You insisted to Papa that you had to put that rock in the wagon." Fanny dabbed Jenny's other ear with a bit of whiskey kept only for medicinal purposes.

"You can't have too many mementos, I say." Shirley wiped the needle with the liquor, then put it back into her fabric sewing kit attached to her bodice.

"It's more than a memento. Earrings and rocks and a cut of hair, they're all ephemera, items of the historical record that are neither documents nor maps," Jenny said. She touched her ear and winced.

"I'm sorry." Kate leaned in.

"What's a little smarting in memory of our momma who endured so much bringing us into the world, and then had to leave it so prematurely? She didn't want to leave Illinois, you know. I heard her tell Papa that they'd always lived on a frontier, and now civilization was catching up to them so couldn't they stay and enjoy it. Papa said no." Tears welled in her eyes while her stomach clenched with anger. It wasn't fair, it just wasn't.

14

"Will you take some item for . . . your friend too?" Fanny asked. Her voice was gentle. A boy Jenny had met on the trail had drowned not long after their mother's death.

"One earring for Momma and the other for him. And then no more." She took the mirror Shirley handed her, turned her head from side to side to admire the earrings. "No more sadness. I've had enough." She stood and with conviction declared, "I will control it."

Their brother Harvey sauntered by as Jenny made her declaration of sending grief away. Harvey, with his good looks and opinions, walked backward away from them then, saying, "You can't control anything, you females. Not a thing. Lucky for you us men protect you."

"Ha!" Jenny shouted after him as he turned his back to them, striding off as though he owned the land, the stream—his future. "No one knows what they can accomplish until they undertake it." Fanny, Shirley, and Kate nodded agreement.

And so Abigail Jane "Jenny" Scott set forth to do the best she could to prove her brother—and all men—wrong. Girls had power too. One day, she'd show them.

PART 1

The things nearby, not the things afar,
Not what we seem, but what we are,
These are the things that make or break,
That give the heart its joy or ache.
INSCRIPTION IN AUTOGRAPH BOOKLET

ONE

Making Her Own Map

April 1853
Willamette Valley, Oregon Territory

A spring rain pattered on the shake roof of the schoolhouse near the little settlement of Cincinnati, six miles south of Salem. To Jenny, it sounded like the clapping of children's gloved hands connecting in a steady, soothing rhythm. Jenny shook her thick curls of the mist she'd ridden through to get to the structure before her students arrived. Her first day of teaching had begun with fixing meals for boarders at her father's inn, then riding several miles warmed by the congratulations of her sisters. Despite less than a year of formal schooling back in Illinois, she'd passed the teacher's test and been hired. She'd board out with a district family who paid their child's fees by offering a bed and meals to the teacher during the week. She'd ride home on Friday to help again at the inn.

Her mother would be proud. It had been her mother's snippets of wisdom offered through the years while cornbread baked or she stitched a pantaloon that created Jenny's educational foundation. Either due to illness or her need to be home as the third oldest child, Jenny had been less than a year inside an Illinois schoolhouse. It was her parents' love of reading, the many books and newspapers available to peruse, and her mother's conveying facts and figures through stories that had prepared Jenny for this day. Some of the newspapers, like the *Lily* that promoted women's issues or Horace Greely's *New York Tribune* that railed against slavery, were considered unusual for their frontier family to acquire, but the Scott children had all been allowed to read them as soon as they were able.

For Jenny, education was critical for boys and girls to grow to make good choices and be wise citizens too. This schoolhouse was her arena to awaken minds to the possibilities of their lives even when others appeared to control their destiny. She controlled what would happen here, the minds she'd affect, yes, but personally, this job granted her a chance to draw her own independent map. It gave her a level of freedom she never saw her mother have. Anne Scott had birthed twelve children, lived to bury two, and once told Jenny she was sorry she had brought girls into the world, as their lot was harder than the boys and would always be. It had been a warning. As a respected teacher, Jennie would chart her own course. It was one of the few professions allowed a woman outside of the home. Operating a boardinghouse or a millinery made up the only other two. That *Lily* editor had risked more than her design of the bloomer costume by running a newspaper. Jenny was grateful her father let that broadsheet into their house, or perhaps he didn't realize a woman was at its head. But her mother did and she'd made sure Jenny knew it. Another snippet of sagacity perhaps.

A chill in the air moved Jenny to set the kindling to fire in the little stove. She was grateful that someone had not only chopped and stacked wood outside but had tented dry sticks over bits of pine needles and forest duff so the flame took without effort. Part of her teaching contract was that from now on, she would split the wood and stack it, start the fires, and remove the ashes as well as maintain the inside and the surrounding grounds outside, sweeping pine needles from the stairs and even the roof if necessary. Cobwebs drifted from the corners, and she grabbed the straw broom and swept them and the floors. As she worked, she remembered the interview with the board of education. She'd kept her tongue when one of the farmers asked her if she had a beau or was using this opportunity to find a husband—as though that were the only goal of a woman's life.

None of your business, she'd wanted to say but smiled instead. "With one woman for every one hundred men in this Territory, I doubt I'd need a schoolhouse full of other men's—and women's—children to attract a husband. No, I'm delighted to teach little minds and to have a few coins to call my own." She thought her mother would be proud of her for controlling her sometimes intemperate tongue. Truth was, she was torn about marriage. She liked the idea of falling in love, being swept away, but only wished to marry a man who saw value in a partner and not just be a "hand" in the drudgery of women's work that took so many women's lives at such a young age. Her parents had loved each other, she felt sure—but she'd wished her father had paid more attention to her mother's needs and waited a little longer before remarrying after her death. But he ruled the roost, as her mother often said. And because she'd let him, she accepted their journey west and it had taken her life.

Marriage could wait. Jenny had brushed off a few offers already, determined that they were more land-based than promising love. If an Oregon man married within a year of reaching the territory, his new wife could bring 160 acres into the marriage in her own name. Of course, as soon as she married, the control of it became her husband's. But it did expand the spouse's holdings. She made light of most of the proposals, encouraging them to seek a less willful mate. She didn't want to offend, but she certainly wasn't interested in expanding a man's wealth without at least a little love to go with it.

Dawn pushed its way into darkness, announcing she had time yet to scan the lessons she'd prepared using the one primer she'd snuck along on the journey west. Her father had restricted what the women could bring—including books and dishes—and never knew until they arrived that her sister's beau had bought their auctioned dishes—a set of Spode—and given them back to Fanny before they left. With tears, Fanny, her oldest sister, had sewed the butter plates, dishes, and cups into a feather bed so their father never knew that he slept on them. Jenny's book had survived, buried in the barrel of corn meal. A woman needed a little piece of home. At least their father hadn't broken the dishes when he discovered they'd defied his orders, as she'd heard some men had. He hadn't complained about the schoolbook, either.

Jenny rubbed her hands to warm them at the flame, reset the combs in her hair to control the curls. She counted the slates piled on the crude table that served as her desk. There were six, so if all the children attended, they'd have to share. With her first paycheck she'd buy two more. She'd have the students work on writing their names today so she could learn who they were and assess their skills. She planned to tell them stories and weave the lessons into them to hold their attention. It worked for her siblings. It had worked for her.

The sound of stomping boots on the pine stairs took her from the primer. *Must be an older student.* She straightened her back, ignoring the pain that lived in her spine.

She expected twelve students. At least that's what the board had told her she'd be responsible for, though she remembered one man's caveat. "Some days you might have more, if they bring a little brother or sister usually too young, but maybe their ma is sick and there's no one to look after them at home. Can you adapt?"

"I've six younger siblings—no, only five now." She swallowed. Willie had died in the Blue Mountains the year before. "Like any good western woman, I can corral them without a rope."

Today she'd see if that was true. If students arrived this early, she'd have to rise at 4:00 a.m. to stay ahead of them in their lessons.

"Welcome," she said as the door opened. Now she'd see what a day in her domain would hold and what kind of a creative map she could draw.

TWO

Courting or Confrontation

"Harold Bunter," the man said. He hadn't removed his hat. "I come to press my case to you, Missy."

Rigid as a fence post, he was a big man, well over six feet tall, with a ruddy face and a broken front tooth. He stood too close and she backed up. "Excuse me?"

"Time's a-wasting, Missy. I've got until December to find my bride, and I hear you're a hard worker helping at your father's inn. He don't serve spirits, only beer and wine, so I guess you're a teetotaler, which is good for me. And you must have common sense or the board wouldn't have hired ya. So I'll court ya proper-like, but we both know the end result. Glad to see you're punctual too, getting here long before the babes arrive. I think an August wedding would be fine, don't you?"

"Mr. Bunter, I am working here. I'm sure you understand the need for my full attention to be given to preparing for my students. Your offer is generous, of course, but I can't entertain it today and likely not tomorrow or the next day either."

"I'll give you time. Until August, like I said."

"I'm barely of age, Mr. Bunter." *Holy cow chips. What was the man thinking?*

"You're almost nineteen. Many a girl at fourteen is marrying in these parts."

It bothered her that he knew her age. It was true that young girls were being handed over by their parents to willing men to help expand their farms and be extra hands. She prayed that some of those girls found love in the process. "You've done your homework, Mr. Bunter."

"I know how to woo a woman." When he grinned, that broken tooth gaped at her.

"Oh, I see another early bird may have arrived." She looked beyond him to the misty dawn. "If you'll excuse me, I must get to work and make my students welcome." She'd looked out through the open door and hadn't seen anyone but hoped she had distracted Mr. Bunter enough for him to at least stop talking about marriage.

"I'll come back after class and we can confer more," he said. "That's a good educated word, isn't it—'confer'? My farm's not too far away, so I can get here easy. I know all the board members. They can vouch for me. I'll let 'em know they'll need to be looking for a new schoolmarm, as they won't let a married woman work out, you know. A woman's place is in the house."

She turned back to him. "Mr. Bunter, I'm sure you're a very fine citizen and your farm is very fine too. But I'm new to the territory, I've just

26

begun my job, and I really can't think about marriage at this time. With you or anyone. So please don't speak for me to the board."

"Now, don't get too frazzled, Missy. I can wait. I got 'til December for my year to be up. Only April now."

"Mr. Bunter, you're not listening to me." *Am I being too rude? No, I must be firm.* "I am not interested in marriage—to anyone at this time. So please, spread your charms to another missy, as you'll be wasting your time with this one."

He took a step closer, inhaled deeply through his nose like he was trying to inhale her. She moved back. Her heart pounded like a butter churn. He was big and could hurt her if he chose to. She shouldn't give him any fuel for his fire by suggesting they would discuss it later. That would only lead him on. But she couldn't think of anything else to do. "Let's talk about it over the weekend," she said. "I'll do my homework too. And find out about you."

"Good for you, Missy. I'll come by your father's inn on Saturday. We can confer then. I'll be sure to tell the board about what a loyal teacher you are, not wanting to mix pleasure with work." He grinned, showing a mouth of tobacco-stained teeth, touched his hat brim, turned his back to her, and clomped down the steps.

She'd deal with him on Saturday. She couldn't think about it now. She took a deep breath, inhaling the new-lumber scent of the building and the desks.

Before she'd returned to her chair, more step noise, and a man's voice, singing. "Holy cow chips," she said out loud. She stood to confront Mr. Bunter once again.

But instead a small child appeared, holding the hand of a tall man with sky-blue eyes and curly hair that matched the child's, with just a hint of ginger to the brown. He'd been the singer. He removed his hat and nodded to her. "Ben Duniway, ma'am."

"And this is . . . ?"

"Josie. It's her first day."

"Welcome, Josie. I'm Miss Scott. How old are you, sweetie?"

"I'm six. We're having a sister or brother. Momma said she could tell me which it is when I got home. I guess she went to town to pick it up."

"That's lovely."

"Her mother would have brought her, but she's, uh, feeling poorly today."

"Yes, I can see how she might be." To the child, she said, "Would you like to put your lunch pail on the entry shelf?"

"Uncle Ben bringed me. He and Momma are sister and brother. Like I'm gonna be."

"Ah," Jenny said.

"I see you've already met Harold," Ben said. "Courting, is he?"

Jenny felt her face grow warm. "He might call it that. I wouldn't."

"Discouraging him could be a full-time occupation. He's made many a proposal, and I hear he's getting desperate to find a wife before his year is up." He let Josie's hand loose, and the child stood beside him, a thumb in her mouth, lunch pail in her other hand, her eyes moving back and forth between the adults. "I brought a slate for Josie. Figured you might be short."

"Thank you, Mr. Duniway."

He removed the chalkboard from his loose shirt.

"I appreciate that thoughtfulness. Josie, would you like to pick one of the front desks? You'll sit with another student, but since you're early, you get first choice. After you put your pail away."

"Yes, ma'am. Thank you, ma'am." She scampered to the entry.

"If you need a rescuer from Harold, let me know," Ben said. "He can be as cantankerous as a green broke horse. And for the record, not that you've asked, I've got my 320 acres and didn't need a woman's 160 acres to make it so. When I come courting, it'll be for the woman's heart and not her land."

"You're right, I didn't ask."

"But you don't mind knowing, now do you?" His grin slid across his attractive face, and she felt a glow inside.

I believe he's flirting. She'd keep this professional. "I'm an educator, Mr. Duniway, a seeker of information for its own sake," she said. "One never knows when one will need it to advance a cause or carve a path forward."

He grinned as he put his hat back on. "I'll be back at three to bring you home, Josie. You be good now and mind Miss Scott."

"I will." The child reached up to him, and he squatted down to let her wrap her arms around his neck. *Children like him.* And he bent to them, didn't stand above them. That was a good sign. "Bye, Unc," Josie said.

"Don't forget to sing when you leave to go outside," Ben told her as he stood and brushed the top of her head with his wide hands. Two honey-colored pigtails poked out on either side of her head.

"I won't," she said.

He turned back to Jenny. "Singing when they face the world is a good way to calm the stomach wiggles. There's lots of them when you're a child."

"And when you're a grown-up too," Jenny said.

"Indeed."

He replaced his hat and headed out, singing a song Jenny didn't recognize, about "seeing Nellie home." It was a happy tune, and Josie giggled as she skipped her way past Jenny and found a front desk. Jenny watched as the man patted her horse's neck and checked her grain bag. Jenny had her mount at the hitching post where other children's ponies would soon be tied. Her horse nickered to him. *Animals and children like him.* He turned and waved at her and she blushed. He had known she'd be watching, the scamp.

She witnessed horses and their child riders coming up the trail, dismounting and tying their animals to the post, filling grain bags, then walking up the stairs.

She was the queen of her domain here, and as she greeted each child, she felt a lifting of her spirit. She didn't know if her joy came from this being her first day as a teacher or if the meeting of Ben Duniway played a part. She couldn't be sure. She just hoped he wasn't a diversion on her map to independence.

THREE

The Hesitating Heart

Ben Duniway had returned to pick up his niece and continued to bring her back and forth the entire week.

"This is the longest child-birthing in history," Jenny had joked to him on Friday.

"I figured she told you she has a little brother. I'm still helping my sister out. And I'm hoping we might have a conversation longer than a blink one day. Perhaps while riding to the dance at Lafayette this Saturday night. Would you consider going with me?"

Her independent self was a bit annoyed that she was so easily swayed by those blue eyes looking right into her heart and the way he listened without interrupting when she spoke. The man asked questions and didn't give orders, though they had only short opportunities with her students her priority. "I'd be pleased. Of course, my sisters would need to come along."

"Understood. I wouldn't want to tarnish your fine reputation."

Thoughts of knowing she'd be seeing him twice a day distracted her studies, and she had to force herself to concentrate on reading and arithmetic rather than his warming smile. She wasn't ready for love. She had too much to prove about taking care of herself and being there for her sisters and youngest brother, Little Toot. Her brother Harvey seemed well able to care for himself. She wasn't sure she could trust Ben's courting kindness, either. People changed. Husbands became domineering once they'd won over their wives. Ben's presence gave her comfort now, but would he always? Her heart hesitated. Back to her lessons. When in doubt, work.

"Put the creamer on the table," Fanny told Jenny. "I'll get the biscuits. You'd think there was a wedding going on with all the people here today." She winced at her own words.

"Travelers," her father said. "Though a good wedding would be in order. Right, Fanny?" He held the door open so Jenny could use both hands to carry the heavy ironstone pitcher to the table.

"It's too heavy, Papa. Let's put it into two smaller jugs."

"Ah, you're right. Give it here, Jenny." He turned to the pantry to make the exchange, and Fanny mouthed "Thank you."

Jenny had wanted to rescue her sister from any wedding discussions. Fanny had been forced to leave the love of her life behind in Illinois. He'd proposed but had an ill mother he needed to care for, and then John Tucker Scott—the family patriarch—said his entire family was heading west, true love left behind. Fanny still reeled from the heartache she carried from their arrival last fall. Work at the inn had not taken the pain away. The tavern, as inns were often called, had been operated by an uncle looking to farm instead, so Tucker Scott had taken over the duties. It provided a good space for his children and his new wife and her two young ones. For Jenny and Fanny, his remarriage seemed hasty, not giving much grieving time to their mother and little brother who had died on the trail. And his new wife was already with child. That their father had also insisted that Fanny consider marrying a well-known man in the territory twenty years older than she was had added to the family strain. "I want you girls married and safe so there are no reputational issues. Unmarried women can be the heart of scorn without even trying. Safety is when you're under the roof of a husband."

Jenny wasn't so certain of that. She had argued that if she married, she wouldn't be able to teach and there'd be fewer coins to help meet the family's needs. They'd left Illinois with a cache of money, but it had been stolen on the trail, the culprit never found nor confessed to it. Jenny had decided she needed an untarnished reputation, and she'd do that by focusing on slates and schoolwork. When she thought of introducing Ben to the family, she found her stomach hurt the tiniest little bit. The feelings she had for him had deepened in such a short time and they'd never even been alone. She hadn't spoken to her father yet about the dance, but she'd told her sisters and they were ready to chaperone.

Ben's introduction would come later—if he even showed up. And how would she feel about that if he didn't? She set her mind on cooking, serving, splashing suds on plates, and scrubbing linens for the guests who had spent the night.

She'd just swirled her skirts through the dining room door to bring out a platter of ham and eggs when she saw Harold Bunter standing at a table. She made a quick turn back into the heat of the kitchen where she told Fanny, "You need to rescue *me* now. That farmer I told you about is out there."

"The handsome one?"

"No, that first-day one who proposed marriage so he could get his 160 acres. I forgot I told him I'd do my homework and we could talk on Saturday. I wanted him to go away."

"Well, let's see. I'll take the platter out and treat him like he's here to eat and nothing more."

"What'll you say when he asks to see me? Or worse, Papa?"

"I'll say . . . that you're not here. That you've . . . stepped out. Go." Fanny shooed her out the back. "Stand on the porch steps so I'm not lying."

River mist rose off the Willamette as Jenny

pulled her shawl around her and shivered on the back porch. Why had she told him to come here? How had she forgotten it? Ben, of course. She'd been distracted by his company. Still, this wasn't right, her hovering like a scared rabbit, forcing her sister to speak for her. She needed to let Mr. Bunter know she was not interested before he talked to her father and the two of them came up with some scheme to marry her off.

She took in a deep breath and walked back into the kitchen, then through the door into the dining area, where her heart sank. Her father was already talking to him.

"Jenny. Mr. Bunter here is asking for your hand in marriage." Her father said it loud enough for other guests to hear, and she felt her face grow hot and her palms get sticky wet. "Said you told him to come by today and speak to me."

"She's quite the missy."

A general murmur of approval came from the diners, with a couple of the men actually applauding.

She nodded to Mr. Bunter, then said, "Papa, may I speak with you? Alone?"

"Now, don't you go all shy," Bunter said. "We're going to be family, so you can say whatever you want in front of me."

"We're not family—yet," Jenny said. "Papa? Please."

Why she had to gain the approval of her father

to make such intimate decisions was a frustration. Men always seemed to have the upper hand in a woman's life. But it was the way it was and no changing it at the moment. "Please. If Momma was here, she'd want you to talk with me about this privately. You know she would."

Her father nodded. "We'll be back in a moment, Harold. You enjoy a meal now, on the house."

"Oh, well, that'd be good then." He took a seat and asked for the platter to be passed to him while Jenny turned on her heel and headed to the kitchen, her father behind her.

"Did you direct him to come by today and talk with me?"

"I told him to stop here, yes, to get him out the door. He came early to the school that first morning, didn't want to leave, and I said I'd do some asking around about him and we could discuss it on Saturday. But I totally forgot because, Papa, I have met someone else. A young man."

"You've been off on your own, have you?"

"No. No. He brought his niece to school, and we've barely had a conversation what with the children there. He's Ben Duniway. He's already got a farm and wouldn't qualify for my 160 acres because he's been here since 1850. He's from Illinois." She took a deep breath. "I'm not even sure about him, but I enjoy his company and he's coming by to take me and Mary Francis and Catherine to the dance. With your approval. I haven't had time to ask you. But I know I'm not interested in Mr. Bunter's proposal. He's only interested in the land I'd bring to him. He even sent me a letter of proposal. It's embarrassing, Papa. I did nothing to warrant his attention."

"I see."

"And I do have a little more information about him. Mr. Duniway said he'd made a number of proposals already and been turned down."

"If you don't want to accept his proposal, you have to let the man know. I won't do that for you."

She clasped his elbow in gratitude. "Oh, Father, thank you so much."

"You got everything settled then?" Harold had walked right into the kitchen. Fanny stood behind him, signaling that she'd been unable to stop him. "We can set the date then?"

Jenny swallowed. "I'm glad you've come." This way he wouldn't be humiliated by her refusal being witnessed by a room full of guests. "I must decline your proposal."

"What? You leading me on and then saying no?"

"I didn't intend to lead you on. I simply needed time to consider, and now I have, and I am not interested in your marriage proposal."

"What do you want? Pretties? I can buy you some nice things to flatter you. Consider it wedding presents. Not something to expect often though."

She could see that she had created her own problem by not putting a stop to it that day in the school. But she'd done what she did to protect herself from him. Instead she'd given him fuel to make the decision an affront to him rather than honoring her own right to her choices. She'd remember this. Don't make excuses or put someone off. Face the music. Hook your corset and stand tall.

"Mr. Bunter, I know you mean well and your offer will be accepted one day, I feel certain. But not by me. I'm sorry I led you to believe a little time to consider would change my mind, but I did tell you I wasn't interested in marriage. And I'm not. Now. Or ever, with you."

"I won't give up. I'll come a-courting."

"Then you'll be wasting time better spent seeking another."

He looked around. The color drained from Fanny's face, turning it white as her starched apron, and fourteen-year-old Catherine—the most beautiful of the Scott girls, at least in Jenny's mind—backed out the door into the dining room, her blue eyes wide as biscuits.

"Court other than a Scott girl," her father said. "My daughter has spoken, Bunter. And I back her."

Jenny felt a warmth of gratitude toward her father for his defense.

"She leading you by a nose ring, is she, Tucker?"

Her father bristled, and Jenny reached to put her hand over his. "It is a woman's right to make her own choices," she said. "Men's laws give that God-given right to other men—their fathers and sons, brothers sometimes—and certainly to husbands once the vows are said. I happen to have a father who believes a woman can make some decisions on her own, and this is one of them." She thought of another argument. "I'm actually saving you from a life of misery with me. We'd be at constant odds."

"I'd break you."

"No, you wouldn't."

He arched his back, looked down at everyone in the room, his eyes landing on Jenny. "I wouldn't want you anyway, though breaking you from a wild filly into a steady mare could be a worthy effort. But not worth it for 160 acres. Woe to the man who does win you. He'll never get a word in and be henpecked for certain."

Don't defend. Don't add fuel to his fire. "I hope you enjoyed your meal," Jenny said. "Now if you'll excuse me, I need to see if the chickens have given up any more eggs."

She spoke a prayer of thanksgiving as the door closed behind her and she heard Mr. Bunter say to her father, "I don't envy you trying to find a mate for that missy. You got yourself a spinster on your hands."

And what would be so bad about that?

FOUR

The Timing of Love

The quartet walked. Sisters Maggie and Kate trailed Jenny and Ben to the dance, meandering a discreet distance behind. At the last minute, her father had told Fanny she needed to remain behind to tend the inn and spend time with her father's choice of beau for her, Amos Cook. *Poor Fanny.*

Jenny's younger sisters giggled behind them, and Jenny found herself apologizing for their silliness, even as she remembered the intensity of the confrontation with Mr. Bunter. He'd frightened her with his bluster, and while she was grateful her father had stood up for her, it also troubled her. Would she always need a man to buttress her decisions before they'd be taken seriously? And how fortunate she was that her father supported her, though he'd done the opposite for Fanny's preferred suitor. How unfair to Fanny.

"Giggling girls is a happy sound to me, so long as they aren't giggling at me," Ben said, bringing Jenny back to the moment.

"They're happy. We've had such grief in the past year with Momma's and little Willie's deaths.

It seems happiness has escaped us." She put her arm through his, and he patted her gloved hand.

Maggie said in her still childlike voice, "Be careful up there." Maggie was her pious sister.

She turned around and put her finger to her lips to signal silence adding, "I'm eighteen, Maggie."

"A body has to come up for air in a world where there are always floods and fires and family feuds," Jenny told Ben as she turned back, her elbow securely attached to his. "That's one reason I like teaching so much. If I ever run a school of my own, I'll call it Hope School, because that's what I think education does for people—gives them hope to get them through the hard times, to try for higher things. Some things are worth doing regardless of how they turn out. That's my thinking. What do you say to that, Mr. Duniway?"

"Good thought. I headed to the gold fields in Southern Oregon a few months after I arrived in Oregon. I hoped I'd become rich. Instead I mined enough to buy a donation land claim but not enough to operate it like a manor boss. It's hard work but worthy work. It'd be more fun to have a wife and family to share it with. Not the work so much, but the outcome of it."

She didn't feed his fire, either. She wasn't certain about a married life, and a week of courting ought not take her there. Risky decisions should be made with caution.

They reached the dance hall, and Ben helped her step up the stairs to the music flowing out the open door. It was a balmy evening. Ben motioned her sisters to come ahead, the chaperoning now reversed with Ben and Jenny looking after them in this jubilant crowd. He directed them toward the punch bowl beyond the coatroom.

"Got my little flock to look after," he said.

"We Scott girls can look after ourselves," Kate said. "Can't we, Jenny?"

"I think it's proper to have a man watch out for our welfare." Maggie spoke up.

"Let me get you all a cup of punch while you nestle yourselves by the wall there."

"He's nice," Kate said, as Ben drifted to the refreshments, stopping on the way to talk with friends.

"And handsome." Maggie settled herself on a higher chair and swung her legs back and forth.

"It is nice to be waited on, isn't it?" Jenny said. "We do our share of serving at the inn. I wish Fanny had joined us."

"It's a woman's place to serve," Maggie said. "Scripture admonishes us."

"Scripture also shows us we should learn at another's feet and not always be working." Jenny recalled the verses about Mary and Martha. She tended to behave like Martha but wished to be able to rest and learn like Mary.

Ben brought the drinks back and sat beside

her. "So you want to open your own school one day?"

"Possibly. I want to be able to support myself or contribute to a family if I have one. But I like having coins I get to spend the way I want. I can do that now, after giving some over to Papa, of course."

"That seems reasonable." Ben took a sip of his drink, wiped his mouth with the back of his hand. He waved at someone across the floor, returned his attention to Jenny. "I think a wife ought to have a say in how monies are spent, though when in doubt, it's the man's duty to make the final decision."

"Hmm. What if it turns out he made the wrong decision?"

"Might teach him to listen more closely to his wife. But then, we all make mistakes. Can't let the count of them hammer too long and hard at your chest, or it'll break your heart. Won't go far with a broken heart. You'll have to find a way to mend it or be miserable for life." He took another sip. "I'm good at fixing things. You might give me a chance."

"This is getting too profound," Jenny said. "Are you fixin' to dance with me?"

"If you'll have me."

Jenny took another sip of her drink. It had a fizz to it. From the sassafras, she imagined. She let Ben lift the cup from her fingers, set both of their cups on their chairs as though to hold their place, and they took to the cornmeal-polished wooden floor. Jenny thought she might not be able to breathe, his gentle touch, the way he held her eyes as they moved around the room. *Of course, the man can dance.* He could sing, and the rhythms moved casual as a lazy stream through his lanky body. Jenny lost touch with what was happening around them, could only see those blue eyes holding hers. She felt herself lifted—not physically, but like she'd been carried to a mountaintop where the air was thin and she had trouble catching her breath.

Then she did have trouble catching her breath.

It might have been the activity or perhaps the heat of the room, but she lost her balance and found herself sagging into Ben, who put his wide hand around her waist and glided her from the floor to their chairs. The girls quickly picked up the cups to let them sit.

"What happened?" Maggie asked. "Are you all right?"

"I'm fine, really. Holy cow chips, it's nothing." She didn't want to bring attention to herself.

"First time I ever literally swept a woman off her feet. Let me get you a little water."

"I'm glad of that," Jenny told Ben. "I just need a moment's rest."

Ben settled her on the chair, frowned, but succumbed to her suggestion that he dance with her sisters. Watching them ease across the floor, she thought it must have been the passion of the day that weakened her. She'd gone from anticipation to confrontation to Ben's kind ministration, all leaving her reeling. It was happening too quickly. She wasn't ready to fall in love. *I wonder if this is how it happened for Momma.*

Then it was time to leave. Papa had been strict about when they had to be back. He would have come himself, except that his wife was pregnant and it wouldn't do to have her there nor to leave her home alone. And he had to chaperone Fanny, after all, left behind with her not-chosen beau.

On the way back, Ben suggested the girls walk in front of them, and they concurred. The moon lit their way. He held Jenny's hand, spoke softly. "I'd like to do this every Saturday night with you. Even midweek. Or every single day."

That shortness of breath caught her again. Her legs ached, her back hurt. Only her fingers wrapped by his were warm as though she held them before a fire.

"Take your time, Miss Jenny," Ben said. "But my mind's made up. And I don't think you'll find anyone who could love you more."

"You barely know me. I have a caustic tongue at times. I can be officious, bossy as a herd cow. Aspirations drive me, call me forward, for opportunities my mother never had because she was pregnant nearly all the time and had to endure both hard births and too-soon deaths. It broke her." Jenny remembered her mother's tears once when she learned she was pregnant again. "She was so kind, so gifted, and so tired all the time. I don't want that."

"But you'd like a babe or two?"

"Or three or four. One day. I want to be able to raise them in safety, without worry over debt or illness we couldn't afford to get a doctor for."

He shouted to the girls ahead. "Not so far out there. Your pa will shoot me if you fall in a puddle or worse." To Jenny he said, "I like the 'we' word you used."

"I'd want a marriage to be a team."

"Good thought. I train horses to work as a team."

"Are you comparing us to horses?" She laughed as she said it.

"Might be a few factors in common, most important is that they're certain they're headed in the same direction." He cleared his throat. "May I speak to your father? We wouldn't have to marry right away. Take our time."

She liked the idea of taking time to see how their walking side by side might work—and she'd have time to savor her independence before giving it up for love. "Let's wait until after the school term is over. You might change your mind the more time you spend with me and my family."

"Not likely. But I can wait. Just don't let ol' Harold slip in and steal you away." He had a deep voice he raised when he teased, although she didn't think what he said was totally in jest.

"There'll be no chance of that. My father has affirmed my interest in another." She squeezed his fingers. "Once Papa decides, it's pretty much a baked pie." She could only hope that a life with Ben Duniway was the sweetness to the soul she wanted.

Spring brought its high step to the region, buds bursting, the fragrance of wild roses perfuming the air. Jenny still rode to the school early, leaving the family she boarded with before dawn each day. They were a kind couple with one young child, who paid the school fee by providing room and board for the teacher. Ben no longer brought Josie to school. That child rode her own horse. Instead, Ben joined the Scott family each weekend, went to church with her, and they became a pleasant gossip whisper long before Ben spoke to Tucker Scott about his daughter Jenny's hand. She found not seeing him all week long was a greater distraction than looking forward to a morning and afternoon short visit at the school chaperoned by children. *Is this what I want?* She posed the question to herself a dozen times a day when thoughts of Ben interrupted a math lesson where the children measured their desks or shared a biscuit to figure out fractions. She was just getting started with her profession and believed her work was important. But so was the work of a wife and mother. At least Ben wasn't pressuring her. He waited for Jenny to set the timing.

As sometimes happens, though, timing is often taken from us.

FIVE

The Vagaries of Choice

"It's this way. I'm sorry, but you girls cannot remain under my roof with . . . my wife's indiscretion. Fanny, you must marry Amos and you two can take over the inn. Maggie and Harriet can remain with you, as can Kate and Sarah. Jenny, is it Ben, or are you wanting me to find you someone else? There's always Harold."

"You can't stay married to her, Pa," Harvey said. "She dishonored you."

It was June, the summer heat beginning its rise in the Willamette Valley. They sat in the parlor, the coolest room of the inn, darkened by shades that made Jenny think they were at a wake. Perhaps they were. They all spoke as though Jenny's stepmother wasn't even present, but she was, sobbing with a broken heart. Her remorse was genuine, Jenny could see that. But they'd all recently learned of her indiscretion before she ever married their father; the child she now carried was not Tucker Scott's. If word got out that the child wasn't her father's, it would be worse than the divorce he was contemplating. Either way, it would be scandalous for marriage-aged daughters to be living in the same home as a fallen woman or a divorced father.

Jenny was torn. His wife had made a poor decision, but she shouldn't have to have her life destroyed by gossip and rumor when the man who caused it had no repercussions. And a divorce— such an act would spill down on all of them like water over a ridge, splattering everything below it. All the girls were in the splatter. She supposed her brothers were too, but they'd at least be able to decide for themselves whether to stay with their father or go live with one of their married sisters—as soon as the girls found husbands.

Her stepmother had written a letter at her father's request where she apologized and revealed how she'd been duped by a previous proposal following the death of her husband. Widowed and desperate, she'd accepted the man's word of marriage and succumbed to his advances. But she hadn't known she carried a child when the man abandoned her, and she met Tucker Scott and fell genuinely in love with him. She begged for forgiveness, and why shouldn't she have it? Wasn't that what Christian compassion was all about, making space for healing from the hardness of life?

"Jenny!" Her father barked her name to bring her back to the tension of the room. "Ben hasn't officially asked me for your hand. I imagine you've told him not to."

She nodded. *And he's honored that request.*

She had wanted the decision about marriage to be hers and Ben's alone. She could stay on at the inn with Fanny if her sister was forced to marry Amos. Or try to rent a room somewhere. She couldn't go with her father, with her stepmother's mistake becoming known. Her father's indecision about divorcing her—she could see he still loved the woman—caught them all off guard. It was the close of the school term, when she planned to take on more sewing in her spare time, help at the inn, and get to know Ben. It was all a swirl, and her growing feelings for Ben were in the middle.

If only her father had waited to remarry! If only she'd had more time to pursue her profession. If only Ben's farm were closer to civilization so she could consider a fee school operated out of their home. *If only.* The most useless words in the English language.

"I asked him not to talk with you until I was ready," Jenny told her father. "I'm still not sure I am prepared." She didn't add how dismayed she was that despite her father having made the decision to marry so quickly, it was all the women who would pay the highest price for having choices rushed or made for them.

"Not much time to spare," her father warned.

"Yes, time's a-wasting and we with it," Jenny said. "I'll advise him to seek your permission." As had happened for her mother, John Tucker had taken a choice from her.

• • •

Jenny and Ben married on August 2, 1853, in the town of Lafayette. She wore a dress the color of daffodils, with a white bow that trailed down her back and showed off her tiny waist. She'd sewed the dress in between making one for Fanny too, who two weeks later married Amos Cook, a well-regarded pioneer of the Territory but still twenty years older than his new wife.

"It isn't fair," Jenny told her sister as she pulled the curling iron from the coals, tested it with her spit to make sure it cooled enough to not singe her sister's hair.

"Some things aren't." Fanny dabbed at her eyes with the blueberry-dyed handkerchief.

"But Papa married whom he wanted. Men get better choices not because they're wiser—but because they're men." She thought of Harold Bunter and the law that aided him if he found a wife in time. "And because they make the rules. Why is that?"

"Oh, Jenny. You'll frustrate yourself wishing it weren't so. We're girls. Men aren't. We have to make the best of it."

There didn't seem any other option but to accept. Still, Jenny's tears as her sister spoke her vows came from both sadness and guilt—because Jenny at least had the luxury of love. Fanny had to learn to love her husband if she could.

• • •

At Fanny and Amos's wedding, Harold Bunter showed up. "Holy cow chips," she told Ben when she saw his brooding scowl as he dismounted and tied his horse to the rail. Oddly he said nothing perverse to Jenny or Ben nor anyone else. He stood at the edge of the crowd, spitting his tobacco juice into a cup, while he stared at Jenny.

"Don't worry," Ben said. "I'll always protect you."

She nodded, took her serving platter of beef dodgers, and set them on the sawhorse table between the vases of wildflowers dotting the crisp white tablecloth. Fanny had served the same foods—beef dodgers and beans, blueberries, and pies of various nature—at Ben and Jenny's wedding. Jenny had waited for Harold to show up on that day and decided, when he hadn't, that a woman could waste a lot of time in worry. Better to think of what to do if trouble did appear and have a plan of action for then but otherwise focus on the moment. At Fanny's wedding he was less imposing to her with a husband by her side. He did nothing but stare, and Jenny could abide that. She turned her back to him, welcoming Ben's assurance that he'd be there to take care of her should the need arise. Many husbands weren't so protective of their wives and daughters—her father included—but she had hope in Ben.

• • •

The yo-yo of "yes or no" about Jenny marrying or not had ceased, and there was relief in that. The vows—for better or for worse—rang true. This was a lifelong commitment, and having made it, she prayed their union would be blessed and gave herself wholeheartedly to loving Ben.

Little Josie attended their nuptials, along with her parents and new brother, and Jenny met all Ben's family for the first time that August day. She heard stories about his growing up in Illinois, about his waddling to the barn and petting the nose of a big draft horse shortly after his first birthday. "Horses were his first love," his father told her. "But I'd say he's found their match in you."

"Come here, my new wife." Ben held out his hand to her and asked her to sit before the gathering on a rocking chair brought to the outside from the inn. "I've a little present for my bride." He strummed the guitar strings. "I wrote this myself." Jenny blushed at his attention and that of the guests. The words of his song praised "a girl with the eyes of kindness and a heart of hope" and went on to tell a story of a strong-minded woman who ultimately "determined she'd fall in love and marry." She applauded and the crowd with her. *I should have written a poem for him.* She'd do that, she decided, and read it to him in the privacy of their cabin she had yet to see.

They spent their first night at the inn and rode to Ben's ranch the morning after, the sweet scent of honeysuckle bursting in the air. They stopped to pick blackberries, filling a basket, laughing as they fed each other the warm, plump fruit that stained their fingers and lips.

"I couldn't be happier, Jenny," Ben said, his naturally white teeth a faded blue.

"It's a good day, Ben Duniway." And so it was. Perhaps not the sweeping romantic fantasy she'd thought of when she read those novels her mother slipped into the house, but sweet and safe nonetheless. This man beside her loved her, and while she wasn't sure what love was, she knew that when he touched her hand to help her from the wagon, then held her to his chest, she felt warm and wanted, and worries over the past and of the future sank like the sunset, slow and easy from their view. Surely if that was not love, it was close.

"I'll think of it as *our* claim." Ben swept his arm before them. He tried to see what Jenny did: tall firs thick as weeds covering the vast expanse except where he'd worked so hard to clear ground. Would she see the potential? He'd built a small cabin and acquired horses for breeding and riding. He had two cows, chickens, and sheep for wool and mutton.

Ben thought of it as "their claim," even though

he'd farmed it an entire year before he even met Jenny. Besotted, his own father had said of him, and Ben guessed he was. Her acceptance of his offer of marriage sent him spinning his hat to the wind in gratitude. He suspected he loved her more than she him, but he was a persuasive man and he'd convince her in time that no man would ever love her more. She would come to love him deeper. He knew that she cared for him but also that he was a good way out of a bad situation in her family. He'd appreciated her honesty in her acceptance.

Today, he walked behind the mule plowing the rock-peppered earth. John Henry, her little brother—the Scotts called him "Little Toot"—picked up rocks and made cairns of them beside the field. Ben knew it was hard land and he might have made a better purchase, but it was his. It was also beautiful and green, though as Jenny pointed out once or twice, it wasn't as good a cropland as farther west in the valley. He hated to hear disappointment in her voice, but most of that land had been already claimed by the earlier arrivals of the 1840s. Still, this farm was much better than the Boonsboro land of Kentucky, or Pike County country of Illinois where his family came from.

Ben had managed to bring his father west in '51, a year after his own footsteps onto Oregon soil by way of California. With earnings from the gold field, he'd paid his father's way out west and operated his own farm from those gold nuggets too. He'd made some lucky strikes but preferred farming to mining any day. Shoot, if he hadn't come to Oregon, he never would have met Jenny, and what a great loss that would have been.

The jerk of the shoulder harness as he split the earth brought him back to the field, but his mind soon wandered to Jenny. He'd first seen her as part of a relief team sent out to meet the wagon trains in the fall of '52. Locals had heard several Illinoisans were headed that way, and like his father's company of '51, by the time they reached the Willamette Valley, people had slim pickings for food and other provisions. Ben had helped organize rescue parties. Well, relief parties. People liked that term better and were more willing to accept the beans and bacon and blankets the settlers had brought with them. He'd seen but a glimpse of the slender brown-haired beauty. She was sitting on a rock beside a stream, writing in a book, waiting for others to get their beans and bacon before her. Something about her made Ben look longer than a stranger should have, and she raised her baby blues to him, he guessed because she felt him staring.

He tapped his fingers to his hat, nodded. She stared back, didn't acknowledge him at all, and soon returned to her book. Ben turned his horse away, not wishing to interrupt the lady, and looked instead for someone to tell him who she was. He couldn't see who her family might be, as she was off by herself, and when she wandered back to the cluster of folks, he noticed her handing out biscuits to anyone who came along. He guessed she saw everyone as her responsibility—once she set her scribbling down.

Then one day in the rainy winter of that year, Ben learned about a new schoolteacher in Cincinnati, a little burg in the Oregon valley. She was boarding out—what teachers did, living with parents of students a month or term at a time. One of Ben's neighbors said she was a popular guest at parties, well-chaperoned by her father and sisters, and a sought-after sweetheart, though she turned most suitors away. "Her tongue's got acid on it, so be wary," one of Ben's friends said, punching him on his shoulder. He'd taken the courting from there and didn't mind, when he later told her, that she had no memory of that gaze exchanged back on the trail. Now here they were, man and wife. God was good.

A late-afternoon breeze dried some of Ben's sweat. He felt he had a few virtues to offer. His hardscrabble farm, for one, with its tall timber and horses. He trained them to ride, gentled them rather than broke them, and they'd taken to the harness too, with his whispering words to their twitching ears. He'd even worked a few to tricks and sold a pair for circus horses. He'd begun a breeding program and hoped for matched white teams one day or a pair of trained pintos to prance at Fourth of July celebrations. For now he'd limited his breeding to help farmers needing animals ready for harness. He had a good reputation for hard work and won loyal friends, and his word meant something. He offered Jenny that.

And he could read. That was a virtue, though he wasn't prone to it. Words didn't hold the same reverence that they did to his wife. She'd even insisted on leaving the word "obey" out of the marriage vows. He'd gotten a kick out of that and how she'd talked down the Methodist minister's objections. Ben preferred to sing and play guitar and talk to friends or work beside them if they had a need. Giving was an important virtue in this young country, and Ben knew how to do that.

Ben had had a gal or two say he was good-looking, and he'd never been in a fist fight. He hadn't had to defend himself, because no one wanted to take him on, being six feet by the time he was twelve. Hard work had filled him out.

Another virtue was his desire to be a matched team with his wife, not one pulling in different directions, so he didn't tell her what to do and she didn't direct him. At least that's what they'd agreed to that day in August. And though they were newly wedded, he hadn't minded a whit having her ten-year-old brother John Henry move in with them after two weeks. The boy liked the horses and the hardscrabble place too, though he was of slight build and tired as easily as Jenny. Her back hurt her often "from an old injury," she'd told him without her usual detail.

Ben unharnessed the plow mule and led him out to pasture. He washed up at the pump, taking water from a shallow well. He wiped his tanned arms as he surveyed his land. Their land. God had been good to them, bringing them together and to this place, an area bordered by split rails to fence the mule and horses in without having to be hobbled. Ben was a good rail splitter too. Another of his attributes along with being a bit intuitive when it came to women's needs, he hoped.

They'd been married a little over two months. It had been an ongoing education. He walked to the log house, stopped at the garden to pull an October carrot. He'd planted these vegetables, but next year, with Jenny here, they'd have a better garden with potatoes and pumpkins and maybe even a little popped corn.

He kissed Jenny and inhaled the scent of supper on the table he'd built. He tried to remember to call her "Abigail." She said a married woman ought to give up any childhood nickname—but it wasn't easy. She'd always be Jenny to him. He took the platter she handed him, set it on the table, then lifted his leg over the back of the chair to sit. Little Toot, not yet ten, was already there, smiling.

"What are you grinning about," Ben said. The boy swung his legs beneath the bench. Ben reached for the fresh bread. Heavens, he loved this married life. How blessed he was and more to come, once they began their family. "Come on, Jenny. I mean, Abigail. I'll say grace over the food for the three of us."

"Make that four," she said as she took her seat.

"Who's coming for supper?" He put the steaming bowl of potatoes she handed him on the table as she sat. "Should we wait?"

"Already here." She patted her abdomen. "He—or she—will be joining us in May in person."

"Well, I'll be. She tell you first, Little Toot? That why you're grinning big as a canyon?"

"Yes, sir, she did. I'm gonna be an uncle."

Ben rose and took Jenny in his arms. "Thought I couldn't be happier with getting you as my wife and now this. All that laboring not in vain."

She laughed and pushed against his chest, but not before he kissed her. "We have children present," she cautioned.

"More than one. I'm happy for us, Jenny."

"I am too, though I'd have liked a little more time to get this cabin into shape, perk up the chickens into better layers, and make and sell more butter. A baby's going to cost, Ben."

"That I know, but it'll also give back twice its weight in joy."

"I hope it's a boy," she said after Ben had spoken a table grace.

"Do you? A daughter would be grand."

"Yes, but she'll have a harder life than you boys have. Girls just do."

"We'll love her like a son, then," Ben said. "And do all we can to make it easier on her. And on you too. What can I do to help?"

"Me too," Little Toot said.

"Well, aren't you versatile men," Jenny said.

"But another of our many virtues," Ben said. "Just know, I doubt I'll ever learn to cook, so give me something else to commandeer."

"Laundry," Jenny said. "It's more work than planting corn and twice as arduous. A babe will bring on more."

SIX

Early Storms

1853 to 1856

She hadn't remembered the winter being so drippy and dark. So much had happened their first months in the Territory—her teaching, her father's marriage, the work at the inn, the dances, her sisters always present—she guessed she hadn't noticed the heavy downpours, broken now and then by shards of sun. "Sun breaks," the locals called the half hour or so when the rains stopped long enough so a girl could jump the puddles and head to the privy without getting wet. Maybe it was a wetter winter. Or perhaps the weather wore on her without the joy of her sisters' voices or the children from her school to invigorate. Morning sickness didn't help.

It was just the three of them at Hardscrabble, as Jenny thought of their 320 acres. Ben often rode off to drum up potential breeding contracts or sales. Little Toot would go with him, so she had hours alone, never hearing another voice while she mended torn pants or churned butter she put in molds to sell. The chickens gave in to winter and ate more than they gave back in eggs. "We're both gaining weight," she told them as she reached beneath their warm plumage seeking one or two eggs instead of their usual four or five.

She'd sewed festive curtains from the feed bags, embroidering flowers onto the gray material in the evenings by candlelight when she'd rather be reading or even writing, but she needed color to brighten the rainy days.

When her "boys" were gone, she spoke to their child, thinking of the baby as a boy, and she told him stories about how to treat a lady. "When your poor momma says she needs a little help with the chickens, you come running," or "You consult your momma and later your wife about big decisions, like where to move to or what to buy. You remember that, now." She spoke as much to advise as to hear a feminine voice.

When the afternoon waned, she would pull out her foolscap paper and write. She thought it a luxury she might not have, once the baby arrived, and since Ben was off doing what he loved, and furthering their livelihood as well, she'd take the time to advance her own. While she stitched, she thought of words to write down, starting with poems that had a hint of humor to them.

There once was a farmer's wife.
Who worked hard to avoid marital strife.
She kept her tongue still
When handed a due bill . . .

"What's a good last line?" Jenny asked her baby as she picked dried eggs from the dishes. Later, while spinning carded wool, she tried to come up with that final line. "I'll give up writing limericks," she said, or not write poetry that needs something to rhyme with "wife." Still, the effort filled her days and she found when resentment over Ben's absence or, worse, when he brought his single friends home in time for her to add a plate to the supper table, that word-seeking was a good way to keep her tongue in check. At least until their "guests" had gone. Then she'd spill a few thoughts to Ben about the extra work his "generosity" brought her.

"I'll help with cleaning up," he said.

"As though that's the only effort." She slammed a frying pan down a little harder than intended, and Little Toot jumped.

"I'll help too, Sister," the boy said and shot from the stool, swirling around looking to see what he could do. "Polish the lamp? See to the pigs?"

"Good idea," Ben told him. "I'll check on the chicks." At the door, he turned and said, "You can out-argue me anytime, Jenny. But you'll never out-love me."

They both scurried out of her way then, which wasn't what she wanted. She wanted them to ease her loneliness. And, like Ben, to be able to love fully. She didn't know what held her back.

There once was a farmer's wife.
Who worked hard to avoid marital strife.
She kept her tongue still
When handed a due bill . . .

Knowing payments are a part of life.

She'd settle on that last line , though her hope for humor had escaped her.

Spring arrived along with labor pains. Ben patted Jenny's hand. "I'll get my sister. Will you be all right while I'm gone? Should I leave? Oh Jenny."

"I'll be fine," Jenny said. "Just go." But as soon as he was gone, she wished he were still with her. Little Toot stared. "I'm all right," she told him. *I have to be brave for my brother.* "Having a baby. Women do it all the time."

"What can I do?"

She laughed. "I don't know. We're two lost pups, aren't we? Oh, oh, oh!" Another contraction. *Pain. Good pain.* "Bring in kindling," she directed. He was panting along with her and would pass out if she didn't give him tasks. She wished she'd had Kate come, at least. But her sister-in-law Mary had delivered two children and would know what to do. Jenny had been there for her siblings' births, but now that it was her body bringing forth a babe, it was as though she couldn't remember the sequence of events. She waddled around the room, stopped to pant with each contraction. Urged Little Toot to read his book. In between the pains, she filled and heated up water in the cast iron pot. *What do we need hot water for? Bathe the baby maybe?* She gathered up cloths she'd set aside. She walked to the barn, inhaled the wild roses growing next to the log structure, and her brother helped her haul in the old feather mattress so as not to stain their good one. She had covered it with a pieced quilt, made ready for this glorious May day. She didn't much care what happened to the cover; she wasn't much of a quilter, knowing her big stitches would never rival her sister Maggie's tiny ones. Besides, quilting hurt her fingers while writing did not. *I can write about this.*

But she couldn't. "Holy cow chips," she said to the log walls. She was an emotional train rushing forward with no way to stop.

She lay on the quilt, panting through the pains, sending Little Toot out to get the eggs. *Where is Ben?* "Go feed the chickens, check on the sheep too."

"I already did, Sister."

"Do it again."

"They'll be awful fat chickens," he mumbled as he opened the door.

Anything to get him away so she could groan at the pain and not alarm him, all the while wishing

Ben were there for her to yell at and at the same time wanting his hand to squeeze.

Am I strong enough for this? Will this baby be all right? Can I do this?

She remembered her mother saying, "Women have been doing this for centuries," and yet it was her first time and she wasn't sure she could. *I have to.*

"Everything will be all right," Ben told her.

"Thank God you're back."

"You've everything ready, I see," Mary Gibson said. She was tall, like Ben, but more commanding. It was the first woman's voice she had heard since New Year's Day.

Ben remained in the room, holding her hand while she snapped at him, silencing his utter joy at what was about to happen while she groaned in misery. "It'll be over soon, Jenny, it will. You're doing great."

"Easy for you to say."

"Push now," her sister-in-law said. She had a high-pitched voice that had once annoyed Jenny, but now her words gave her strength. "You can wail to the moon. Go ahead."

Jenny took her advice and shouted, though she didn't remember her mother ever doing so. But Jenny did, and then the child arrived, ripping its way into the world with a pain nearly as great as the labor pains.

"I'll stitch in a minute," she heard her sister-in-law say. "Ben, you cut the cord. We have to wait for the afterbirth."

"Oh, help me," Ben said, his words a prayer. "My hands are shaking."

"Is he all right?" Jenny tried to sit up as Mary placed the wet weight onto her belly.

"She's perfect," Ben said. "It's a girl, Jen. A beautiful baby girl. We made a girl."

"A girl." She sighed and gentled her hand on the still wet crown of her child's head. *A girl.*

She felt another contraction-like movement. *The afterbirth.* All was as it should be.

But it wasn't.

"This is going to hurt. You've torn quite a bit. Take this laudanum. It'll ease the pain." Her sister-in-law picked up the needle and thread Jenny had laid out. "Think of something else. Do you have a name?"

"We don't," Ben said. "Well, not one we agreed on."

"I was sure it would be a boy." Jenny's words barely passed her lips before she felt herself drifting. *A girl. We have a daughter.* She looked at Ben and saw his tears matched hers. "We'll go with your choice," she told Ben, and then she faded.

Clara Belle joined their lives. Yes, a girl's life would be hard. Yes, her mother had been correct in that, and yet to see the tiny lips, the fingers small as new carrots reaching for her, to nourish this child's body from her own, to imagine a future chattering and exploring with this girl, brought joys she'd never known. She loved her in an instant. In the beginning, she had wondered if she loved Ben as much as he loved her. She had grown to care more for him in the nine months of their marriage. But with Clara Belle, there was no doubt to the depth of her emotion. With the first look into those baby eyes, she was in love. This was unconditional love that only grew deeper in the following days. Clara Belle's presence eased the loneliness, and Jenny vowed she'd do all she could to make this girl's life better and maybe other girls' lives richer too. She didn't know how, but she was committed to educating her, giving her all the advantages that their small farm could bring. She'd teach her about the joy of the landscape, towering trees with needles ever green, help her notice the soft rains turning their log cabin rooftop moss the perfect shade of jade. Clara Belle would see what devoted parents looked like.

When she found herself mumbling at the doughboy, kneading bread while Ben and his bachelor chums waited for her to serve up biscuits, she vowed to see their presence not as intrusions but as opportunities for her daughter to see how men could rest while women worked and how one day, working together, women might change that. She didn't know how. "We need rest too," she told the intense blue eyes of her daughter in the cradle. "Your father works hard, he does. But so does your momma."

She envied the men in her life, that was the truth of it. Ben found a way toward ease that escaped her. He refreshed with the laughter and guitar-playing and singing to his daughter. She'd never learned to rest—she had no practice. Maybe playing with Clara Belle in the middle of the day would bring such pleasure, but there was always work to be done. Eggs to collect. Cream to churn. Butter to place into molds and sell. Laundry.

Still, as Clara Belle grew, Jenny could imagine standing her on her mother's slippers as she shuffled a dance away from the stove and into the higher chair Ben had built her or blowing on her belly while she changed her. Those would be small moments she could savor with her child. Her mother must have had those moments, hadn't she?

Today, that kindred binding would have to wait. Jenny sighed. Washing a mountain of dirty diapers was the immediate future of this mother and her girl.

"Everything will be all right." It was Ben's mantra, and sometimes Jenny resented Ben when he said it. If she expressed concerns about her isolation or how much her bones ached or that their larder needed filling and there were no coins nor eggs to trade, he'd say "Everything will be all right." It felt like he dismissed her concerns. Things didn't always turn out all right. It was what she was thinking as she milked their small herd of three cows while Clara Belle lay in the cradle chewing on a bit of dough Jenny had tied on a piece of string around her toe so her jerky feet would keep her from swallowing it. Chickens cackled, wanting out of their coop. Jenny pressed her head into the side of a cow while she stripped the teats of their white gold. The butter and egg sales were their only income many months. Ben was once again gone to try to sign a breeding contract. He'd taken Little Toot with him. Clara Belle cooed. Jenny loved that sound.

She felt a cooling come across the timber, and the wind picked up enough to move the harness hanging on the hook beside the open door. The barn darkened. Birds had stopped chirping, and the cow's tail twitched and she began to prance. Jenny looked outside. A black cloud had moved in. Her heart pounded as she swooped Clara into her arms. She raced to the cabin door as rain poured and she witnessed the shape of a funnel drop down into the timbers, the wind threatening at the leather hinges of their door as she pushed into the cabin. She threw the slide bar across the opening and raced to the back of the cabin as she heard the roar. Deafening.

Jenny fell to the floor, her baby beneath her as she pushed them both to a corner where they huddled, her baby against her breast. And she prayed, oh how she prayed that they'd survive this tempest, that Ben was all right and Little Toot, too, out in this cyclone. Her words flew to the wind, the clacking of hail against the roof, and then she heard the wrench of logs as the ceiling timbers tore from the walls as easily as an ax splits kindling.

Jenny hovered over Clara as the hail ground onto them, no protection, no roof. Pellets of ice, some the size of new potatoes; more like popped corn but rough as rocks. They shredded the bed linen, tore at the table, cupboards, the stove. Jenny's hands were bloodied, held over Clara's crown; her own head pierced with pain from the ice.

And then a stillness though the rain poured down, the moss-covered roof, gone.

Jenny stood. She shook and looked around her. Trees like children's toys scattered in all directions. She could see them through the missing walls. Fences, gone. Cattle, dead. A timber driven into the side of the house as though it were a peg to hold the clothes of giants. Her teeth chattered in the cold. The barn flattened with timbers sticking up through logs, and a first cutting of grass hay a mass that looked like drenched salad greens. A strip of field crops, vanished. She began crying then, clinging to her daughter.

What if Ben's caught up in this? What if—

She couldn't let herself think the worst. "We'll go to Mary's. We'll go to Mary's."

She grabbed a rag and wiped Clara's face, her own, and her bloodied hands. Rain pelted them. "We'll go to Mary's." She repeated the mantra, a promise of an action she could take. It brought her strange resolve.

The three miles to her in-laws took what seemed like hours through the mud. When she saw Ben's horse and Little Toot's at the trough, she started to cry. They were all right.

She cried out, "Ben! Ben! Oh, you're safe."

Her husband stepped out onto the porch, beginning to welcome her with a question on his face. Then she saw him race toward her, taking two porch steps at a time, catching her as she collapsed. She was so weak, but she had protected Clara Belle. That was all that mattered.

Ben pulled his daughter from Jenny, ran his big hands over the child before handing the crying Clara Belle to Little Toot, who stood behind him. Bruises had formed on the back of the child's palms. "What's happened?"

"I did the best I could. The farm is gone. It's all gone. Wind. Hail. No roof."

75

"It's barely raining here." Ben sounded confused.

"Hail, the size of river rocks. I tried to cover
us."

Her in-laws came out onto the porch, heard her.

"Shh, shh. Hush now." Ben held her in his
arms, his warmth a comfort as he helped her
forward. Clara had quieted as Mary held her.

"You're bleeding," Ben said.

"You won't recognize . . ." Jenny's words
drifted.

"Bring them inside. Goodness. You poor thing."
Ben's sister helped her stand.

"It can't be as bad as all that," Ben said, helping
her up the porch steps. "You're here in front of
me. You're safe and Clara is too. Everything will
be all right."

"It isn't."

"Did you walk down the creek? You're muddy
as the pig sty." He tried to make a joke.

She collapsed on Mary Gibson's bed, and the
men were shooed out so she could be stripped of
the wet clothes by her sister-in-law.

"They'll dry out. You rest now," Mary said.
Little Josie had followed them in. "You've had
quite a scare, I can see."

"I couldn't make it stop. I tried to cover Clara
Belle, but her hands are bruised." Tears welled.
She couldn't stop shaking.

"Don't you worry." Mary directed her daughter

to get Clara Belle a little hat and her brother's night shirt. "They'll be big on 'er." To Jenny she said. "You're safe now. You're through the worst."

"I'll ride home and check on things," Ben shouted behind the closed door.

"No! Wait. Don't go." She felt exposed as a newborn kitten. She rose, pulled open the door. "Please. Stay. We'll go back together."

Ben patted her shoulder.

And so they did. Theirs was the only farm in the area that had been hit, the destruction stunning. "We can re-roof the barn easiest, live there until the cabin can be readied."

The rebuilding will take months. Jenny watched Ben wander through the debris. "I was so scared," she said, holding her fussing daughter close. She felt herself shiver, made herself calm for Clara's sake.

"But you did everything right. Looked after Clara and yourself. I wish I'd been here to help. But no matter. You took care of things. Everything will be alright." He patted her shoulder as they surveyed the wreckage.

Ben's brother-in-law and neighbors, her father and Harvey and her sisters would come to help with rebuilding, the days of work and sharing food a blend of sorrow and delight. And during it, Jenny began her push for them to sell the farm, to find a place closer to their neighbors where a woman could have a cup of tea now and again to ease the troubled times of women's lives.

"It's a campaign, Ben," she told him. "To get you to change your mind about this acreage. Let's sell it to a man with sons who can run it while we find a place more suitable."

"But we've put so much work into it."

"I miss being closer to my sisters. Let's find a place where Clara Belle can one day go to school. Let's consider it at least."

"We'll get more for the farm if we rebuild."

"And be further from where we want to be because we took the time. Let someone else replant it as they'd want. Re-roof the house so it's livable, but then let's find a place we can both love."

"Sometimes one has to cut one's losses. Is that what you're saying?" Ben said.

"Yes." Was it a failure to leave a challenge? Or wisdom to face another? Was that the reason her father had moved west, even against her mother's wishes?

SEVEN

A Clearing in the Fog

1856

Ben patted his hat down, mounted his big bay gelding, and rode into the fog. It wasn't that he didn't want to go for the doctor. It was that doing so meant leaving Jenny in a bad place. He trusted his sister and the women who had arrived for the birth of this second child, but ever since the tornado, he'd been worried about her. She was more fragile than he'd seen her be, jumping at small sounds, jerking away when he touched her shoulder from behind without first announcing his presence. She was short with Clara Belle too, snapped or sighed in frustration. He hoped it was the child-carrying attitude of easy annoyance and impatience. He didn't want to think her irritation was because they still lived at Hardscrabble Farm and, now with a second child, might find it even harder to afford to leave it, even if he did find a good place for them.

He felt a chill and pulled his wolfskin coat around him. Jenny had sewed the coat for him from the hides he'd brought in. He'd gotten a bounty—which helped their finances—but she'd insisted that he hold enough hides back for his coat. In this kind of weather, he was glad for it.

He realized he had ridden beside the barn when he thought he'd headed out toward the trail to the main road. It was still daylight, nearly dusk he guessed, but the fog made everything unfamiliar. He kept his eyes on the trail now and found the main pathway toward Needy and the doctor.

She was larger this time than with Clara, even he could see that. And his sister wasn't one to rush to worry, so her insisting that they needed a doctor wasn't just a plan to get him out of the way. A second child in less than three years of their marriage. Maybe they were pushing it. He felt her urgency, even if Jenny had minimized it. He did know she'd like having womenfolk around. He'd thought he'd be enough, but she missed her sisters and other women. He guessed he could have taken her along when he headed out to neighbors. But women's work never quit, as Jenny was fond of reminding him. Farms gave the ladies no rest. His lady. Truth was, he didn't want to move. They owned this land, had built it up together. One day she'd understand.

He started singing to keep himself company and to set a pace that would get him to Needy. "Camptown Races" and its line "gwine to run all night" was a favorite tune, and the sound of his voice in the fog echoed with a deep resonance.

He crooned out "Home Sweet Home" and "Old Susanna" before belting out the "Alphabet Song," a move that made him laugh and think of Clara, whom Jenny sang it to as much as he did. Then the fog lifted and he pulled up Biscuit's reins. The treetops were still misted, but he wasn't on any trail. "Where are we?"

He felt a clenching in his gut. "How can a man who lives on horseback and knows this country right and left not be sure where he is?" The horse shook his head, jangling the bit and bridle rings. "Yeah, I don't know the answer to that either." He'd have to pick a direction and hope to intersect the trail or come upon the town or another farm or something familiar. He pressed his knees against Biscuit's sides and reined him to the right. They rode through the timber for an hour or more, easing around treefalls and deadwood. Ben watched in despair as the fog descended again and he could barely see his horse's ears. He'd been gone at least two hours, and he wasn't anywhere near the doctor. He didn't know where he was. He heard a wolf howl and hoped it wouldn't be answered by a pack. As long as he could take another step, he'd be all right, but the best thing he could do would be to sit tight, build a fire and stay until the fog lifted. But how would he explain to Jenny or his sister that he sat by the fire while she suffered and maybe . . .

Women died. Jenny told him that childbirth was the greatest cause of death for women. The plight of women was her favorite topic.

No, he'd have to keep going, even if it was like riding inside a duck.

Blood everywhere on the bedclothes despite the women's efforts. "He must weigh ten pounds," she heard Mary say. *So, a boy.* She also heard her son cry, and the women oohing that he was healthy as they washed him and laid him on her breast. But they didn't leave him there long, needing to tend to the hemorrhaging. Anticipating possible problems, Jenny had made a mustard pack and directed Mary to it. She could hear Little Toot talking softly with Clara under the lean-to roof, entertaining her on the child's feather bed. Their voices soothed her, though they came from a distant shore.

"It'll be better after the placenta comes, surely." One of the neighbor women massaged her abdomen to release the afterbirth, while Mary placed the mustard pack, then removed it with the rush of blood and tissue.

"You should sew me up." Jenny panted. "I know I tore. Again."

She saw the women look at each other. "I'll do it," Mary said.

"I've done the sewing before," one of the midwives said. "It's a very large tear. The doctor would be so much better. And he'd have something . . . for pain."

"We don't have a doctor." Jenny's breath carried worry over what could have happened to Ben. He'd been gone for hours. She kept her mind from racing to all the possible tragedies, like accidents or wolves or who knew what all. Hadn't they had a miserable past year with the storm and rebuilding? Prices for wheat and apples were down. Miners in Jacksonville and California were less dependent on Oregon goods. And the Duniways had fewer goods to sell. *Why does my mind go to money worries? It's stitching up I need.* "Just sew. There's laudanum on top the pie chest. I wish I had chloroform."

"Or that laughing gas," Mary said. She had a kerchief tied at the back of her neck, holding her thick hair in check as she ministered to Jenny. "I saw it used at a forum once. Ten boys volunteered. They didn't remember a thing afterwards, they said, even when the host poked a needle into their fingers and drew blood."

"Not the image I'm needing right now," Jenny moaned. "Give me a small dose of the laudanum and then sew quickly. I want to be able to nurse that boy. Willis, we'll call him. After my little brother William who died on the trail. He even looks like him a little."

The conversation depleted her. Mary dipped the tincture onto Jenny's tongue. The neighbor put a rag in her mouth to bite on, and the older midwife began to sew within seconds. Jenny remembered little after that. She woke hours later to Ben, looking haggard, leaning over her.

"What happened to you?"

"I—the fog was so dense that I got lost. I . . . I still can't believe it. I finally gave Biscuit his head and the gelding brought us home, though hours it took. I'm so sorry. I—" He knelt beside the bed.

"Did you meet our son?"

"I did. And massive he is."

Jenny winced. "I'm still bleeding."

"Not as much, though it's likely to continue." The midwife didn't look at Jenny when she spoke. She fiddled with her instruments she'd placed in the pan of water no longer boiling. "It's a clean wound, but there'll be seepage and you must stay down. No heavy work at all or the bleeding will begin again in earnest."

"When the fog lifts, I'll go fetch your sisters."

"Until then," Mary said, "I'll stay." She saw another look pass between Ben and his sister.

I am worse than I thought. She patted Ben's hand. "Kate will come and Harriet. Neither have seen the rebuilt cabin."

Her sisters would laugh together and tell stories, which is what they did in a week, when March brought on the Willamette Valley spring and the doctor arrived too. He pronounced the sewing a fine stitching. "Any number of folks got discombobulated in that fog, Ben. You shouldn't feel bad about it."

"The outcome was all right," Ben told him. "I'd never have forgiven myself if Jenny had . . ." His voice caught and he couldn't finish.

"Bad things happen to the best of men," the doctor said. "Things work out."

"And sometimes they don't," Jenny said.

She had survived another birthing, but this child left his impression. Jenny spent weeks propped up in bed, frustrated with not being able to do the work that needed doing. After her sisters returned to their homes, Ben served as a good nurse and not a bad cook either, despite his having said he wouldn't be.

"My father didn't lend a kitchen-hand with babies around," Jenny said. She'd never seen her father pour hot water onto oats for his children to eat nor cut up venison for stew.

Ben washed their dishes. "He'd be missing out."

"You think so?" Household chores were mundane, repetitive, even though she knew they were essential tasks. "I haven't minded not being able to sweep or scrub."

"That's because you're destined for bigger things," he told her. He handed Clara Belle a tin plate. "Wipe it like this." He showed the child, and the toddler beamed.

"I help," she said.

"Yup, you do."

Jenny pondered Ben's offhand remark. "Destined for bigger things?" *Such nonsense.*

"It's true. You've got the kind of mind that thinks past the moment," he said. "Once you come out of this post-baby fog you've been in, you'll be pondering again. You're always ponderin' on something, mostly about women you don't even know."

"You've as good a mind as mine."

"Don't think so. Mine is content to brush a horse or scrape dried eggs from the pan." They turned together toward a crying Willis, lying in his cradle. "I'll leave it to you to change the world. I'll just change his diaper."

Writing helped ease Jenny's healing, but what she couldn't seem to regain after Willis's birth was her sense of hopefulness, that as Ben said, things really would work out all right. He'd point to how the children thrived, how neighbors had helped them recover, how she healed—though she still bled, often grabbed the table corner, and placed chairs equal-distant so she always had something to hold on to as she moved around the house. *Will this be my life now?*

"It'll get even better once you're able to let go of all the way stations," Ben said. "And can join in the neighborhood doings. Go to the horse races, pie fests. You know, participate."

"I haven't felt much like being out. Besides, we need new farm equipment, and I'd love a labor-saving device for washing clothes. And we could use an addition built onto this cabin if we're going to stay here. We stumble over ourselves. Besides, I've no energy for neighboring."

"Sure, you do. Being around people feeds you, rubs away some of your cranky edges."

"I'm not cranky without reason," Jenny said.

"Not arguing that." Ben held his hands up to ward off her sharp words that could rise as quick as a wind change. "I'm merely seeking a way to buff it into something that restores your high spirits."

He'd persisted in his gentle way, and on a Saturday when Willis was a few months old, the Duniways took the buggy to Needy, past the little school Jenny had taught at. They stopped by the Aurora Colony where the communal colonists played music on Saturday afternoon and there were stores the general public could buy from. It was said they had their names on ledger sheets recording what they brought or bought but didn't need to bring cash or trade. And that women were taught Greek and Latin like the men.

It was a glorious day in early October and hop harvests were in full swing in the valley, the air fragrant and leaves magically turning green to vermillion. Jenny ran into friends who commented on how well she looked (*Do I?*) or how they'd missed hearing her side of issues in the cloakroom while men discussed potential statehood at the local schoolhouse. She had to admit, she missed those conversations too, especially when they spoke of subjects of import and not only about the value of packaged yeast over sourdough starter.

Heading home with a bit more grit, she realized Ben had been right about her getting out. She did appreciate the compliments about the children looking well and healthy, and she liked hearing Ben's laughter as the men exchanged stories of horseflesh or hunting. There was life beyond the cabin walls harboring wet diapers and the daily drudge of churning. She breathed in the soapy smell of Clara's hair as the child leaned against her on the buckboard seat. Willis reached out to pat his older sister's arm and rocked himself back and forth as he sat on Jenny's lap. "Gentle," she cautioned.

She wondered if all women in fact found sustenance not only from things nearby, like the hug of a child, but also from things outside the domestic realm. Both near and far were necessary to withstand daily demands, she supposed, and vowed that evening to write about it, to continue to fill up on a day that had reminded her of her resilience. And friends. The future wasn't so bleak after all.

Ben chirped the team forward as dusk settled

onto the roadway. Jenny leaned her head onto her husband's shoulder.

"That was a good idea, Ben, to get out."

"I have a few now and then."

"That you do." She needed to remember that.

After the inspiring day, they drove the wagon up the last incline, and Ben held the team back as they started down the grade. He sniffed the air. Jenny did too. *Smoke.*

EIGHT

Brooms of the World

1857

Their cabin was a pile of burnt timbers and black rubble.

Things don't always turn out well. "Now we have to move," she said.

Jenny was insistent, and so they moved—temporarily—into the barn.

After locating the andirons, arranging for how they'd cook and sleep, and while she nursed Willis, Jenny gave her requirements to what a new farm would need. "Within a mile—no more than two—of some kind of village where I can sell eggs and butter, take in some sewing. And horrors be, laundry."

"I'd suggest land with fruit tree possibilities," Ben said. "A place for the sheep and horses of course." Ben's requirements were of the soil, the land, Jenny's of connection, family.

"And a southern exposure," Jenny said. "I need sun whenever it appears."

"I have your list branded in my brain," Ben told her.

"When you've found one, come get me before you make any offer, all right?"

"Agreed."

He had found a farm in Yamhill County, and when Jenny and the children rode up to the gate in the wagon, her spirits lifted. The sun shone on the cleared fields, and at the top of the hill, a two-story frame house with a covered porch beckoned them to this harbor on the hillside. She named it Sunny Hillside Farm and it was all she'd ever dreamed of, she told Ben.

Moving day arrived and her sisters—minus Maggie, who had delivered her second child on the Oregon coast—arrived to assist. Even her brother Harvey came. He drove one of the teams and a wagon to the new farm about twenty miles distant from their old one. Harvey had enlisted to fight in the Yakima Wars and would leave soon. She was grateful Ben hadn't decided to go with him. The danger seemed far away and he was needed closer to home.

"Two moves are as good as a fire," Fanny told Jenny. The sisters raked up ashes, seeking anything of value that might remain. Ben had determined that it was a spark from the hearth that caused it—who knew what had been left close enough to catch aflame. The stone memorializing Jenny's mother was black as tar pitch.

Several brass buttons appeared through the swept ashes. A pair of earrings—not the ones

Shirley Ellis had helped push through Jenny's ears on the trail, thank goodness. Those Jenny had worn the day of the fire. Her *Primer*, the book she'd managed to sneak along on the trip west despite her father's wishes, was stored in a trunk in the barn along with pages of a manuscript she'd been working on. When they'd arrived to what was left that day, she went into the barn to make certain the trunk was there. She pressed two poems to her breast from it, pieces she'd written during her convalescence after Willis's arrival. She'd stored old newspapers there too, including an issue of the *Argus*, an agricultural paper that she thought could use a woman's touch. She had a poem in mind to send the editor. There must be other women who suffered loss and struggled, who might find comfort in her words.

Writing something for publication caused a small conflict for her, which had kept her from submitting her poems. Her words in print would make her both a public and a private woman. She hadn't yet shared that concern with anyone, including Ben. Writing had become a balm, different from being a reader. Hadn't she found solace and been challenged by Shakespeare or that *Lily* woman, Amelia Bloomer? Amelia also edited a newspaper, something a bit scandalous for a woman to do. Yet when Jenny was a child learning to read, her parents took subscriptions to such newspapers. And the world had become more than simply a home on the frontier.

At the same time, her father had impressed upon her that respectable women ought to keep themselves from public display. "A woman's reputation is all she has," he said. *And a man can ruin his without consequence because he is accepted in the public arena.* Her father had cautioned all his daughters about avoiding public spheres. Women were to be unnoticeable, subservient. She'd carried that attitude like a proper platter served up for herself and younger sisters on how they ought to best behave. What would happen if she wrote something controversial, not that she was intending that. Just a little poem. Yet words put into the open could arrive as something unintended by the poet.

But when she watched Clara Belle prance around the room, singing, she wondered why such joy should be kept only in the kitchen or in a church choir. Why were women with gifts not allowed to show them? And she could hear that her daughter had a gifted singing voice.

"It's good that Ben found a claim so quickly, one with a frame house bigger than your log cabin was anyway." Kate's words brought Jenny back to the cabin ruins. Kate removed her work gloves. The women all wore wrappers to protect their day dresses. The Scott girls liked color, and each wrapper was dyed differently: yellow from daffodils, blue from berries, red from blood, and if Maggie had been with them, bleached white as a baby's tooth with embroidery around the edges.

"It's the perfect time of year to move," Kate continued. April daffodils dotted the pathway between the barn and their former house, and Kate had dug up the bulbs for planting at the Duniways' new farm.

"Take a few for yourself," Jenny said. She entered what was left of the house, swept the old hearth once more. "You can plant them in pots until you know where you and John will settle." Kate planned to marry a steamboat captain in June.

"Give yourself time before you start your family," Fanny advised her. "It'll be easier on you, believe me."

"Believe her," Jenny added. "Any news, Harriet?"

"We want to wait." Harriet had married her own sweetheart.

"It's good you and William are of one accord with that," Kate said. "John and I have discussed it." She blushed. "And he doesn't want to interfere with nature."

"That's my Ben too," Jenny said. "What they don't realize is how repeated pregnancies deplete a woman's body and interfere with nature too. Look at Momma."

"Twelve of us. And there'd have been more if

she had lived," Fanny said. "Father being who he is." She wiped Eda's face. The child always had a runny nose and a frequent cough, especially in the spring. Fanny inhaled. "How does a mother survive the death of a child? At least she didn't live to witness William's lonely grave on the trail."

"Birth and death. It's a woman's lot to mark her world by those bookends." Jenny sighed. "But," she perked up. "I think we've done all the damage we can do to what's left here. The wagon's ready as soon as Ben and the men return with the teams. Let's have a cup of tea."

Harriet found the tea tin and lifted the pot from the iron over the outdoor fire they'd built. "I'm glad you found Clara's silver spoon though. Momma snuck that along."

"I could write a poem about all the things we brought that Papa never knew about." Jenny laughed.

"Do that," Fanny said. "I managed to bring needles, right out in the open. Father never said a word."

"He knew you'd need them to patch his pants," Kate said.

Copies of the *Argus* Jenny had stacked and tied were ready to be put into the wagon.

"Are you saving all those issues?" Sarah Maria, the youngest sister, asked.

"They can be cut up for dress patterns. And

they'll be useful if I ever teach again," Jenny said. "The *Argus* deals with hide prices and women's recipes, so the men think we can't get into too much trouble reading it. But the articles that stimulate the mind is what people need, even farm wives. At least I do. So I read *News of the World* and the *Spectator* too. I just don't accept everything as gospel." She lifted her eyes in time to watch a breeze flutter across the field, brushing bachelor buttons, grasses, the movement easing toward them like an invisible wave until it reached the girls and cooled Jenny's face. She looked up at the sky. No sign of a storm. "Did you see that?"

"See what?" Sarah Maria asked.

"The way you can watch weather change. All was quiet, and then with barely a flutter, the entire field began to wave and carried the breeze right here."

Kate—the beautiful sister, as Jenny thought of her—stared at the timbers.

"Never mind," Jenny said. "I suppose I'm twisted as an old oak, finding metaphors where no one else does. It's that change happens so invisibly at times, one hardly notices. Like Clara Belle. One day she was babbling as though she carried on a conversation with inflections and bursts of sounds that made no sense, and then within a day, voilà! She said, 'Where's Pa?' "

"Your teaching gifts are showing then," Kate said.

"Maybe. Time is moving. The world is moving."

Jenny kept her gaze at the field where all the foliage whispered and aspen leaves fluttered. She decided then to write something down about what she'd seen, how change crept up on people when not expected, how the language of the landscape spoke as loudly as words sometimes.

Jenny shook ash from the straw broom. She'd swept through this mess soon after the fire, and they hoped the spring rains might have washed up other treasures. But she thought they had taken all they could from this hardscrabble place.

"Do you want to keep that?" Sarah Maria reached for the broom. She had celebrated her tenth birthday and looked up to her older sisters, whom she didn't get to see much as she lived with Fanny and Amos. She appeared to relish being brought this time to help out. Jenny watched her grasp that broom, a woman's tool, and stand the way men held rifles in studio photographs as though they were a defense as well as a stabilizer.

"An ode to the broom," Jenny said, using her teacher's voice. "It sweeps up dirt, then gets put back into the closet until the next mess. Not unlike a woman. Brooms of the world we are."

"We all have something of Momma's, I think," Fanny said. She shifted baby Eda to her other hip. Eda had her mother's deep-set eyes and looked sober and wise beyond her almost three years.

And she had full, arched eyebrows like Sarah's. She looked pale, Jenny thought.

"I've got Momma's thimble," Kate said. "And you've got the spoon and her stories."

"Being sickly kept me inside a lot, so she talked to me. But I also saw how hard she worked, how tired she was, all the time." Jenny saved the tea leaves in a small linen bag. She stuck it in her apron pocket. There might be another cup inside it.

"Having children every other year didn't help."

"Let that be a lesson to us all," Harriet said. "I have a twist of her hair I wove into my bridal veil."

"I remember that. It was lovely," Kate said.

"If you want to wear it, you can. It can be your something borrowed."

"Or something old," Fanny added.

"It's nice you've had time to plan for your wedding, Kate." Jenny sounded wistful and she knew she shouldn't. She'd made the choice to marry Ben as soon as she had. It wasn't like there was a mass of suitors. Well, that one—Bunter—who had written her a letter and acted like he was doing her a favor in proposing. He'd since written letters to the *Argus* editor about strident women and how he was as eligible a bachelor as any and the government made it hard on him to compete with other landed gents who could snatch up an Oregon woman who brought land with her. Land was all that man had wanted. Ben had wanted something more, and she was grateful for that. If she hadn't loved him to begin with, how would she have endured these past years as they struggled together?

"It has been fun to be courted by a captain over time. But he's quite certain of his preferences," Kate said. "He picked out our house with little say from me. Not like your Sunny Hillside Farm you and Ben chose together. I like the name you gave it. It has a happy tone to it."

"Near beautiful Lafayette. The French would be so pleased," Jenny said. "It is a good part of the valley. Orchards abound." Lafayette was the county seat, so stores were but a few miles from the farm. "Maybe it won't be so lonely during the rainy season. We women can get together now and then, even in the rain."

Ben and her brother Harvey and others brought the teams and empty wagons back and chatted to her sisters while Ben harnessed the horses to the wagon the women had loaded.

"It's a good place, Jenny," Harvey said. "You'll thrive there."

"Women thrive wherever we're planted," Jenny said. But she knew the soil, the tending, and the exposure to the sun made all the difference in how well one flourished.

She turned back one last time to look at the burned-out carcass, witness the rebuilt barn and fences after the tornado and all that had happened at this hardscrabble place. She wished the new owners good fortune. They had a nice barn and fresh-peeled logs for their cabin to begin with anyway. She hoped for better things at Sunny Hillside Farm. Give the neighbors something good to gossip about the Duniways now, instead of clucking their pitying tongues at their tragedies.

She faced forward on the seat and watched the wagons ahead, carrying harnesses, shovels, forks. "Wait! Let's take the broom."

"I'll get you a new one," Ben said.

"No. That one is my symbol of endurance."

Ben pulled up the team. "Little Toot, ride back and get your sister's old broom. Where'd you leave it?"

"Leaned it up against the hearthstones." Jenny pointed.

"I'll have it for you in a minute, Sister."

Little Toot kneed his mount and rode back to bring her symbol of a woman's work—and maybe of her life. Old brooms swept away dust and disappointment, but both came back.

NINE

Ora et Labora

November 1857

"They published it. *The Burning Forest Tree* by Jenny Glen." Jenny put the newspaper on the table while Ben drank his morning coffee. "What do you think?"

The sun had peeked its nose above the horizon, casting long shadows over the green. It promised to be a pretty day, fluffy clouds pushing November gray away. The babies slept, a moment of reprieve. Little Toot had grown into "Jerry." After Harvey returned from the war, Jerry, now a wisp-of-whiskers teen starting to shave, had gone off to live with their father and stepmother, helping his father farm and work at the sawmill near Forest Grove. Jenny had resisted Jerry's leaving, but the appeal of his being able to go to school in Tualatin Academy won her over. Education was critical for all people. Harvey was right about that but wrong that he thought it less critical for girls, and that if someone wanted schooling for their children past the eighth grade, they should pay for it and not expect the government to do it. Her argument—exchanged over the meal the evening of Harvey's celebratory return—was that it was in the country's best interest to have educated, critical thinkers, and providing for it for free with all citizens helping to pay for it, for as long as someone gained from it, made sense to her. Their siblings present had groaned at the rising level of voices, and it was Jerry who had eased the temperature down and said, "Let's just eat."

Harvey worked now too for their father in the sawmill and took college preparatory classes—that he paid for himself, he reminded them all. He'd been hardened by the war, living in harsh conditions, and didn't have much room for looking after those Jenny saw as less fortunate through no fault of their own. She knew firsthand how a storm or a fire could set a family back. Jenny watched her youngest brother eat. Thin as a bird he was. He'd lost weight since leaving Sunny Hillside. Like her, he tended to frailness, and like her, he would push himself to exhaustion to prove he could. She knew he dreamed of becoming a lawyer, taking on cases to help others. She'd do everything she could to help make that happen. She knew about dreams.

She'd burned the midnight oil to write that poem and had overcome her fears by taking it to the *Argus* editor. He'd accepted it.

"Abigail Duniway. That's how it'll be attributed," the editor said.

"Oh. No." *What will people think? If they don't like it, it'll bring ill repute onto Ben.* She should have thought of that before. "No. Ah, let's say Jenny Glen wrote it." Her pen name. The editor had shrugged and wrote it on the copy she'd presented.

"You're Jenny Glen?" Ben's blue eyes gazed up at her, held surprise. He read the poem again. "I like the part where you talk about the air being like no other. And 'I feel no loneliness.' I like that best." He handed the *Argus* back to her. "I don't want you to be lonely. That's why I invite friends over. But why didn't you use Jenny Duniway. Or Abigail Duniway? Are you—"

"No, no. I thought it might bring negative attention to you if people don't like it. To us."

"Naw. It's a little poem. The womenfolk will like it. Well done, Wife." He changed the subject. "We finished planting those five acres. Apples soon. This land is perfect for it." He stood, tipping back the chair as he lifted his leg up and over on his way to grab his hat, kiss Jenny, then head out the door.

"My moment of glory," she said as she lifted Ben's chair back up and pushed it under the table. "Your father did like it though," she told Clara Belle. "Now we'll see if anyone else does." Willis woke and she soon lost thoughts of poetry as she washed his face of mush and took him from the high chair. Clara made her way out the door to wave at her father in the fields and sing a little song to him. "Later I might show your father my column they call 'The Farmer's Wife.' They published it anonymously." Willis looked back at her with inquisitive brown eyes. "Pretty soon people will be talking about that, if not my poem."

She had begun with the anonymous letters to the editor and did a little jig around the wooden floors when she saw the first one in print. She'd signed it *The Farmer's Wife*. It recounted an episode when Ben had offered to help her with the laundry that turned into a tale of stumble and trouble, resulting in more work than either of them planned. She made light of Ben's awkwardness—she referred to him as "the Farmer"—and yes, he was the misery of the episode, but she had wanted to show that a woman's work took coordination and effort and could be as complicated as that of planting a field of straight rows or operating a sawmill safely.

After supper, Ben picked up the paper. "Did you read this, Jenny? The Farmer's Wife is quite a cutup. Looks like we weren't the only ones who had a bad washday, though she makes it funnier than ours was."

Jenny remained silent, her heart pounding.

"Say." He looked up at her. "Did you write this?"

"I did. Are you upset?"

"Me? No. It makes hay out of straw." He laughed, tapped his finger on the page. "I bet you get some letters though."

And she did. People said they liked the Farmer's Wife and hoped she'd continue her stories. During the long rainy months, she'd written of isolation and how their being closer to a town had made the showery days less dreary, knowing once a week they could traverse the muddy roads to go to church, if not to market. She planned to slip in a few words about the value of women's work and such—if the editor allowed it. The copyeditor started putting a block around Jenny's letters, to make them stand out, as though they were a column.

She speaks my heart, a reader wrote. It was then Jenny knew that words had power. Her words, at least, got others to respond. Wasn't that the purpose of words—to get movement, to share the burdens and even joys?

She got braver. She wrote not about who visited whom or of church events. She left those topics to others. Jenny's subjects pushed toward the fate of women, how hard they worked, how some men took better care of their horses than of their wives and daughters. She charged that once men gained wealth to hire workers, they never thought to bring such hired help to their mates (Kate's husband John's hiring help excluded) and how they acted like they didn't want to tax a woman's constitution by allowing her to attend public events with men. And certainly many men did not want women to vote—heaven forbid, and a few men thought heaven did actually forbid a woman's vote—but it was fine to treat a woman like a beast of burden.

"The Farmer's Wife is a peevish, ill-natured, irritable, fault-finding common scold." The letter wasn't signed. She wasn't surprised. She didn't mind being called a scold, but a common one? She was better than that, and she wrote as much in her follow-up letter to "anonymous upset reader."

Who is the Farmer's Wife, advising men how to treat their families? She should stop her malicious babbling at once.

Her husband needs to set her down and teach her a thing or two.

Most responses were anonymous, but Mr. Bunter had written that such a witchery point of view had no place in a family press and he was canceling his subscription.

She'd purposely not shown Ben those letters nor the responses the newspaper had printed either. Ben didn't read all that much, and some comments made her cheeks burn when she saw them referring to her as that "common scold" and even a "hag."

Those words stung, but they also fueled. How could simply pointing out the importance of treating women like people and not beasts of burden create such an uproar? She wasn't sure what they'd say once she got her novel published, and she would. But whether she'd use her own name or not, she wasn't sure. How far could she go using words as brooms to sweep up trouble and even stir up more trouble that needed stirring up? She'd taken a risk and now would have to face the consequences.

When Jenny wasn't finding respite in writing, she worked and often mused of what other women did to overcome the drudgery of their days. How did they build their spirits up? She'd think of loftier things, but then the daily regimen would take over.

It being Monday, that included laundry. "Why Monday?" she told Clara, who chased Willis around the table as the toddler squealed in delight. "Why not do laundry on Saturday when clean clothes can be worn on Sunday, the very next day," she told her children. And when the following day a woman could have respite in the pews, laundry being the hardest of labors. *Ora et labora.* Prayer and work. Harvey had given her that Latin phrase. He was teaching himself Latin and Greek. *How fortunate for him he has the nights to study.*

At least today it wasn't raining, so as she

moved between their frame house and the laundry cottage at the farm, she wouldn't get doused and the clothes would dry faster.

She heated the water on the cookstove, lamenting that she didn't have the strength to lift the heavier cast-iron pots and instead had to dip pitchers into the scalding water, then carry them to the big wooden tubs where she'd add the lye soap and stir the sheets and mud-stained jeans with a stick as wide as an oar. Then into a second tub of rinse water before hanging them with split pegs on the line. Before the children were born, Ben built fires beneath the cauldrons so she didn't have to carry the water, but she'd heard tales of children falling into the tubs or tripping into the fire. Twice in her own childhood she'd rescued both Kate and Harvey from laundry fires. *I must remind Harvey that I once saved his life.*

At least here she stoked the cookstove, feeding it kindling, and it took the chill off the laundry cottage in the fall and winter; heated it to a misery in the summers. Despite the work it took—and how Monday always ended with her joints aching worse than any other day—she preferred this safer method. In the distance, she could see Ben and his workers planting apple trees and wished she had help as she pegged the sheets.

The truth, she told herself, was that she'd rather be teaching or writing, almost anything except laundry or other "domestic arts." Her sisters were so much better at them than she was. Fanny could whip up a meal for a dozen with hardly a second thought, even with her Eda's runny nose and Lillian's weepy eyes. "Something in the air bothers them," Fanny had written in her latest letter. Maggie had two children as well, but her boat-house-store dodging in and out of ports on the coast was still as tidy as her quilt stitches. "Clean house, clean heart," she said. "You only need what's functional."

"I'll decide later about the clutter," Jenny had told Maggie. "The children don't mind and the floors are clean. Cobwebs grow overnight. Can't be helped. Spiders get free rides inside on the logs."

She supposed it was some small comfort knowing that all of her sisters—and women everywhere—were washing clothes on this day of the week as she was. Kate would be doing laundry too, but John had hired help for her, and it was only the two of them! Such a small basket of dirty clothes. Envy stuck out its tongue.

Laundry was such a thankless task having to be done over and over. She'd told Harriet's inventive husband that he ought to come up with some way to make laundry easier and not just spend his inventive mind on doodads like punched patterns in tin lanterns. She'd told Ben that too, and he'd said, as he often did to her suggestions, "I'll think over it."

When she wasn't composing poems or articles while she spun wool or churned cream, she worried over money. Teaching had once given her currency to call her own. Ben listened to Jenny at least. He still thought though that men were entitled to hunt and fish and "jaw" and visit and offer undiminished hospitality as respite from their labor no matter the season nor their income. Women had no such hope to interrupt their daily demands. He didn't always know how inventive she had to get to spread their cash or trade in ways that kept the family—and the many friends Ben brought around—fed.

He let her save a little of her egg-and-butter money for her books, papers, and lead, and she had proposed they buy a small house in town where they might spend winter months so the children could attend school. "A man should be responsible for financial matters," he'd said, but he went along with the Lafayette house purchase. "It's how we look after our women, protect you." But what of those men as she imagined Mr. Bunter was? Who protects those wives? And widows? A woman needed control over her income, but laws would have to be remade to make that so. And men made all the laws. How would that ever change?

Her hands were chapped by the harsh lye soap she used to launder clothes. Jenny prayed while she folded the "underlings," as her mother had called the unmentionables. She wished she could find peace in the everyday work instead of resentment of its daily-ness, its weekly-ness, its constant-ness. The domestic arts did not make her thrive. Instead, they were bars on a window women had to look through to accomplish anything. She stood and pressed both hands on her lower back. She'd need to stop and prepare a noon meal for Ben and his helpers. She walked toward the house, checking the line to see if those clothes were dry enough to remove and she could prepare to hang up others after the cleanup from the noon break. She felt a trickle between her legs. She still bled, especially on Mondays.

Jenny finished the laundry as the day waned, bringing evening cooling. She rested her body on a bench Ben had built outside the laundry cottage. Clara's clear voice belted out the alphabet song to Willis, who tried the same but babbled an up-and-down rhythm instead. "Clara, you have your daddy's voice, and poor Willis, you got mine."

Why she pondered women's labor so much, she wasn't certain, but women spent so much time in work, praying for ease. Except for childbirth, she'd had no time to lie and rest. There was always something more to do. She had written that ode to the broom, singing its praises as a sign of what women were—laborers in the never-ending fields.

"A woman should get paid for her housework." She said it out loud to Ben.

"How would that work?" Ben asked. He settled on the bench beside her.

"If her husband paid her, she could hire others who liked to sweep and clean and tend, women who did that well. And she could do what she was called to. That would allow a woman to take on work more meaningful to her, like asking questions. Why couldn't a woman make her way doing what she liked to do as much as a man? Why shouldn't she get land in her own name even without a husband? The Farmer's Wife might need to take on that subject."

"I hope it doesn't become too obvious who the Farmer's Wife is, Jenny."

She turned to him. "Does that worry you?" She didn't want to make his life complicated nor somehow tarnish the Duniway name.

He was thoughtful. "I suppose not. Must be a sign of a wise farmer if he can allow his wife to speak her mind. At least you're not up on some stage like I hear those Eastern women sometimes do."

"Yes, public speaking is the realm of men. My father always says that." She watched the sunset turn the world a rosy hue. "But something might be so important that it would be worth risking a woman's reputation to speak her voice in public, as a man can, don't you think?"

Ben sat silent. "I'll think over it."

TEN

Life, Death, and What Is Sure

1858

They'd endured more than celebrated the Christmas holidays. Her niece, the sickly Eda, had passed. For Jenny, the very thought of the death of Clara or Willis caused such heartache that she sometimes couldn't catch her breath. Her mother had grieved her firstborn, and then another son died when Jenny was eleven and the boy only one month old, followed by their sister Alice, born and died the same day, the autumn before they left Illinois. The work hadn't stopped for her mother with any of those deaths, and it wouldn't for Fanny either. But neighbors helped. Families brought food and talked softly while preparing Eda for burial, putting all the hopes and dreams for her gentled into the wooden casket that the Lafayette furniture maker crafted. There was nothing more forlorn, Jenny decided, than an empty child-size casket being brought into the house—except one holding a child when it was taken back out.

It made Jenny want to grab up her two children and set them inside a fleece-lined basket and hold them there, prevent death from reaching its greedy fingers into their lives. But of course, living held risk, the very act of breathing meant another step into the unknown. How one took those steps would shape the character of those around you—Fanny's other children, her husband, Amos. Men had their own struggles with such a loss. Women suffered differently. Jenny vowed to visit Fanny often, help her with the daily tasks that must go on, and put her own struggles and fatigue aside when she was with her. And she wouldn't mention a word about the restrictions placed on women to mourn in silence and not too long, as though there were a timeline for grief to close the cracks in a family's foundation.

She must also include such loss in her novels— for any frontier reader would relate. There wasn't a single family who hadn't experienced a death of some kind. She would attempt to capture life inside her stories . . . give new meaning to the tragedies they couldn't control.

"It's something you're good at, Fanny. It will give you a sense of accomplishment, when right now you likely can't feel much of anything except anguish."

Fanny sighed. "I have no skills. I couldn't even keep my girl alive."

"You did everything you could for her. Illness

. . . there's so much we don't control, Fanny. Only how we respond to what life hands us. And you have a talent I desperately need. Please."

Jenny had opened Hope School in the Lafayette house. She'd thought of the idea while washing clothes and wondered if mundane tasks might indeed be the catalyst for creativity. She got Ben's agreement with the promise she'd be back on Sunny Hillside each weekend with the children and all summer long.

"Not much of a married life though." Ben had chewed on his pipe stem. He never put tobacco in the bowl.

"Men go off to the mines. Or they work large ranches East and leave their families to operate their farms. It's what people have to do. I'll make up stews, and you can fix potatoes and bacon easy enough. You'll have plenty of eggs. I'll still make butter to sell."

She could out-argue him, and he'd agreed, so Jenny had her subscription school she called Hope, and now Fanny was enlisted to help with the school's Christmas pageant.

Jenny admitted to herself that she liked the drama, the rehearsals, hearing children read the lines she wrote telling a story of a lost present and how it had been magically found and everyone lived happily. And then the grand performance. She had actors for the Bible story, and each student had a part. After all, the

Christmas story was for everyone. She dressed Willis up in a fleece, and he moaned "Baaa! Baaa!" even when he wasn't supposed to. Clara sang. One of the tallest boys was Joseph, and her youngest sister with the beautiful eyebrows, Sarah Maria, acted as Mary, who had to shout above the bleating sheep. The others were either shepherds or angels, and they had more than three wise men, who also had to yell above the bleating ram. Everyone laughed, even Fanny and Amos, grieving parents finding comfort in the family and friends who walked beside them as they were reminded of the story of Christ's birth and promise.

Jenny accepted the congratulations from her students' parents and that night sank into bed happy.

Her best work had been convincing Fanny that her labor was worthy and that there was life after grief. She loved seeing Fanny enjoy herself. As she told Ben, "She accepted my few coins to reimburse her for her stitching too."

"Always working to honor women's labor," Ben said. "Well done, Wife."

Spring was approaching, and Jenny knew she'd have to close the school down and be available for the farm work, especially cooking for all the men. Ben had enjoyed the winter, coming into Lafayette midweek and fixing meals so

116

Jenny had more time for lesson preparations. He told of ways that other families adjusted to the challenges of frontier finance.

"There are gold strikes in Idaho." Ben turned the bacon and the aroma filled the large kitchen. Jenny sat at a day desk he'd built for her. "I was thinking this fall I might go there and make a strike like I did in Jacksonville before I met you."

"We'd be separated even more than this past winter." She looked up from her foolscap.

"If I made a strike, you wouldn't have to have the school. We'd have enough with the farm."

He doesn't see how much I love the teaching, having a part in contributing to the family through more than just laundry.

He smiled at Clara, who sat waiting for the bacon. "I'd miss my pumpkins, that's sure."

"I'm no pumpkin, Pa," Clara said. "But Willis is a squash."

"Am not."

"Are so."

"Children." Jenny's voice stopped the fracas. Ben did enjoy his time with Clara and Willis. He was a good husband, despite his tendency to visit and bring back friends—at his leisure—for her to serve them supper. And he didn't mind cooking for the family, which was a boon to her, though she couldn't imagine him frying potatoes for his guests or hired men.

Once they'd had a row over how his "guests"

were treated. Two of his bachelor friends had stopped by Sunny Hillside Farm after the supper hour when Ben wasn't home. Jenny had been quilting—not her most favorite activity—and she kept on as the men chatted with each other about whether Oregon would become a state, how they'd lose their autonomy as a territory able to make their own laws once Oregon joined the union. They talked around her, didn't ask her opinion. Eventually realizing there would be no food forthcoming, they made some comment about it.

"Oh, were you waiting to be fed? Had I known that's what you stopped by for, I could have told you an hour ago and you could have made your way back to your own kitchen." Which they then did and later told Ben about it. He'd been livid.

"You provide when you can, knowing that someday someone will help you," he had told her, his voice raised. "Hospitality is the bedrock of this country."

"No. Work is the bedrock, and I was working, but not to prepare their suppers. You get them married off so they can eat at home." *Poor souls who accept those proposals seeking stomach-soothing over love.* "I'd say I'm not alone in my feelings about this. Why should women be expected to take care of everyone? It was the end of a long day, and they expected me to wait on them just because I was a woman."

"They're neighbors."

"Who should eat at home or when invited." Silence. Then, "The Farmer's Wife might have words to say about such frontier hospitality. It's the pioneer women who are expected to be hospitable while you men make the rules about what that looks like."

"As it should be," Ben said.

"Maybe one day it'll be different. Ouch." She had poked the needle into her finger, sucked on it. Her Farmer's Wife gave her an outlet to express her upset, but it didn't change anything for the lives of women and that had been her intent and still was.

Her finger bled.

"Let me kiss that and make it better," Ben said.

She let him. He said he understood that women got little rest and that she especially didn't seem to know how to play.

"We women have no time to play."

"You need to laugh a little more," he'd told her and kissed her hand again. "Try to be a little more accommodating."

"Holy cow chips. One more task to put on my list." She had sighed. "I'll think on it."

"Good. Now let me hold you and kiss that pain away. I hate arguing with you."

"Because I almost always win."

He had grinned at that, and she let him pull her close.

Come spring, they were expecting another Duniway.

ELEVEN

Surety

January 1859

Jenny listened. She'd been busy stuffing duck feathers for comforters while frying potatoes for their supper. She was as big as a washtub, carrying this third child, and her belly bumped against the table, so her back hurt as she stretched to fill the comforter. She wasn't sure how she felt about another child so soon, but Ben wanted a big family. She blew feathers from her nose as she heard Ben say to yet another guest in their living room something about "surety." *Ben is offering to secure something?* When she later recalled this day, it would be with the scent of bacon swirling around the house, children chattering, and her hands inside the softness of feathers, while her mind pondered uncertainty.

She didn't know well the man who'd be staying for supper. He'd stopped by and talked apple markets with Ben previously, as she remembered. Since the time she hadn't been hospitable to two of Ben's bachelor friends, she rarely said anything about the surprise meals (as she called them) that she had to serve.

She peered into the room and saw something legal-looking in three folds lying on the slab table in front of them. *This is not good.* She put the feathers aside, sneezed—as she often did around duck feathers—and moved the frying pan off the burner with a scraping sound, then entered the room where Ben watched the children and "jawed" with Mr. Markham. *Yes, that's his name. Bob Markham.*

"What high finance is happening in our living room?" She kept her voice light. "I heard the word 'surety.' We can't afford a cosigned note, Ben."

"Like good Oregonians, we look after each other," Ben said. His eyebrow twitched. *He's nervous about my interfering.* "We're helping Bob here make his investment in the field. Don't you like my pun, Wife?" Ben beamed.

He's trying to distract. Her heart started pounding a little faster. She reached for Willis and plopped him on her hip. He squirmed. Her belly got in the way, so she let him down.

"And how are we helping Bob, here, become outstanding in his field?" She heard the sarcasm in her voice and saw Ben frown.

"Shouldn't your little lady be protected from thoughts of business and investments?" Jenny heard the challenge to Ben's "head of household" status in those words.

"I'm signing a note at two percent per month, Abigail."

He's called me Abigail!

"They'll be compounded semiannually until paid, but Bob can then get his loan. He's good for it. You'll manage your money well, won't you, Bob?"

"No question about it."

She could feel bile rise beneath the baby she carried. "That's a hefty interest rate." She turned to Ben. "If Bob"—she emphasized his name—"fails to pay, we could be ruined meeting that kind of obligation in his stead."

"Now, Jenny, let's not air our underlings in public."

He's offended that I bring up a concern? She was offended that he hadn't.

"You'll always be protected, don't you worry now. Is supper ready? I think I smell that bacon frying but no rasher of potatoes as yet." He used his fingers to gesture her back into the kitchen the way she clucked at the chickens. She forced a smile, returned to the kitchen, helping three-year-old Willis onto the bench. "Clara, sit. I'll serve you now." She banged the pans on the stove, prepared the children's plates, fed them, and cleaned their faces, and when the men came in, she served them but chose not to sit with them while they ate, going to her bedroom to write and await Bob's departure. She was as frightened as when Ben got lost in the fog.

Ben signed three notes for Bob. And they

argued, fear fueling her words until Ben yelled, actually shouted at her. "Cease, woman. I can take no more. It's done."

Their words led to nothing but them curled with their backs away from each other—after Jenny bathed the children and Ben read to them, followed by Jenny cleaning up the table and the kitchen. What could she do? *I'm powerless.*

"It's a lot of money, Ben," she said in the morning, not wanting to challenge him nor return the argument to its burning state.

"He's good for it. Don't you worry. Apple markets are excellent. Wheat is too. Remember that proverb. 'He who waters will himself be watered.'"

She considered that. "I'm not sure watering our neighbor's field means we should risk our own supplies though, and just expect God to deliver our water from somewhere else."

Ben patted her crossed hands as they sat at the table. "You worry over much," he said. "Haven't we done well here on Sunny Hillside Farm. And your Lafayette school, in season? Everything is turning out fine."

"And I'm grateful. But my egg-and-butter money is our only cash until fall. And Californians are planting again, so not buying our wheat. Several of our neighbors have opted out for schooling, lacking the cash for tuition, they say. It's worrisome. Something is happening all around us. It makes me nervous. I feel . . . vulnerable and—"

"You're oversensitive. It'll be better when the baby comes. Work on your story. You always do better when you've had a time to write—even those farmer's letters."

"I get to blow off steam like our kettle," she said. "Writing helps turn the heat down. But it doesn't ease my worries."

"You'll always be sheltered," he assured her. Then added, "First lamb was born last night. We need to start the watch."

"So much for my writing," she said, though she'd get a few lines in—memorizing them— while she huddled in the lambing shed awaiting the arrival of lambs whose mothers often needed help. All mothers did. She would trust Ben. What else could she do?

Oregon's status changed from territory to statehood on Valentine's Day 1859. In March, Hubert arrived. He was a smaller baby than Willis had been, and though she bled again, the doctor had been there and stitched her up. "Three babies," she'd cooed to the round face. He was a plump child. "My best delivery yet. Don't tell the others." His eyes followed hers.

A month later, Jenny made another delivery— her book. *Captain Gray's Company or Crossing the Plains and Living in Oregon* was published.

"I did it, Ben." She handed him the book. "Turns out it's the first published novel in the newest state. Will you read it?"

"I'll think on it," he teased, then realized she couldn't decide if he jested. "Of course I will. I'm married to an author. How about that?" She beamed. "Not right now. But I will read it."

That night she watched him while he turned the pages, then left him to put the children in their beds. She sang to them one verse, then stopped, saying, "Singing's not my talent, is it?"

Clara Belle answered with her own sweet notes. "We all have our gifts, Momma. You always say that."

"Singing is one of yours."

"And you write, Momma."

"Yes, I do. I hope your father likes my story."

"Is Papa in it?" Willis asked.

"Hmm. Maybe a little of him is. As are each of you. It's hard not to include the ones we love in a story." She lowered her voice, whispered, "There's a villain too."

"What's that?" Willis tucked the quilt around him so Clara Belle, lying next to him in the featherbed, wouldn't touch him. "What's a 'vill in'?"

"Someone the heroine of the story has to fight against. It wouldn't be much of a story if she didn't have someone to fight against to win her cause."

"So it's good when Willis and I fight? It makes a better story?"

"Not all tales need arguments." She kissed their foreheads. "And sisters and brothers should never fight. They should look after each other. Now get some rest."

Her sisters applauded when she handed a copy to them at a family gathering after church. She hoped to be invited to the Presbyterian academy, though novels weren't exactly a preference of the literary crowd.

"Congratulations," Harvey told her. "After I read it, I'll place a copy in the school library. If it's suitable."

"Why, thank you. I think."

"There are few novels in the collection. They're somewhat of an anomaly, more of a curiosity than anything learned, of course."

"Are they checked out?"

"Oh, of course. By students studying fiction as a format. And by what I call simpering women who are somehow engaged by such. They have to make sure it's suitable for our students."

"I would expect nothing less. If you reject it, of course, as not good enough, I'll have to take an ad out in the paper and mention that it's banned. That'll make my sales go up." *Might they reject it? Could it be so bad?*

He grunted.

Jenny waited for the reviews, but no one wrote

a one. Except for her family, it appeared that her book landed like a stone in a pond, making no waves at all.

Her father told her the family back in Illinois would love it, as it was a story of the Scott crossing with the sadness of the widow's death, "being your mother's, I assume" and poor "Effie—I guess that's you? Having to work so hard once they arrive."

"It's not me, Papa. It's a novel."

Her sisters said little after they'd had time to read it. She'd sent a copy to Shirley Ellis in Sacramento and hadn't heard back from her friend, either.

Ben had deemed it "interesting," and then added, "You'll get your saddle under you with the next one."

"So it's not appealing?"

He shrugged. "What do I know about novels and such? And firstfruits aren't always the best."

Then the reviews came, and she knew why her sisters and friends hadn't known what to say. Newspaper editors did. "Bad taste" and "slang language"—"simplistic plot full of sickening love stories." Tears seeped from her eyes as she read them. Harold Bunter wrote a scathing letter lamenting "Poor Mr. Duniway" married to such a wretched writer. *Poor Ben!*

The *Argus*, that had sold more advertisements and increased subscriptions from the letters from her "Farmer's Wife," wrote nothing at all. Not a single word of praise or piercing. They simply carried the ad and the price. It was the first commercially published book in the new state, and the *Argus* didn't even do a story about that?

Ben stroked her arm as they sat side by side on the divan while she nursed Hubert. "Maybe it was your strident letters about men and their treatment of their women where you used your own name now and then, maybe that's why people haven't taken to the book."

She wanted to blame someone for the disappointing response. *I hate to hear what Harvey thinks, if he even reads it.* "But my characters, at least one of them, is the proper wife, the one who wouldn't speak in public or challenge her domineering employer, and eventually the lovers find each other again and marry. It's a happy story. The husband's not the villain, the employer is."

"But the men don't come out so well."

"She has failures too. And her brother sends her to school. Some of the men are good." She cried now—for the wasted hours writing, for the time away from the children and from Ben, and for what? "It's all rubbish."

"Jenny, Jenny." He pulled her closer. "Celebrate that you not only delivered a child, a 'little man,' a future voter in the cradle as you put what mothers do—"

"That might have been too forceful," Jenny said. "About women making voters and not just giving birth. My last 'Farmer's Wife' might have turned some readers away."

"I think you write better about real things than imagined ones. You birthed a book while teaching and taking care of the little ones and me. That's quite an accomplishment, Mrs. Duniway. Quite amazing indeed."

"Everything didn't turn out all right, now did it?"

"It's what comes after that matters," Ben said. He thumbed her lashes and brushed her cheeks of tears. "Best thing to do when you're bucked off a horse is to get back on. Ride another one."

"You think so?"

"I do. You found satisfaction in the work, didn't you? Isn't that part of your scribbling? It can't be all about how others like it or don't. You'll learn from this."

She wiped her eyes. The pain ached, made her wince as she took a deep breath. "Will I learn something from this?" The scathing reviews cut like a knife, but the wounds would heal and she'd see what she could do differently in the next novel. She might have to publish it herself and anonymously write a good review. But first she'd read those rotten rejections to glean what she could learn from them. *Yes. That's one way to make things turn out better. Learn.* It was the only surety she could count on.

TWELVE

The Farmer

1860

Sunshine warmed the earth, and early plantings ensued throughout the region. Abigail—since the publication of her novel she went by her official name, Abigail Duniway—loved her view on Sunny Hillside and only wished she had more time to sit and enjoy it. Or had a chair that felt better on her back. Or didn't have the morning sickness. Again. This child would be due next February. Abigail wrote now too for the *Oregon Farmer.* Her essays included information about the economics of the area, advised women to "buy local," and took on California merchants who had complained about Oregon butter costs. She proposed a union for women who "do the work and get little of the profits." She advocated for hired help for farmers' wives; urged women—and men—to save; and preached about the value of staying out of debt. She winced when she wrote those words, knowing that Ben had signed those notes. She still signed her columns "The Farmer's Wife" and often gave examples of what "the Farmer" himself had been up to, personalizing her pieces. She was paid small amounts for her articles, whose topics continued to garner interest both from the ladies of the region and also at men's gatherings. *Words have power,* she told herself more than once. But did they really have the power to change a woman's lot?

The extra money, though, felt good in her teapot bank, so words were changing their financial lot. It wasn't much, but if disaster struck, she would have a next step to take and a little money to make it.

Her sister Kate gave birth "with ease," she told Abigail. John was an attentive husband, and Kate's life seemed more sublime than Abigail's. She was happy for her sister but a bit wishful for those hours Kate had to read or simply sit and spend time with her baby. "You have time too," Kate told her when she commented.

"Holy cow chips, when?"

"Early morning. But I suspect you're writing then."

"I am. And during school days, I'm preparing lessons."

"We all make our choices."

"Yes, we do." Writing was one of Abigail's. Becoming financially secure was another.

The summer eased its way into their lives with daily toils. Maybe Kate was right and she wouldn't know a moment's leisure if it washed her with warm water in a copper tub. Work consumed, though she did find joy in attending meetings at the Butte Creek Store, startling the men when she and a few stalwart women showed up not to speak, mind you, but to listen to the conversation about the fall election when a Republican had a chance to become president—an Illinoisan whom they had known as a lawyer from their small town back east.

Their wheat harvest that year was abundant, filling the warehouses along the Willamette River so ships could take their goods afar. Ben was happy and Abigail was too when America did elect its first Republican president in Abraham Lincoln. Abigail hoped he could stop the spread of slavery. All people should be free, in Abigail's mind. Regardless of race—or sex.

Close to home, Sunny Hillside Farm proved productive too. Abigail thought there might be enough to buy a few household conveniences like a self-propelled butter churn and decent chairs, but Ben informed her that he'd spent $500 on the purchase of an adjoining farm. "We wouldn't want someone else to come in under our noses and take that good property."

"I could have used a new wringer. And I've read that a carpet sweeper has been patented. I'd like to have such a thing. Honestly, Ben, the hardest housework I do is sweeping. It agonizes my back no end. Couldn't the needs of the farmer's wife get a little attention?"

"Your back is likely worse now because you're expecting."

"Whatever the reason, it's hard labor sweeping the carpets and floors with a broom."

"I'll sweep for you."

"And where will you be when I'm gathering crumbs from beneath the table? You'll be out on that additional farm with your paid helpers while I'm in here preparing food for them."

"Now, Jenny. It's in our best interest."

"Our best interest would be to get out of those notes, to be able to set aside money. We're paying interest and I haven't seen Bob around reimbursing us." She grunted at Ben's silence and returned to her churn.

Wilke arrived February 13, 1861, the day before Oregon's birthday—and right after six more states seceded from the Union. Abigail worried there would be war, but there was nothing she could do about it. Instead she delivered another boy for Ben to cuddle as he loved to do. Clara, at seven, was old enough to help by looking after Willis and Hubert the way that Abigail—as an older sister—had looked after her siblings while her mother gave birth. Clara, with her dark curls and puppy-dog eyes, big and brown and round, followed Abigail's directions, then got out of the way when the midwife arrived.

"Good girl, Clara. Momma will be all right."

Abigail prayed even as she held her newborn in her arms that all her children would grow up healthy and able to spread their wings toward safety and goodness.

A few days after Wilke's birth, Ben brought in the mail, including a large envelope with no return address. "This was in our postal box."

"What is it?"

"A valentine perhaps?"

She looked to see if Ben had a glimmer of tease in his eyes.

He brushed at his copper-tinted hair, then bopped his forehead with the back of his hand. "I totally forgot. You give me another son for a valentine, and I get you nothing. I am a clod of a spouse."

He bent to kiss her while she opened the envelope, not sure if he was the conveyor of the missive or its originator.

Looking inside, she knew. It was a drawing of a hen-pecked man with children crawling all over him, crying, clinging; and a disheveled woman, snaggletoothed and worn, holding a rolling pin like a weapon over the man's head. The handwritten words were "Fiend, devil's imp or what you will / you surely your poor man will kill / with luckless days and sleepless nights / haranguing him with women's rights."

"You . . . you gave me this?"

"What is it?" He stared. "Never. Jenny, no. Forget it."

The sobs were as deep as they'd been when she'd read the horrible book reviews. "Have I ever given you reason to say such a thing?"

"I didn't send that card to you, and if I'd realized that you'd take it seriously, I wouldn't have brought it home. It's from one of those 'Farmer's Wife' readers. Bunter maybe."

"Bunter. No, it's too creative for him." She paced. It scared her that everyone knew who the Farmer's Wife was. "There are others out there, Ben, men who hate me, who besmirch you. I . . . I'm so sorry." She set Wilke in his cradle. *Will they threaten my children?*

Like the reviews, the image was difficult to set aside. She didn't want people thinking Ben was hen-pecked just because he loved his children or because his wife had opinions. Perhaps she should be a little less strident in her columns. Maybe back off from some of her suggestions, even though there were other writers—men—who advocated paid household help for farmers' wives, and others—men—who wrote of women's health and the depletion that came with too many children too close together. Even the *Oregon Farmer* carried articles now about family planning, they called it, and wrote discreetly of contraception. The economists—men—recognized the role of farmers' wives in the successful weathering of the vagaries of markets. The moneymen saw how women marshalled attacks against everyday challenges of cooking, cleaning, and laundry. Of course, laundry.

Ben had told her of a man seeking a loan to build a bigger barn, and the lender had said unless he improved the condition of the house first, they wouldn't make the loan. "A happy woman can make all the difference to the success of a farm. The lender said that."

"Smart man," she said.

She'd have to build stronger armor and not let such things as a mean-spirited valentine set her eyes to sprouting wells. Maybe having delivered a "new voter" to his cradle, she was oversensitive. Yes, she'd pony-up, as Ben told her when he wanted her to ride with him and go forward, forgetting past disasters.

At least she didn't have the fate of the nation to deal with. Poor Mr. Lincoln would be inaugurated in March while a Confederate government had already installed its own. *What do I have control over? Think on that.* It became her new mantra.

War news dominated the summer. Harvey had had his fill of combat from the regional conflict, and he now slept in a tent in Forest Grove so he could attend the university there. Heavy snows fell early that winter in the Cascade mountains, and once or twice a foot or more at the valley floor.

"It'll be good for the soil," Ben said, though

tromping the snowy mud through the house did little for their hardwood floors. More scrubbing on hands and knees ensued. More meditation with the broom.

Then it turned cold. Bitter cold. Rivers that had never frozen did. Cattle died for lack of feed in the eastern part of the state. Even in Lafayette, ice in water troughs had to be broken daily.

Abigail shivered as she rolled out egg noodles, looking with longing at the teapot, hoping she wouldn't ever need the money inside to see them through.

At first when the warm rains came that November, people were relieved to have the snow melt. But it kept raining, for days, weeks, then months, off and on, through Christmas holidays and all of January 1862, pouring on them harder than any could remember. "Ark Rain," the old-timers called it. Sheets of silver so dense Abigail couldn't even see the fruit trees from the window. What should have been more snow in the mountains turned out to be early snow melt, the heavy snowfall in the Cascades earlier in November now swelling rivers and streams. The news from California and Nevada, too, reported heavier rains than usual and flooding. Rivers swamped the storehouses on the Willamette, carrying buildings and trees and bloated animals all the way to Astoria and the sea. The Duniway home stood above the waters with no risk of flooding—but getting across bridges to town proved a challenge, so eggs and butter remained unsold; letters for her column couldn't be sent; no one was able to attend school; apples failed to reach their California or Chinese markets.

Abigail learned that the little town of Canemah—where her sister nursed her baby— had four feet of water running through the streets. People climbed to their rooftops, and John Coburn, Kate's husband, was one of many ship captains and crew sent to rescue overwhelmed settlers onto steamships. Abigail hoped Kate was on one of those ships and not waiting in her attic for rescue. Towns that were a part of Oregon's young history, like Champoeg where the vote to become a part of America one day and not Britain had taken place, were washed away with nothing to show for what had been there except the memories of the survivors.

And Lafayette's new warehouse holding 80,000 bushels of wheat—including the Duniways' bumper harvest—was washed away, along with Amos and Fanny's store and much of the business district. Abigail sent word when she learned of it, and communication resumed that the Coburns and Cooks—Amos and Fanny—should come to Sunny Hillside where they'd welcome them high above flooding streams.

The warehouse loss devastated the area, but Ben had already lost on the sale of his wheat when he was forced to sell it before the flood for fifty cents a bushel. It was less than the going market rate. But he had to pay that surety debt at 2 percent interest. Abigail wrote of it in her 'Farmer's Wife' column, though she never mentioned Ben by name. The subject was always "the Farmer." She wrote that the merchant who had purchased the Farmer's wheat at a bargain price (because the Farmer had a debt to pay) hoped to resell and make a profit. That merchant had lost now too—to the flood. In her column, she wrote of the devastation, how people lost cattle and how surging waters kept them all from beginning repairs. Water. Flooding. Waiting. That was the real force of nature, worse than tornados or fires, because after those, one could begin cleanup and start over without having to wait and obsess about what one would do in the aftermath and what might be salvaged or lost.

They called it the Great Oregon Flood of 1861–62, but Abigail's trail friend, Shirley Ellis, wrote that a boat was required on K Street in Sacramento and that people had died, washed away, their bodies never found for burial. It was more than an Oregon flood.

"Such a tragedy," Shirley had written.

"In so many ways," Abigail wrote back, and didn't even mention wondering if her novel had ever arrived.

Abigail became even more specific in her next column. She told her readers that the Farmer's debt amounted to $240 a year and his farm only earned $500 on a good year, so there was little left to support his family. She also complained that the typesetter had made many errors in a previous column but added that "My husband says I ought not to complain about the printer, because he probably couldn't read my scratchings. I advise the Farmer that people often compliment me when they watch me write before them. He says, 'They're looking at your handwriting upside down.' Perhaps he's right," she conceded and hoped the interchange between the Farmer and the Farmer's Wife brought a bit of joyful relief as people came out of their badger holes to assess what had happened to their landscapes and their lives.

"That last column was a little too personal," Ben told her. "You ought not mention our debts, and so specifically." They had put the children to bed, and Abigail worked on another piece to submit to the paper.

"I want people to see that they aren't alone." She looked up at him.

"And poke your thumb in my eye?"

Was that why I was specific? "Details give authenticity to a writer's work."

He grunted. "A little less truthfulness at my expense could be pleasant."

She did consider whether she was being unfair or not and decided that she wasn't.

"It shows that the Farmers, the men, are in charge, and they make the deals, for good or bad," Abigail said. "Every man and woman can relate to that."

The flooding aftermath attacked the economy. Jobs disappeared, households split, forest trees fell over roadways, their roots loosened by inundated soils, blocking transports and deliveries. Steamships on the Willamette maneuvered through waterways clogged with debris and changed channels. The school where Jerry and Harvey attended closed down for the term as it tried to recover. Everything wasn't working out all right. Harvey's camping site had been swilled away by the greedy river. Damaged sawmills like her father's hindered rebuilding, both getting logs to the mill and out to building sites. Abigail's little house in Lafayette had water to the third step leading to the porch but hadn't been washed away. Her sisters' families could stay there while they rebuilt.

"At least no water in the basement like there would be back in Illinois," Abigail said.

"No basements in Oregon," Ben said. "Another western innovation."

It was a few weeks into March when her brother Harvey rode up the hillside to the house through a field of daffodils at dusk, a drizzle of rain dripping off his hat.

"You're not bringing bad news? Jerry and Father are all right?"

"No bad news. Nothing you haven't already heard," he said.

"Come on in. Get yourself dry. I'll tend your horse." Ben spoke, motioned for Harvey to dismount while his brother-in-law led his mount to their barn. Abigail heard him talking to the animal on the way, then start singing a little tune.

"I read that 'the Farmer's Wife' gave her permission for 'the Farmer' to head to Idaho," Harvey said as Ben returned and put Wilkie in the high chair, his one-year-old legs sticking out like little stumps. His hands reached out to pat his father's cheeks as he bent to the boy. The men took their seats with Clara, Willis, and two-year-old Hubert perched on a bench side by side. "The Farmer is you, right, Ben?" Harvey took the bowl of beans Abigail handed him. She kept ahold of it just a second longer than she needed, making him pay attention to her and not talk about her as though she weren't there. Harvey gave her eye contact, said, "Thanks, Sister," then to Ben he said, "Does it bother you that she's always putting private things out there for the world to read about in her column?"

"I don't mind it much," Ben said. He moved his

peas around the plate, didn't look at Harvey. "It gives Jenny respite, as she calls it, to scribble."

"Still, a little delicacy wouldn't hurt. Or a letter informing the rest of the family of the Duniway-doings before we have to read of it in the paper."

"I never write about you," Abigail said. "Are you envious?" She set a platter of rice and a chicken she'd butchered onto the table. She cooked it up with dried herbs that Harriet had given her the last time they were together.

Harvey snorted. "At least your farm wasn't damaged." He forked a chicken thigh. And 'the Farmer' managed to pay his debts."

Ben winced then. "The Farmer will pay his debts," Ben said. "Why I'm heading to Idaho to the mines."

"I wondered if that was true, what the Farmer's Wife said."

"The Farmer's Wife always writes true things," she said.

"Just not always factual."

Before Abigail could object, Harvey continued. "I thought I might go with you to Idaho. I'm not taken by the war effort. I think those Southern states have made a mistake, but I don't think dying to end slavery is the right answer. Negotiations makes more sense. But I thought I'd take a year while the school gets back on its feet and students can return to create needed capital so I can go through the university without having to work at the sawmill."

"Will you study law?" Ben asked. He passed the platter to Abigail, who had at last sat down.

"Maybe. First a general degree in economics. Then math, English, the usual advanced courses."

"A woman wouldn't know 'usual' when it comes to the higher education she's deprived of."

"Not now, Jenny," Ben said.

She sighed. No need to be strident at the table. There'd be time for her and Harvey to wrestle over issues later—if either had the energy for it.

Ben said he'd be glad for the company in the mines, though he worried about leaving Abigail with the children, and hired workers to run the farm.

"Send the money," Abigail said. "We'll be all right, though missing you more than all the water in the Willamette."

"I'll miss you more than all the water in the ocean, Pa," Clara said.

"Where are you going, Papa?" Willis asked.

"On an adventure, Son." Ben squeezed his daughter's shoulder and made his voice light for his children.

For the first time since they'd made the decision for Ben to leave, Abigail realized how much the children would miss him, and they didn't have the luxury of knowing why he was leaving, sacrificing home and hearth in order to help them all, and yes, make amends for his poor judgment. She let herself feel the pain of the coming separation, then vowed that she couldn't let those feelings intrude or she would be a puddle when he left and that would upset the children even more. In the same way that she brushed by little joys that she didn't think she deserved, she tamped down sadness by getting to work.

"Finish up now," she told the children. "Take your bowls to the sink."

While Abigail washed the dishes and Clara dried, Harvey caught them up on the news and told tales of daring rescues during the flooding, stories of people helping neighbors, free blacks and Asians helping whites and vice versa, the vitriol of race and politics diminished for a time.

"Disasters bring out the best in us," Abigail said. "It's that pioneering spirit, how we have to try new ways when the circumstances force us into different channels."

"And give a man permission to make mistakes," Ben said. "I'm told by my carpenter friends that the mark of a true craftsman isn't that he makes no errors but how well he covers them up so no one notices, that's the key."

"A little difficult to do when the carpenter's wife spreads the error in the newspaper," Harvey said.

He held a teasing voice, but Abigail noticed

145

Ben's bearded face turned a little redder, and she thought in the future she ought to increase the good tales she told of the Farmer. Surely his sacrifice of leaving home would be worthy of a column. Maybe even two.

THIRTEEN

Going On

1862

Abigail sent Ben off in March, hopeful for the
benefit of this needed separation. But with him
gone, she realized how much she relied on him,
even when he merely sat and jawed with friends
in the other room. Buttressing in a relationship,
she realized, came in many shapes and sizes. He'd
never complained about the Farmer stories she
wrote, except that one time when she'd harped
about the loan. But maybe Harvey was correct,
and flapping the Duniway "underlings" in the
newspaper winds wasn't the best use of her time.
She'd write of less personal things or use those
personal events to be symbols of wider concerns.
She penned a column in the spring about the
death of someone "dear" and how alcoholism had
shredded the promise of his life. It was an uncle
she worried over, and she used the occasion of his
downfall to urge Oregonians to wage war on King
Alcohol who is "if possible, a worse enemy to
progress than the dire hallucination of secession."

She wrote about missing her farmer. Anonymous said she'd driven him away. She penned a

sad tale of her children crying for their farmer-father. Anonymous said she was a poor mother to let her children suffer so. Without Ben to put the nasty reply letters into perspective, she dwelt overmuch on negativity rather than on hope. One needed others to nurture optimism, or at least she was finding that she did.

So far there'd been no gold strike in Idaho, and her Hope School hadn't restarted due to the regional flooding aftermath. Ben wrote of his longing to be home and encouraged her that if she had some idea for income that would bring him home, she should pursue it. So she did.

"Forty dollars a month," she wrote to Ben, *"is at least a sure thing."* She'd taken a position teaching in a private school. *"Some people still have capital to pay tuition, but it's a relief to not have to manage the collection of funds and just take my salary at month's end. Clara and Willis can attend for free, so there is that added bonus. Soon you'll strike it rich, God willing, and I can buy new shoes for the boys who are so badly in need."*

Like the two tracks of a wagon wheel through tall grass, she sent him dual messages: shared stories of how much the children missed him, next to expressed concerns about their fragile pecuniary state. Her letters gave him details, too, of the spring at Sunny Hillside and the glorious blooms on the apple trees, a blanket of white fluffs floating on a sea of green. *"I wish you could see it, Ben. The farm is so beautiful."* Then she'd consider striking out those very words, writing a new page, not wanting him to feel homesick. *"Save these letters, Mr. Duniway, that I might draw upon them one day when I have time to work on another* improved *novel or two. They'll help me remember what was happening for us during this* temporary *separation."*

She decided to hire a bit of help for herself and put a small portion of her income toward a woman to care for the children while she taught. *"It puts money into the economy so don't say I'm wasting it."* She wished Jerry still lived with them. He'd lend both happiness and help, but schooling was more important. She knew that.

Clara Belle had taken an interest in the piano, and Abigail traded laundry work for her lessons. One day she'd buy a piano for her, she would. She gave Willis the task of sweeping every day, told three-year-old Hubert he had the important work of watching fifteen-month-old Wilkie while she soaked the more well-to-do neighbors' duds. While the clothes dried, she worked the spinning wheel, turning their sheep's wool into thread she could mend with or sell. She had to remind herself to relax her shoulders, take little pauses in her labor, because Ben wasn't there to remind her. She read to the children before bedtime, though she could barely stay awake. And each evening when she fell onto her own feather comfort, she longed for Ben, prepared a celebration for when he'd come home, and prayed for a bountiful harvest in the fall on Sunny Hillside Farm. And each evening she turned questions over in her mind. *What do I have control over? How can I make everything be all right?*

"It's Jerry. He's very ill and he's asking for you."

"The flu?"

"We don't know . . . he collapsed at the mill." Jenny's stepmother's voice caught and anguish flooded her face. "Tucker's with him. He may not make it through the day. Come. I have the carriage to bring you back."

"No. You take the children to Fanny's. Let her know what's happened and to bring them and her own." Abigail turned to the children's nanny. "Please let the school know I won't be there, and catch Clara and Willis and bring them back."

"Of course."

Abigail raced to the paddock behind the house where they kept one mare. The breeding stock and other animals stayed at Sunny Hillside. The horse recognized Abigail and came trotting across the field to get her treat. "We've a twenty-mile ride, Bonnie. I hope you've eaten your breakfast. Poor Jerry's down." The tears came as she saddled and mounted up.

Anger and frustration were the reins she held

as she kneed Bonnie toward Forest Grove. Why did her father make Jerry work so hard at the mill? At nineteen, he was still a frail young man, competing with Harvey. She chastised herself for not having found a way to have Jerry stay with them instead of being under her father's thumb. She should have insisted he remain with them. Shearing sheep was tiring work but seasonal. The sawmill was heavy, demanding, year-round labor. Wind dried her tears as she pushed the mare, slowing only when she felt the horse might falter if she didn't.

In the end, it didn't matter. By the time Abigail reached Forest Grove and dismounted a lathered horse, her father stepped out of the house. His face told her everything she didn't want to know. She'd never missed Ben more.

Abigail rinsed the cloth she'd used to wipe Jerry's eyelids, his thin face. "No way to avoid it," Abigail said, answering Fanny's longing to sweep away grief as so large a part of their daily lives. "We have to plow through."

"You're always so strong, Abigail," their step-mother said. Their hands touched when Abigail gave her a wet cloth.

"Strong? No. I've found a way to push the pain under. Get angry at the world, at . . ." She started to spit blaming words toward her father, but she didn't.

"May you never lose a child," her father said as he leaned against the doorframe, shoulders drooped, watching the women. What they did was women's work.

It might ease his grief to participate. Why couldn't men perform such ministrations as women did?

"Love helps," his wife said. She left Jerry's body to go to their father and stroke his crossed arms. "Love always helps."

Her father held her hand as she leaned her face against his shoulder. The shared grief was visible to Abigail, and she felt a new appreciation for Ruth as the woman returned to rub Jerry's body with fragrant oils.

Perhaps, Abigail thought, love is the only real balm to pain. Perhaps that was why her father had remarried so quickly. They could say "time heals all wounds," but it wasn't time, it was courage. It was being willing to risk love, after love had disappeared, after sorrow for whatever reason caught the heart up short and pierced it like an arrow. Her stepmother grieved Jerry's death too. He'd been her stepchild, but she had loved him, done his laundry, cared for him, fed him. And Ruth's mistake those years before had happened after her own husband died and she sought comfort, thought she'd found it in an irresponsible man but had encountered only fleeting warmth. Love had come into her life again through Abigail's father. Abigail thought of Ben and how fortunate she was to have someone who loved her so very much.

She vowed to love her children more deeply, to give up her insistence to work so hard, to *make* things happen as she wanted, to change the world quickly. She knew that vow might not last long, but it was still good to make the promise to her children, to herself. And to Ben. She would write to him and Harvey of this terrible grief and how the Scott descendants would once more gather at a grave.

And she prayed that she would never have to learn what her father knew: how to go on after the death of a child. For him, Jerry was the fourth.

FOURTEEN

Refresher

1862

"You are a godsend, Captain John. And where did you learn how to shear sheep?" Abigail handed her brother-in-law a jug of water.

"Not on board a steamship, I can assure you." John Coburn had agreed to help the hired man, Sam, shear the animals at Sunny Hillside.

"It's good physical work, and Sam's a good instructor," Abigail said.

"Even without my chew," Sam grumbled. The hand was testy that day because Abigail had told him she didn't have the money to buy his tobacco.

Kate watched the children with Clara's help and waddled as she walked, expecting the Coburns' second child in September, a month away. "He's a good sport about so many things," Kate said.

"Yes, that laundry help he hired for you is an envy of many, including me," Abigail said.

"Hold 'er tight," Sam said. "They like to squirm on ye."

The ewes were in good shape, had dropped their lambs in the spring. The hired hand and

Abigail had shared the long night hours watching to make sure the ewes didn't by mistake roll onto their babies or reject them as though they had no idea such a thing had come from their bodies. Some ewes needed assistance in letting the lambs suck, and more than one baby sat warming by the cookstove at the house. Now they were being sheared and separated, and the bleating was incessant.

"It reminds me of Willis at our Christmas pageant," Abigail said to Kate. It would be a long day with the women preparing meals in between stomping down the fleeces. Canvas bags hung down from a platform like giant hummingbirds' nests. The fleece was dropped down into the bags around the women who stepped into the canvas, allowing new fleeces to fall in beside them and be pressed into tight bales. The women grew closer to the top as the bags filled and stepped back onto the platform while the men tied the canvas bales. Men below unhooked the packed fleece and carried them off on their shoulders to the wagons for transport.

"You'd better not stomp, Kate," Abigail said. "And be careful of the wood floors. They get slippery from the lanolin."

In all, they had several bags the hired hand would take to the market. "It might be enough to buy coffee," Abigail said, lamenting the poor harvest.

"More than that, surely." Kate fanned herself with her fingers.

"At least the chickens are laying well and there's the butter money and my ever-optimistic hope that Ben will return healthy, wealthy, and wise. Refreshed, perhaps, but with emphasis on the wealthy."

"Oh, Abigail. It can't be as bad as that, is it?"

"You know about those notes Ben signed? I told you, didn't I?"

"Not directly. The Farmer's Wife did, though."

"I don't know if we'll make the payment this year. It scares me to death. I've been trying to confer with Dear Bob, but he's nowhere to be found."

"Maggie says the Lord never gives us more than we can handle," Kate said.

"Then the Lord has to work on his estimation of my capacities. I'm reaching the end of my already frayed rope."

"You're missing Ben."

"That I am. I told him in my last letter how the children wake with 'Pa' on their breaths and how Clara sleeps with me now and moans 'Pa' in her dreams and how I think I will surely die if he doesn't come home soon, that I'd rather have him here healthy more than wealthy. I miss him terribly."

Kate patted Abigail's hands. "That lanolin really makes hands soft, doesn't it?"

It was Kate's way of saying she'd heard enough of Abigail's laments. May as well speak of hand care than of longing, homesickness, and worry. She'd just have to wait for Ben to return for things to get better.

At dusk, John took Kate home, and then Abigail saw their wagon stop just at the corner at the end of the lane. *What's wrong now?*

It was nothing wrong; all was right. Ben had come home.

The children climbed all over him; Abigail hugged him tight. She didn't care that he hadn't written her of his homecoming. He'd read between her lines and come back to them all.

"I'm sorry I'm not bringing bags of gold," he said.

"You're my bag of gold."

"I'll remind you of that when things get tough," he said.

She held him close all through the night.

Harvest went easier with Ben there, directing the hired men, conferring with them about tobacco costs and whether such was included in their wage. She didn't even mind cooking for the crew or the extra visitors Ben brought home with him. Her eyes would catch that now-empty teapot, but she imagined putting egg money into it again someday. She still taught at her private school, but with Ben back, she handed her wages to him. At least they talked about how to spend them. Abigail knew other wives who handed over their laundry wages or brought resources into the marriage and then their husbands drank up any profit at the local tavern. Her life was so much better than that. Best of all, he was home. Safe.

In the evenings, they talked about public things—the war, the commissioning of the 1st Oregon Cavalry and whether Ben might join them.

"No. You're needed here," Abigail insisted. "Don't even think about going off again."

It was pleasant to have a sarsaparilla while they watched the sun set and shared opinions about the area's rate of recovery from the floods. She was grateful they had similar views about slavery and how the state appeared conflicted, having entered the union as a free state but having an exclusion clause in its constitution meant to keep out free-black people. She didn't see many of that race, but they had hired one or two, and they'd been good workers, pleasant to the children when they sat together at the table for their noon meal.

Yes, she loved having Ben back, but when he rode off to spend an evening with his friends, or when he bought a new hay rake with money she'd earned, she realized how much she missed the singular command she'd had while he was gone. And he'd insisted she let the hired woman go as soon as school ended for the term.

"Hazel could have helped with the housework,"

Abigail pointed out. "She was also very good at getting the children to make their beds and pick up after themselves."

"You're their mother and I'm their father. We can sway their behavior better than an outsider."

"Perhaps."

"Don't you worry." He tapped his pipe, tidily cleaned the bowl. He'd begun to smoke it now. "You're a wise mother."

"It isn't my wisdom I need help imparting. It's saving my back and body so my mind can work."

"You know I can help."

"When you're not otherwise occupied."

"I can take care of them—and you. It's what husbands do, Wife." He smiled, looking at her with those big blue eyes that had won her over those years before. "Trust me."

They'd left the conversation there. It was a woman's role to step back and let herself be taken care of. Abigail had grown up with her mother imparting such wisdom. There were roles men and women played that kept society in order and moving forward. Still, when she remembered her mother's reluctance to go west and what not challenging her husband's wishes had cost her, she wondered if some roles didn't just need to be changed. She glanced at the teapot while Ben smoked his pipe, a habit taken up in Idaho. It had been her mother's china pot; one *her* mother had given her with the birth of the last of her mother's twelve children. Something to celebrate, she supposed, was that she wasn't expecting another baby. And she had another idea for making money. She had to run it past Ben.

In the spring of 1863, they attended Harvey's graduation in Forest Grove—the first graduating class of Pacific University founded by that feisty Tabitha Moffat Brown. Harvey was the single student receiving his degree. Mrs. Brown had broken the rules of roles for men and women, Abigail thought as her brother received his diploma. *I should think about going to the university.* She'd let her character in her novel go on to school and even start a magazine. But that was fiction. Besides, what would such a degree give her that she wasn't already able to do with her teaching certificate? Garner a bit more respect? Or disdain that she was moving too far outside her expected lane? Harvey had been successful in teaching himself Latin and Greek, and while she wasn't sure if those languages had gotten him the job as a librarian in Portland, at least it had earned him employment where he would use his mind instead of his back. She envied him that he wouldn't need to help slaughter a pig or ever again have to plow a field as they had back in Illinois. But no amount of advanced education would enable a woman to rid herself of backbreaking laundry. It was a woman's fate.

Later, back at Sunny Hillside Farm, with Ben off making arrangements for their stud to travel to a nearby homestead, she mused that momentous events seemed to happen at dusk, when one was already tired and had not yet time for the contemplative evening prayer, the *labora*—work as prayer—having filled the day. It ought to be a time of calm, recounting the successes of the day. Instead, bad news took the whole day to arrive, it seemed.

She had heard a coyote howl near the sheep pen and started down the lane to yell at it to protect her sheep. Ben had been away the whole day. They'd acquired a dog—Hubert had named it Buffy—and she told the dog to "Stay!" She thought when Hubert named him, he was trying to say "Fluffy," as the mixed breed of black and white with a roly-poly body and long tail looked like a ball of wool when they'd gotten him as a puppy a few months back.

"You stay back there, Clara. Hold Buffy. I don't want him to get called out by the coyote."

That task finished, she returned to the house, when she heard a horse clopping at the front. She recognized the sheriff as he dismounted, and her first thought was that something had happened to Ben. She felt a weight in her stomach. "Everything all right with Mr. Duniway?"

"Yes, ma'am. After a fact." He didn't meet her eyes, pulled a folded document from his pack. "I've this summons to give you, Mrs. Duniway."

"Summons? For what?"

"For nonpayment of your notes."

"My husband's notes." Her heart pounded harder now with Ben safe somewhere but her having to bear this catastrophic news. Alone.

"Your notes too, missus. The law sees you as responsible too."

"Even though when he signed it, I had no say. Ah, yes, justice is a man's name."

"Sorry, Mrs. Duniway. You've missed the last payments."

Are you really sorry? Enforcing laws that turn people's worlds upside down? The Duniway state of being was known, of course, in part because of "The Farmer's Wife" columns. But she hadn't known that Ben had missed the last payments. She noticed he was gone more often but thought his absences were because he was making money with his horse breeding, a task that took "jawing" and politicking to get potential customers ready to pay the stud fees. He hadn't shown her the books. But she as well as he was now responsible.

She didn't invite the sheriff in. He went on his way as she read the word "Sale," her stomach churning. She slammed the frying pan against the stove, wanted to lift the stovetop and throw the summons into it but couldn't. She'd had no say in Ben's decision. She warned him and he patronized her, assuring her that Dear Bob was good for the money, that pioneer hospitality meant helping out a friend. Who would help them? Her face felt warm. She rehearsed what she'd say to him and wondered if this was what her mother felt when her father had to file bankruptcy back in Illinois. He too had signed a note for another man who had failed to pay. Had that been the real impetus that sent the Scott family traveling west?

"Why are you crying, Momma?" Willis asked.

"Just a little sadness. I'm fine." She forced a smile. "Have you finished your work page? Arithmetic is important to learn, you know." *Especially for a male child.* "Though it seems your father could use a refresher."

"What's a refresher?" Clara said.

Wilkie started to climb up onto his chair. "Not yet," she told him. "Wait until Pa comes home. Then we'll eat." Then to Clara she said, "A refresher means breathing new life into something forgotten." She changed her mind. "We'll eat now," she said. "Let me get the potatoes on. Willis, put aside your papers and get the ham from the smokehouse, please." *If he's like his father, he'll need a math refresher before he turns fifteen.* Why make the children wait on their father's timing? It was something she could do—feed her offspring. At least for the moment.

Vulnerable. That was how she felt as she

waited for Ben to come home. Harvey had told her once that the word *vulnerable* came from the Latin word meaning "wound." And what healed a wound? She wasn't sure.

The day waned into darkness. She fed the hired hands and sent them off. While she served the children their ham and washed the dishes in the pan, she stewed. While she read their bedtime story and listened to their prayers, she fumed, waiting, planning all she'd say to Ben when he finally got home, beginning with "I told you so." She'd remind him of the thousand times she'd scolded him about their financial worries, how he needed to take them seriously and not always brush her concerns aside, and now it was too late. They would have to sell the farm, have to. *Sheriff's sale.* It would be in the newspapers, the shame of it for all to read. And whoever bought it would know that they were forced to do so, and the Duniways would be required to take whatever high bid was offered, even if it was lower than a sow's belly. The bulk of any profit—if there was any—would go to pay the notes. She had no idea what might be left, or once off the farm, what on earth they would do to support the family.

Ben arrived. He took one look at her. "What is it? One of the children?"

"No. They're safe, thank goodness." She took in a deep breath. "The sheriff came by." She slapped the summons in his hand and started her rehearsed spiel. But his face turned pale as he read. He sank onto the divan, folded up like a broken ladder. She saw tears in his eyes when he lifted them from the paper.

"What will we do?" Ben's words came out as a whisper.

"Sell Sunny Hillside. It's all we can do, and hope there's enough left to, I don't know, find another way to make a living." She'd been pondering that. "I'll have to do something more than take a teacher's salary. You . . . your horse breeding, well, without a farm—" She opened her hands in dismay.

He hung his head. "You're right, of course. You've been right all along. I'm . . . I'm so sorry."

"Of course I'm right. And of course you're sorry, after the fact. That's always the case. You always feel badly. It's never your intention." *Of course. Always. Never.* Acidic insults, nails for her hammer. He deserved them, didn't he? Righteous outrage fueled more words. She had more to spit out, but she watched his face— pale and grief stricken—and the disdain drained from her. She suspected anger wouldn't long stay away, that with every dish she packed she'd resent him—but she could see his remorse in that nearby moment; could almost feel his humiliation, not from her words, but from what he told himself.

Anger had always been a secondary emotion anyway. That's what her mother had once told her, that fury rode on a fast horse charging through a relationship, trampling right over loss, disappointment, and grief. And if one wasn't careful, wrath crushed love too. *"Pay attention to those forgotten feelings when you lose your temper, Jenny. Those are the trio of emotions that if not recognized and dealt with, will surely bring a soul down and make ire the driving force in your days. Wounds must grow new flesh."*

Jenny rose from her rocking chair and went to Ben, his shoulders hunched over the trifold document he held in his trembling hands. She sat on the wide arm of the divan, slightly above him. She put her arm around his shoulder, and he gentled his head into her side, the summons falling from his fingers. She felt his body shudder as he tried to hide his sobs. She'd never seen him cry before.

She felt the disappointment and the loss, but he felt it too. Perhaps more. "We'll weather this storm," she told him. "Take a refresher course in how to start over. And we'll make it."

He nodded. "I'll do better."

"It'll all turn out all right."

It was a prayer as much as a promise.

FIFTEEN
Moving and Moving Forward

1864

"Hang that linen a little closer," Abigail told Ben. "We want to get as many girls in here as we can but still give them a sense of privacy."

"Yes, Jenny—Abigail."

She heard him trying to accommodate her request to not be called by her nickname, one of many adaptations he'd made. Ben didn't go very far from home these days, no visiting his bachelor friends. At least they had a roof over their heads because Abigail had invested in the Lafayette property, and now the attic was finished and would be a dormitory bedroom for boarders. Ben built a pen behind the house for the chickens so that they still might have egg money. They kept a cow. The dog had stayed with the farm and she missed him. But he would have disheveled the house with his bulk. Another sacrifice they had to make.

Ben gave up the breeding stock, selling his beloved stallions he'd been building a solid bloodline behind. He did so without a word of protest. *Penance. Self-imposed.* She chastised

167

herself when she snapped at him. She found she liked living in Lafayette full-time, closer to family, finding new ways to make money, relieved of the heavy farm work or chasing coyotes from sheep pens. But oh, how she missed the view!

Ben had managed to find a buyer, so they didn't have to file bankruptcy to settle the claim. Millard Lownsdale, the son of a man who had brought apples to the Oregon Territory and had made a fortune because of it, bought Sunny Hillside. He planned to expand the orchard and had the capital to do so. Abigail was glad that the land would be nurtured but resented that some had the means to prosper at the expense of those working hard every day who lived on the edge and by some small mistake could fall to ruin.

"If not for you, we'd be there too, Abigail. Penniless. You work so hard."

She thought to encourage him by saying that the farm brought as much as it did because of his work, his vision of the orchard he'd begun. That she knew he'd sacrificed by going to the mines and that he too had lost dreams along with the farm. But she kept silent, perhaps sending her anger at despicable men, which at that moment included her husband.

Withholding comfort now and then was better than being strident. Even Clara had said once when Abigail snarled at her spouse, "Don't be mad at Pa. He's doing the best he can." Abigail knew he was, and she chastised herself for her attitude, hoped the husband-bashing and self-lashing would not last. She didn't much like herself for her reluctance to prop him up, but she hadn't yet learned that not forgiving Ben hurt her as much as him.

"I've been working on something." Ben stared at the egg noodles he swirled on his supper plate, not at Abigail. It was months since they'd moved and life had taken on new patterns. Ben was gone often in the afternoons, and Abigail assumed he was once again visiting with his friends. That was good. She hoped he'd start singing again too. He cleared his throat. "Something that could help with the laundry."

"One of those Thor washing machines would be handy to have, but we can't afford it."

"I've made a better one and enough different with the wringer attached and two rinse tubs that Capt John thinks it could be patented." Ben's words were tentative.

"Don't forget to scrub that noddle pan, Clara." Then to Ben, Abigail said, "So that's what you've been doing. Why, that's wonderful." *It is!*

"I apprenticed with a cooper back in Illinois. Did I tell you that?" She shook her head that he hadn't. "I'm ready to give it a try here. If you approve, of course."

"Why would you even wonder. Anything to make laundry easier, though saving for one of those newfangled Thors might have been quicker."

"Mine has features." He looked up at her now.

She reached across the table and took his hand not engaged in noodle-shifting. "If you designed it, I'm sure it will be superior to anything on the market. Bring it home. Let me see those features."

"Thank you."

Ben pulled his hand from beneath hers, stood, and carried his dishes to the soapy water in the dishpan. "Are you ready for your story, Wilkie?" he asked their youngest. The child nodded his head. He'd been slower to pick up language, though Abigail wasn't worried. Yet. "You are? Good. I'll read. You turn the pages."

"We do it together. You sing, Pa?"

"Maybe." He smiled at Abigail, kissed the top of her head as he walked by.

"Well, I never," Abigail said. "It works . . . fine, Ben. Yes, it does."

"You say it as though you doubted it would." He'd filled the tubs with water, and a pump heated it so Abigail didn't have to lift steaming pots of water. She still had to swirl the clothes with a stick, but the heavy lifting was gone. Dirty water drained into a bucket he could carry for watering the garden.

"No. I didn't doubt you." *But I did, shame on me.*

"I'll eventually work out some kind of trough so you can do laundry in the kitchen instead of outside or in the laundry house. We can put the wastewater on the garden." He showed her how the rinse tub worked.

"I won't make much on the sale of each one, but it'll bring in something now and then."

She kissed his cheek, dabbed sweat from his forehead with a towel, then wiped her own. "A labor-saving device. It's wonderful, Ben. I'm proud of you."

It looked like he might cry.

Abigail rose at 4:00 a.m. in order to prepare the day's lessons, staying one step ahead of the learners. Ben watched their children too young to attend school, and he'd taken over preparing much of the larger meal of the day. The boarders were fed breakfast and supper. It was a cooperative effort.

"If I'm honest with myself," Abigail told her sister Kate, "It's all been good. I love running the school and the bustle of the boarders and having the children know of current events and giving them wise counsel. My counsel, of course." She clacked her knitting needles, making winter socks.

"A chance to pontificate," Kate said. "Your

forte." The two sat on the Coburns' porch while Ben and Captain John smoked, leaning over the back rail.

"It is my *métier*." Abigail grinned. "And Ben is such a help with the children and the housework. He doesn't bat an eye at that broom. And he's invented a washing machine. It actually is quite useful."

"I hope you've let him know how much you appreciate him."

"In my way," Abigail said.

"Ha! I know your ways."

Kate rose from her rocking chair where she'd nursed her youngest, placed her baby in the cradle where a lace coverlet draped nearly to the floor. "You've turned your loss into something full of gain, Jenny. Perhaps you'll worry less now, enjoy your teaching more. And Ben's assistance. He doesn't appear as sad about the farm sale."

She'd noticed that too. He sighed less and even joked with her now and then, when she let him make her laugh. Perhaps inventing something took him from his cellar of sorrow the way writing worked for her.

"I've another novel rising in the doughboy."

"I don't know when you find the time."

"Ben helps, as you note."

To herself, Abigail acknowledged that despite the loss of Sunny Hillside, she was more invigorated now than she'd ever been, stood straighter, and had less pain in her joints, even found time to work on that next novel—when she woke at 3:00 a.m. and gave herself that hour to indulge in pure writing without regard to lesson preparation or boarder breakfasts.

Ben had undertaken the laundry, and she said not a word when she had to replace a button torn off in the wringer because of how he'd fed the contraption that squeezed water from the cloth. He'd even taken out a patent, with her assistance.

She thought about how one of the worst moments of her life—that wretched sheriff's visit and the sale of that beloved farm—could have resulted in this time of respite. Maggie would have quoted her Scripture, maybe Romans 8:28 about God working for good for those who follow him. Maggie used that verse often enough, even with a brother's or niece's death, events so sad Abigail couldn't imagine how anything good could come of them. But might it mean that even in sorrow, one wasn't alone. Abigail found Scripture beautiful as a language but never held it to be predictive the way Maggie did, she who could spout its words to support whatever view she held, whatever pain she had to bear. But for this day, in this moment, Abigail would admit that something good had come from the disaster of the farm loss.

As they drove back to Lafayette after visiting Kate and the Captain, Ben said, "Capt John's offered to loan me use of acreage he's purchased that I might take up horse training again." Anticipating her protest, he raised his voice. "I could work out some during the day, help farmers with haying, and still have an hour or two to work breeding stock. I've been checking around. Experienced farm hands are sought after."

How hard it must be for him to think of working for others when once he owned his own place.

"There's a market for matched white circus horses. You know I'm good with training." He kept his eyes forward, gave her time to think.

She thought about how he wouldn't be as available to help with *her* ventures if he was gone working horses and forking hay all day.

"Are you up to that?"

"Absolutely. I can still fix breakfasts while you study your lessons and be there for supper too. Willkie's three already. He could sit in on your classes, couldn't he? I sold another of my washing machines, so we could bring in a helper."

"Squeeze another bed into the attic?"

"Something like that. Or I could fix up that small room behind the kitchen stove." He kept his eyes on the road ahead, reins loose in his hands, while the children chattered to each other behind them in the wagon box.

Abigail thought of Kate's words and the good that had come from the sale. Ben was entitled to a bit of goodness too. "I know that working with horses gives you great pleasure." *And he loves to gab. He needs people around. He doesn't ask for much.* "You've earned that, Ben. We're moving forward in this westering place. We can make it happen."

PART 2

In those simple relationships of loving husband and wife, affectionate sisters, children and grandmother, there are innumerable shades of sweetness and anguish which make up the pattern of our lives day by day . . . These secret accords and antipathies which lie hidden under our everyday behavior . . . more than any outward events make our lives happy or unhappy.
WILLA CATHER, NOT UNDER FORTY

SIXTEEN

The Direction of Light

1864

The next year found Ben doing what he loved. He kept a garden at the Lafayette house, nurturing the tomatoes and marveling over the lettuce sprouts unfolding as delicate as a baby's tongue. He spent hours away with horses and farmers while Abigail hired a Chinese cook and housekeeper so he could. In the early evenings, Ben and eight-year-old Willis wielded a saw and hammer and wooden pegs, contributing to the cabinets Ben made to furnish the school. He joked with men who came to him for his advice on horses and found "pleasantness," as he called it, when he worked his young colts, forming teams.

Abigail continued her teaching, but she knew it wasn't enough. Contentedness wasn't a part of who she was, she decided. She began making a few loans to women in need. She didn't always confer about them with Ben, thinking that he didn't run every detail of his days by her, either. She wanted to help them get back on their feet. She'd made a loan to a divorced woman to help her buy furniture to start a boardinghouse to support her children. As soon as she had the chairs and table and beds to replace what her former husband had taken in the divorce, he returned and gathered up what she'd bought and sold them out from under her.

"Can you imagine?" She told Ben as they sat at the table while Clara and Willis cleared the plates and squabbled at the dishpan over who would wash and who would dry. Hubert played with Wilkie. An advantage of having more than one child—they could look after each other. The boarding girls had already gone upstairs for the evening.

"Tragic," Ben said.

"Yes. Tragic and perfectly legal. What was hers, was his. Even after the divorce, he could trot right into that house and take what he wished. She had no say. And now she's in debt, and you can bet no law will make him pay it. She'll be liable for it and still without a pot to sit on. It's so unfair."

She didn't tell Ben that the money the woman owed was to the Duniways. Instead, she wrote a scathing letter to the editor describing the need for changes in property laws so women would have more choices when deserted by unscrupulous men—some of whom were husbands. She wrote letters to help women, supporting changes dealing with unfair practices, like a neighbor having to pay off a debt incurred by a deceased husband, a debt he had before the couple even married.

"What I need," she told Ben one evening while she added a patch to a thinning shirt elbow, "is a wider reach."

"The paper publishes your letters every week now." He drew on his pipe, the breathy air the only sound she could hear above the crickets. "And you and your 'flamboyant' friends attended an open meeting. That sent some tongues to wagging. We men let you."

"But the reporters barely mentioned it. There is no reason women can't attend public meetings and even speak at them. We'll go again. The editor will have to do an article about such a commotion. Editors have total control in deciding what goes in and what doesn't."

"Advertisers influence that, I suspect. There has to be a balance or they'll lose subscribers."

"If I ever run a newspaper, I'll find supporters willing to fund my perspectives. Balance won't be a part of it, because the scales are already tipped toward papers that celebrate men, protect their interests, not their wives or even mothers."

Ben sucked on his pipe again. He'd been giving up actual smoking, just used the pipe stem to chew on in the evening again. Abigail said she didn't like the taste of tobacco on her lips, and she kissed him more since he didn't fill the bowl. He held a sleeping Wilkie in his arm.

"I had no idea you hankered after running a newspaper. When did that happen?"

"Susan B. Anthony owns one, and the *Lily* has a long history. Both are women's rags, and they celebrate how life needs to change and offer ways to do it. Anne Royall ran one in the '30s, and though she was tried as a scold for being so outspoken, she supported herself with it and made a difference fighting corruption and taking on religious leaders who had forgotten that Christians are to be loving souls. My little letters barely scratch the surface to do what that Royall woman did with her paper." She put the thimble down and grinned. "Besides, with a newspaper I could get my novels printed. Serialize them, then bind and sell them later. I certainly haven't had any luck finding a real publisher since my first . . . fiasco."

"You learned from it."

"I hope so, but until the books are in the hands of others with reviews, I'll never really know."

"Oh, you know. You never let a lesson pass you by." He set his pipe aside and motioned for her to put her mending away. "I'll put Wilkie to bed, then let's take a look at the garden. We've a full moon. You can almost see the melons grow."

She shook her head. "I've got a lesson to plan."

"You're giving up a good moment, Mrs. Duniway." His voice had teasing to it, and for an instant she thought she might succumb, allow affection to soothe the tension in her shoulders, the racing of her mind.

"Those melons will grow without my admiration. And the moon will shine as bright. But if I'm not ready to stimulate those young minds in the morning, who knows what ideas they might walk away with." She saw the frown on his handsome face. "I'll only take an hour," she said.

He grunted. "I know your hour. I'll be long asleep by the time you notice you're still working at midnight."

She rose, bent to kiss him and Wilkie too. "Good night, Ben."

And so, she gave up tenderness, let it slip away, turned to thoughts of commerce. She didn't let herself wonder why.

It was late in the year, the children napped, and Abigail sat on the floor, a rare moment of pause as her back leaned against the couch. She'd bought a rag rug from a woman with arthritic hands, marveled at how that widow persevered to feed her family. Abigail ran her palm over the wool braids.

Ben sat above her reading an agricultural magazine.

"I've been battling the unfairness of a woman's life ever since I watched Momma go along with Father's decisions that failed. I hear these stories of women suffering through no fault of their own but from laws that mistreat them—as they mistreat our free-black and Chinese neighbors. It's the laws that have to change."

"You'll have to get men to vote the changes in."

"Fat chance of that." She crossed her arms. *Maybe I could start a cooperative where women sold their work and encouraged each other at the same time.* She sighed. "I thought the West would be a vibrant place for women's rights. Women work right beside their men. But here we are, still chattel."

"You should write about the importance of women securing the vote," Ben said. "It may be that the only thing that will really make a difference in a woman's life is her having a chance to make her mark at the ballot box. Men will have to grant that permission, and our lives might be made easier if we do, though we're a stubborn lot." He set his magazine down, stroked her hair. Tender. "It'll take good wisdom to create that end in Oregon. You could make the case better than anyone I know, if you find the right way to ride that horse."

"Do you really think so?" She turned to him. "I want women to have so much more control over their lives, so many more options to excel with their talents, their economic progress, their education. Removing barriers to either gender's excelling would help both sexes. Why can't men see that?"

"You'll have to show us. Become a suffragist." He smiled.

She turned back to stare at the mirror on the far wall. It reflected her mother's portrait behind the divan. "I never saw myself as being one of those kinds of 'Hurrah' suffrage women."

"Much as I hate to say this, perhaps you've been hiding your light under a bushel." Ben patted her shoulder.

"But back east . . . they hold parades and bang kettles on the streets and are so . . . strident. I don't see that going over well here. I don't want to compromise a woman's reputation. I want to expand it by showing that she can make good decisions, as a man can."

"Perhaps try another tactic."

What might that be?

Ben added, "They could vote out taxes they now have to pay."

"Yes. Women have taxation without representation. I believe the founding fathers had something to say about that. Not to mention the founding mothers. Bless Abigail Adams. But she couldn't get the word 'woman' added in either, though we all thought 'man' meant 'mankind' and not just the sex bearing whiskers."

"Expand that meaning. You can do it."

"I wish I knew for certain this was the best path

to take. And I so wish we had a map to get us there."

"There's little certainty in the world, Jenny. Except attitude and effort."

A beam of light came through the window then as they sat together, the shaft illuminating a circle on the carpet's burgundy-shaded cloth. Abigail's whole body warmed, whether from having the luxury of a husband who understood and supported her or from that light pouring through the window like a period at the end of a most meaningful sentence. And then she did know.

"Do you see that light, Ben? You'll think me foolish, but I think that's God sending me a sign." Maggie, her faithful sister, would say that too. "In women's suffrage lies the answer to women's liberty. I don't know why I never saw that light before."

SEVENTEEN

Misfortune's Middle Name

1865

Abigail's next novel started the morning after that suffrage conversation. It took on the message of freedom for women by building the case for a woman's right to vote. Women were capable of birthing citizens in a cradle and raising them up, so they ought to be hardy and smart enough to vote about a school board position or who ought to be president. She planned to work such arguments into a plot. She was invigorated and gave Ben's sage advice and that directional beam of light the credit.

She felt a new energy in her classroom lessons. She chatted longer with the parents of her students, especially the women, to get a feel for how her arguments landed on men's and women's heads. She started wearing a white silk scarf held at her bodice with a fancy pin to offset the dark clothes she wore. She felt in constant mourning, so black linsey-woolsey made sense, but the dark colors also weathered the tendering in the wash tubs better than the bleached cloth the hot summer sun forced her to don. She posted a sign about her sewing abilities, deciding that stitching other than quilts would be a good way to earn extra cash—but also give her time with women, a chance to listen to their interests to better incorporate a strategy for how to secure them the vote. The idea of a newspaper would stay a pipe dream.

She used her editor letters to start her campaign. Spoke with her next-door neighbor, carefully bringing up the subject of suffrage, and found there were others like herself, contented wives who wished for more. Oh, yes, she had a hundred ideas now that the focus of her energy was so clear. She loved the organizing, the idea-generating, pulse-driving joy of knowing where she was headed and having a path forward, even if she had to push the boulders out of the way herself. Ben's temperament, too, had lightened with his work with his horses again. There was singing in the house. His occasional sales of both washing machines and matched teams took her farther from her fears of poverty. She felt secure for the first time in years.

Through the opening in the glass door, she watched the sheriff walk up the steps. "What now?" she asked. She often made the sheriff a villain in the drafts of her novels. The one she worked on now had such a character.

"There's been an accident, Mrs. Duniway."

Abigail's eyes scanned the room: all children were present and accounted for.

"Ben? My sisters?"

"Ben." He held his hat in his hand and didn't look at her.

"Where? What happened. Children. Class dismissed." She reached for Wilkie, who had been playing quietly in the back of the classroom, something he did when Ben was either in his workshop or at the farm with the horses, which was where he should have been and was now. *Why when things are going so well does disaster always strike?*

"I'll take you to the doctor."

She swallowed the lump in her throat. "Clara. Watch them all."

Abigail rushed through the house, jammed a hat on her head, grabbed her purse, and went through the door the sheriff held open for her. She pressed the silk scarf at her throat, gaining small comfort from the softness. She waited to pepper the sheriff for answers until they were in the carriage. Spring birds chirped.

"Best I know, missus, is he was tossed from a wagon when a team he was working broke loose. They trampled him, the wagon straight across his back. Soft earth from the spring rains might have saved his life."

She breathed her prayers, trying not to chastise a God who allowed these tragedies, over and over. Financial strain. Ben's depression. Her own physical depletion, the joint aches the doctors named rheumatoid arthritis. Now this, when they were moving forward, had found a good routine and rhythm. *At least he's alive. At least he's alive.*

"Broken back," the doctor said. "I've given him laudanum for the pain. He'll need to be kept quiet. Fortunately, there doesn't appear to be any organ damage, just broken vertebrae from what I can determine by the feel of his spine."

"Just broken vertebrae." Her sarcasm appeared lost on the doctor. "Can he . . . will he walk?"

"Time will tell. Healing takes time." The doctor patted her hand as she sat beside Ben's bed at the doctor's office, the distant clank of instruments on metal punctuations to her rushing heartbeat and the patter of his retreating shoes leaving them alone.

"Oh, Ben." His eyes claimed hers.

"Sorry, Jenny."

"I know you are." She brushed hair from his forehead, watched the bruising spread before her eyes on his cheeks, even his hands. He forced a weak smile. She could only imagine what his back looked like.

"What'll we do?" Ben whispered through the laudanum haze.

"Right now, you'll heal. We'll pray your spine will hold you up again and you'll be back fit as a fiddle. I'm sure of it." *No, I'm not.* But she knew that he drew from her confidence. "You rest now. We'll be fine." She put all thoughts of the future aside and laid her head down on the bedside, breathed a prayer of gratitude that he was alive. They'd find a way to work things out, God willing. At least they didn't have Sunny Hillside Farm to take care of.

Ben's pain was like an uninvited guest who came to dinner, had to be accommodated, then stayed well past the promised departure time. In fact, Abigail began to wonder if there would be a departure time. He was a good patient, asked to be allowed to lift hand irons so he wouldn't lose arm strength. He let the nurses help him stand. He joked with them and made them laugh. Then when they left, he sighed to Abigail, leaned on her. "Will I ever walk again?"

She wanted time with that cheerful Ben who made the nurses and doctors grin with his stories. Instead she got needy Ben. Then she chastised herself for even lamenting her frustrations when he was dealing with broken bones and who knew what he might not be able to ever do again. He'd lost—at least temporarily—what he cherished: time with his horses and tossing Wilkie in the air to catch him. He could look forward to . . . what? Neither of them knew.

"John and Harvey have moved a bed into the parlor downstairs. I kept the piano in there so

Clara can practice and soothe you with music at the same time. She's quite good. I think we can stop the lessons. She can even *give* them."

"Hopefully we won't need a disrupted house for long. I'll be up. Lincoln's won reelection. The war is over. Hope is in the air."

"That's the Ben I married." She kissed him. "The doctors say you can come home any time we're ready. There's a chair with wheels to get you around, and John and Amos installed a board nicely smoothed by the boys you can pull on to get you upright and taking those steps."

"I'll miss the nurses offering aid." He smiled at her.

"I'm sure you will. The children can help and I will. When I can." She straightened his bedsheets, smoothed the pillowcase above his head. "I've been thinking, Ben. Albany's a larger city than Lafayette, and with the war ending, business will boom. Albany's got a steamboat stop from both north on the Willamette and south at Corvallis and the Calapooia. Bigger things are happening there. The Presbyterians have started a college and we could live right next door to the Fosters. You remember them? They had a house in Lafayette. And my sister Harriet lives in Albany now too, you remember."

He looked thoughtfully at her. "I've got my friends where we are. When I'm better, I'd have to find a farm to work the horses instead of being able to use Capt John's. Albany's farther away."

She didn't correct him but thought if he ever worked horses again it would be a miracle—if not a terrible mistake.

"There's a Union-leaning newspaper in Albany, giving the southern Democrats a run for their money. They already accepted a couple of my letters."

"Ah," Ben said.

"And we can purchase a bigger house there." She pulled a chair up beside him. The room smelled of disinfectant. "I've been thinking."

"No doubt."

"If we sell the school now, we'll make a profit. I've been looking over the figures. Plus, the extra room at this newer house I've found could be used for a retail operation, and there's . . . a bedroom on the main floor, to accommodate you. Us."

"You've located a house? When did you ever find the time? Oh. Sure. I've been here and you've been, well, carrying on."

"Didn't you expect me to?"

"No. Yes. Of course. It's what you do, thank goodness."

"I hand-delivered my letter to the paper a few weeks back and had time to talk with an agent." She looked away. "The house is perfect, Ben. A much bigger attic space. We could take in six boarders."

"And the retail idea?"

"I've a plan."

"You usually do. But leave Lafayette and our friends? Couldn't your plan involve where we are now?"

"You'll make new friends. You're good at that. Kate says I don't praise you enough for your many gifts."

"Bless Kate."

"I do. You do make friends easily and you keep them. Yes, they take advantage of you—at times." She added that last when he began to protest. "But your goodwill softens my shrill."

"Goodwill over shrill. I'll remember that."

"It'll serve you well in Albany. And we have to do some things differently now, Ben. You won't be able to . . . add to the teapot. At least for a time. We have to take advantage of the market. We must hire a nurse to help. Someone for you to flirt with when your old wifey is busy."

"You're the only one I want to help me walk again."

"I know."

He lifted her hand and kissed it. "Go ahead and get your house. You probably already have."

The teapot was the last of the items Abigail packed as the Scott sisters and their husbands helped the Duniways move. Again. The teapot sat proudly on the mantel over the fireplace in their new Albany home. It had coins in it again.

She might have exaggerated to Ben in a small way. The profit wasn't much from the sale of the school but sufficient to get them started. They'd still have to pinch their pennies, but she wanted to continue her newspaper subscriptions. She needed to see how the rest of the country was working on women's suffrage and how Oregon's campaigns would be different. But in Albany she could have conversations with the instructors at the college. She could debate with friends as well as those who saw the world differently than she did. She did love the intellectual pursuit. She might not have a Pacific University education like her brother, but she could go head-to-head with Harvey on current events around the world as well as at home, she was certain of that. He might have an advantage as he studied law now, too, in addition to having access to every book in that Portland library collection. She wished Ben liked to read more, but his was an oral tradition, telling stories rather than reading them.

Perhaps the move was more for her than for the rest of the family, though the extra space did help Ben move more easily, first with the wheeled chair and then with canes. The children would adjust. They had Scott blood in them and knew how to persevere. The Duniway side seemed a bit more fragile. She had to remember that as she watched Ben sigh when he looked over the financial sheets she'd showed him and told him of loose boards in the attic. The house's foundation was sound, but the roof would need buttressing.

Abigail hired men to fix rafters, put old newspapers for insulation in the walls, readied the attic for additional boarders while she drew out on paper how she wanted the largest room on the first floor converted. "We'll put the glass case here, where one can stand behind it and take out the beaded purses from the back.

"I can build those cases."

"Can you?" She hadn't thought he could do such work. "That would be wonderful, Ben."

"It'll take me a little time." Ben stood steadied by two canes. "Willis can help. And Hubert. I can sit."

"Then we'll have clothes trees along that back wall where we can shape wires to hold the ready-made dresses. They'll be hung rather than folded, giving a better view of the handiwork from the moment people come into the store. Fortunately, there's a separate entrance, so people won't need to tromp through the house."

"I can twist wires into round shapes to hold the hats." Clara showed her parents one she'd made.

"That's perfect. They can be bookends on the glass cases. We need to make the counters wide enough to accommodate the hat stands but also allow people to look down through to see the wares for sale." She kissed the top of Clara's head and gently touched the cascade of curls that fell to her nearly twelve-year-old shoulders. *She's beautiful. We need to be sure she finishes school and make suitors wait.* "My creative daughter."

"I can sew too, Momma."

"Better than me, that's for certain. But I want to hire out seamstresses, give Albany women money for their work. With the war over, we'll have a booming business. Women like to have other women do the fitting and stitching. When you're older." She saw the disappointment. "You'll do well behind the counters, Clara. You could knit a purse or two. That would add to the stock."

"What stock?" Ben said.

"My kind of stock is going to come from my teapot nest egg. I'm taking my thirty dollars and heading on the steamboat to Portland to meet with Jacob Mayer. He's that retail genius in Portland where things are booming too. I'm going to ask for a loan, then head to San Francisco and get the latest frocks and unmentionables, needles and threads, and felted hats."

"A loan."

"Yes. I can show him how I can repay him. I've got the numbers all worked out. You're making progress. It won't be long, and you'll be contributing better than you did before. The pain is less, isn't it?"

"It comes and goes. The laudanum helps."

"At least there's something." She didn't like him taking the liquid because it made him so sleepy. But life was a balance. Without it he suffered; with it, more often than not, he lay in the shadows.

"You're leaving me behind, Mrs. Duniway."

"No, I'm not. I'm moving *us* forward. You're right with me. You checked the figures. I'll build up a way to push for suffrage—my way. No parades or crazy-marching women holding signs. My way is a 'still hunt.' Quiet coercion of men in power and men in general to be less frightened by women. I need capital to do that. I think Jacob Mayer has a nose for investments, and I want ours to be his next. But I can't do it without your approval."

He shook his head. "You can. I wish I could help more. You won't need me in the end."

A flash of anger surged through her. *Why do I have to prop you up? Don't I have enough to do?*

"I'll always need you, Ben. You're my rock. You keep me out of trouble. Well, sometimes. People love you. They tolerate me."

"You're strong enough not to care."

"Oh, I care. But I can't let it deter me from my task."

"Being the breadwinner. Yes. I know. I'm so sorry."

"Making a difference for women, Ben. That's the task. And you help with that by progressing, being there for the children and letting me be me despite the boulders I uncover on this journey we're on. Now, you work on your exercises while I head to Portland. And say a prayer that Mr. Mayer will have the vision to support Albany's newest millinery."

EIGHTEEN

The Stars and Spoils

Abigail loved the bustle of Portland. The clatter of harness and hames—even the smell of horse droppings in the streets near the still unpulled tree stumps—didn't offend her. Good walkways bordered the shops. She might even stop by and see Harvey at the library if things went well with Mr. Mayer. The merchant had begun a new business, Fleishner, Mayer and Co., with two brothers from Albany—of late and earlier from Germany. The Albany dry goods store had closed, and the men partnered in Portland now. Abigail could see why. This was the city of Oregon's future. But for now, she hoped to capitalize on the customers they'd left behind.

Mr. Mayer was a smallish man with bright brown eyes and hair slicked back over a beginning-to-bald pate. She started to introduce herself, but he interrupted. "I know who you are, Mrs. Duniway. I read the papers up and down the valley. You've quite a poison pen—when it calls for. I approve of your support of the downtrodden and the Jews as well."

"I guess I ought not be surprised that you'd reviewed my history, knowing I came to ask you for money. I didn't think my political proclivities would enter into the discussion."

"A man doesn't want to do business with someone he wouldn't introduce to his wife or family."

"I'd be honored to meet your family one day." She was pleased he wasn't put off by her columns that sometimes pushed aside a woman's role as demonstrating solely decorum and a family focus. "For now, I have a solid business plan I want to share with you."

She watched him read her documents. She was glad she'd dressed in her finest black dress worn over the larger bustle that the wind-down of the war allowed. She was up-to-date and as fashionable as any *Godey's Lady's Book* model.

He laughed and she swallowed bile. "Thirty dollars, Mrs. Duniway?"

"Is it—I thought it a reasonable amount."

"No, I won't loan you that."

"I'm good for it." Her face felt hot with embarrassment.

"Your reputation says as much. No, I won't loan you thirty dollars." He adjusted his glasses. "But I will loan you twelve hundred dollars to buy stock in San Francisco."

"That's . . . stunning. Thank you for your confidence in me."

"And why not. You've a good business head, Mrs. Duniway, and you can see what women are interested in, now that the war is over and it's safe to spend again. Prosperity. Yes, I think you are right at the cusp of it, and I'm happy to be of assistance."

She barely remembered the steamship ride back. She told Ben that evening and his proud grin pleased her no end. "Oh Ben, he believed in me."

"Smart man."

"I'll head south tomorrow and make my purchases. I've already paid for an ad in next week's paper. Clara's ready to stand behind the counter."

"And I can too," Ben said. "I'll wear my best coat and collar."

"It won't tire you?"

"Got myself a stool to sit on, but I'm taking steps with only one cane."

She hugged him. "That's so good, Ben."

When she started to break away, he kept his arms around her. "I only want to hold you close for a moment. Kiss my happy retail magnate." He did kiss her then, and she let herself sink into his arms.

"I'm not a magnate yet." She pushed herself away, though he still linked his arms around her waist. "Only on the journey. I hope. One I need to pack for."

"Just so long as I'm on the voyage with you."

"You always will be. Not literally, of course.

You're not up to a steamship ride yet." She patted his vested chest. *He always takes such good care of his person. Tidy.* "I'm not sure I could do any of this without you."

She wished his progress made her as giddy as her success with Jacob Mayer, but she was genuinely pleased he wanted to help and pushed himself to do it. They were a team, though not one exactly matched.

Abigail made the trip to San Francisco, bought her twelve hundred dollars' worth of baubles and beads, fabrics and finery, and returned to sell them. She paid Mr. Mayer back within three weeks and returned to California with a three-thousand-dollar advance from the financier and came back to sell those items too. She'd been at the front of a buying boom and was in the right town to make that happen. Only Lincoln's assassination had slowed things as the country mourned.

"Did you read Harvey's essay about Lincoln published in the *Oregonian*?" Kate asked. "It's quite moving."

Even Abigail had to admit to the passion and the expression of grief brother Harvey so beautifully conveyed.

Then Maggie, their faith-loving sister, died that fall, and Abigail was back to wearing black.

They'd taken in eight-year-old Annie, as

Maggie's children were brought into their aunts' folds. Harvey, with more means than any of them, had not taken on his nieces or nephews as wards. *Where is his generous Scott heart?*

"That husband of hers," Abigail complained to Ben as she packed for yet another buying trip to California. "He took Maggie on that swampy boat in and out of coastal ports selling bread and basics, putting her right in the path of consumption. And then did nothing to help her when she became ill. He didn't even let us know. Just allowed her to suffer." She sat at the edge of the bed, noticed a sock stuck between the mattress and the footboard, and grabbed for it. "She hadn't wanted to go with him to the coast in the first place. How I wish she'd stood up to him."

"She believed a woman must listen to her husband. A God-given requirement of a good wife. You know that."

"But there are other ways to interpret that Scripture. We are all made in God's image, so we are all equal, though different. There's that message too. Her word means as much as his, it does. More, because frankly she's smarter than George Fearnside. Was smarter." Her death was one more on the heels of Lincoln's assassination. It was nearly too much to bear.

But then, Maggie's children were now under the spell of their aunts, away from their father's influence. Maybe it was good that women would have more to say over the little girls and not have them exposed to the restrictive views of women's roles that their father held. Or that Harvey did. Harvey had told sister Fanny that he didn't approve of Abigail traveling so much for business, that it wasn't a woman's place. She'd confront him at some point, but it was so like him to complain to another sister rather than speak to her directly. He wouldn't like at all her decision to have another woman present at the store while she traveled—a woman who would also share the financial load. With Ben's consent, she'd taken on a female partner.

"A prominent family," Ben commented. He straightened a small area of men's hats that Abigail had decided to purchase to see if they would sell in a woman's shop.

"They're good Republicans," she said. "She's operated a millinery out of their parlor on Elm Street so knows that trail all right. She has the social contacts, and as you know, my social skills aren't always the best."

Ben laughed. He sat behind a glass case, his body filling out again as he became more mobile and active and didn't need the medication so much. Nor the canes. But the pain came and went, ebbing and flowing like the tide. He'd wince bending to pull a carrot from the garden. That could put him down for hours.

"With a partner, I can be away from here now and then with fewer worries."

"But the children are devoted to you and really like your being around more. I want to start training again, Abigail. I don't want the accident to keep me from getting 'back on that horse,' so to speak."

Abigail was grateful Ben had improved, but it also meant he had more ideas and sought greater independence that forced her into new arguments to get him to accept her "plans."

She resented the weight of responsibility of being the primary supporter, but she also liked holding the reins. As he got better, he'd have to make different accommodations. "I suppose we could use the extra income if you're successful. But it's risky too. You could get hurt again."

"And you could get hurt traveling so much, alone as you do. I should go with you."

"One of us has to stay with the children. And I'm only gone for a few days at a time." She reset a feathered hat on one of Clara's wire head mounts. "All right, let's give it a try. Maybe a day or so a week?"

"Aunt Abigail, can I help in the store?" Annie's voice broke into their discussion.

"May you help," Abigail corrected. "Of course. What would you like to do?"

"I can draw pictures to put in the window." She pointed to the glass behind a sitting area where friends could wait during a fitting. She showed her aunt a drawing she'd done.

"Very good, Annie. Let's see what you can do for a newspaper ad. Would you like to try that? Clara, can you find lead and wrapping paper?"

"I would." Annie danced her way out of the room, the first time Abigail had seen the girl smile since her mother's death.

"Training needs to be daily," Ben said.

"What? Oh, yes, we were speaking of your getting back on that horse, so to speak."

"I'll spend the mornings."

"Yes. All right. Mornings."

The new partner would increase sales. She would share the costs—but also any profits. Business or personal, there would be a price to pay. Relationships were so unpredictable, and she longed for certainty—certainty she could control.

The family gathered to attend Harvey's wedding at the end of October to Elizabeth, a quiet soul who adored him as she gazed at him with admiration in her eyes. He was quite a catch, Abigail decided, though his domineering opinions about everything meant Elizabeth might have a difficult time expressing hers—especially if they differed. The woman didn't say much, so the sisters weren't sure what she thought about issues of the day. Still, she knew Latin, which probably attracted Harvey to her in the first place. She did say she found it quite remarkable that Abigail traveled so much when she had young children still at home. *I wonder where she heard that?* "Steamships are so full of . . . strangers." Elizabeth dabbed at her full lips with her napkin. "What if something should happen?"

"I find travel quite invigorating," Abigail told her. They were at the breakfast Abigail hosted for the couple at the Albany Hotel when they returned from their honeymoon. Abigail was rather pleased they had the finances to put on such an elegant breakfast for them. She was as prosperous as Harvey was. In a way. At least she wanted him to conclude that.

Rain fell, but it didn't prevent Kate and John from arriving from Canemah. Fanny and Amos sat at the far end of the table, ferns behind them moving gently as the servers passed by. Harriet and William sat across from the Captain and Kate, while eighteen-year-old sister Sarah sat next to Ben. It was the first time they'd gathered since Maggie's death, as Fanny hadn't been able to make Harvey's wedding. She'd been struggling with morning sickness.

"One simply has to let go of having total control when traveling," Abigail said. "There are opportunities for serendipitous moments on a steamship or even a stagecoach."

"I never thought of you as liking the unpredictable," Harvey said.

"I'm quite adaptable."

Harvey coughed and raised his eyebrows toward Ben.

"One has to be," Abigail continued. "That's what wives and mothers do, adjust to the whims and fortunes of their men. Let that be a warning to you, Elizabeth." She raised her fork to emphasize her point.

"Seems to me you do more than adjust." Harvey leaned back to allow the server to place bacon strips onto his plate. "I see you planning the destination, setting the sails, and if the captain would let you, organizing the wheelhouse." Harvey smiled at her, more indulgent than critical, but she took afront anyway.

"I prefer to be the captain, it's true. But I know how to be a good crew member too."

"She runs a tight ship." Ben passed the rolls around. "And she's the hardest working woman I know of. Fingers in lots of pies."

"A sign of a life with misplaced purpose perhaps. Being a dutiful wife and mother is a higher calling than indulging in the business world, rushing off to San Francisco, writing letters to the editor exposing yourself to public criticism, leaving poor Ben to manage the home fires you ought to be tending."

"Poor Ben does fine," Abigail said. "Don't you, Ben."

"That I do. I've got a matched team ready for sale. Not the pair that got away from me.

Someone else finished them. Wish I could have."

"You're back at doing what you love. Good for you, Ben." Harvey turned to his new wife. "He talked of little else when we were at the mines together. Well, horses were second—to Abigail and the children. He both loved and loathed your lengthy letters, Sister."

"Loathed?" She looked at Ben.

His cheeks above his reddish beard had turned a shade of pink. She had been hard on him at times, begging him to come home but not until he struck gold; telling him stories of how the children missed him while listing needs they had and hoped he could meet.

"I told him to overlook your punctuation," Harvey said. His usual downturned lips lifted in his moment of jest—at someone else's expense, Abigail noted.

"It was missing you all," Ben said. "Your letters made me sad and glad at the same time."

"Well," Abigail said. "Words have power. I won't apologize for that. Nor should anyone who writes of truth and heart, even with bad punctuation. Some of us had the benefit of early education, and some of us were sickly and worked our fingers to the bone."

"Have you settled into your Portland home, Elizabeth?" Kate said. "It's a lovely area of the city."

Catherine, ever the diplomat.

"Yes. We have. And it's so much closer now to Harvey's new appointment."

"What's that, Brother?" Sarah asked.

"I've been named the editor of the *Oregonian*. Mr. Pittock liked my essay on Lincoln so much he made the offer. And I accepted." He beamed.

"You're the editor?" Harriet said. "Congratulations. That's quite a feat."

"It is indeed," Ben said. Congratulations were sent across the table.

Abigail bit off her biscuit, staring at Harvey, who smirked at her. She didn't see a newly examined lawyer, head of the Portland library, and now editor of the *Oregonian*. She saw her little brother putting himself above her just because he'd been born a boy.

"If I'd had primary schooling and a college education, I'd have been a newspaper editor by the time I was twenty-one, not waited until I was twenty-seven."

"Abigail," Fanny chastened.

"I didn't realize you aspired to be a newspaper editor," Harvey said.

"I do. And I will be one day." She took a deep breath. "But congratulations anyway, Harvey. You've done the Scott name proud. And who knows, you might be publishing one of my essays one of these days."

"I look forward to that. Make sure you double-check your punctuation."

NINETEEN

An Editorial Option

1866

Abigail waited at the landing called Steamboat Point in San Francisco, her ship having rattled by swamps still visible in a city infused with gold and silver riches. Porters carried trunks off, and others dragged luggage and who knew what all on board, followed by passengers dressed in the finery Abigail hoped to find duplicates of and purchase. She was anxious to do her buying, read the *News of the World* and other local newspapers, and be treated to supper in the ladies' dining room of the Cosmopolitan Hotel. A porter called a cab for her—drawn by a white horse that made her think of Ben—and when the porter helped her up, she saw that another passenger waited inside.

"Jenny Scott? Can that be you?"

"Shirley Ellis? Oh, what a wonder!" Her mind flashed back to the girl who had pierced her ears. A slender young woman smiled back at her, though with eyes that showed more strain than the sparkle she'd been known for on the trail across.

"Jenny Duniway, I mean. What are you doing here?"

"I'm on a buying mission. Dress trimmings, threads, the latest in hats."

"Of course you are. I remember you writing about your millinery. What a gift our paths should pass in person once again. Let me look at those earrings."

Abigail turned her head.

"Still look fine."

"They're my favorite, though I've a dozen pair now."

"How's Ben? Your children?"

"Thriving. What are you doing in San Francisco?"

"I moved here from Sacramento. I'm teaching and just took a friend to the ship. You'll stay with me, won't you? We've so much to catch up on."

For a moment Abigail longed for that quiet supper at the hotel. She liked solitary times when her thinking became clearer, and after supper, she'd enjoy the time to write, free of distractions. Still, seeing Shirley again reminded her of good times the girl—the woman—had brought during hard trials. And she had yet to hear what Shirley thought about the novel she'd sent her.

"Yes. I'd be pleased."

Shirley hugged Abigail as she settled onto the leather seat. She was surprised to feel tears in her eyes. Shirley's presence brought back memories of her mother, the journey across the continent, and her youngest brother's death too. Shirley had helped them all out of their sorrows, made her and her sisters laugh despite themselves. She was also reminded of how glorious it was to have an old friend. They chatted and caught up, and it was as though no time had ever separated them.

"You're limping," Shirley said when they stepped out of the cab.

"Sometimes. After sitting a long time. It's my joints and the strain of childbirth. I think the latter is passed now." She smiled. "Too busy supporting the family to have time to make it larger."

"I'd love to meet your children. And Ben."

"Come and visit but wait until spring or summer. The rains are wretched, the only thing I dislike about Oregon."

"We have our share too." A wet December fog near the Bay had them pull out their umbrellas when they reached the brownstone building where the driver stopped. "I don't suppose the rains do anything to soothe your bones either. Here we are." They climbed the stairs to the third floor. Shirley opened and closed her umbrella to knock the rain off, then unlocked her door, and they entered the tiny apartment, nicely furnished. The umbrellas were popped into the stand.

"It's lovely." And it was, with no clutter, no children's toys lying about, no business dealings mixed in with family. Abigail set her carpetbag down. She loved tidiness but couldn't seem to manage it in her own life. A wreath of grapevines with peacock feathers accented with burgundy bows hung over the fireplace. "That's gorgeous. Did you make it?"

"Oh, no. There's a collective, a group of women who make crafts to sell, to support themselves and their children. My women's group helps them. Will you buy Christmas items this trip?"

"Most seasonal items were commissioned before September. But if there are more of those, I might take a few back. They look so festive. Your entire apartment does."

"It's big enough for our women's gatherings. Now that the war is over, we can put our hearts and hands into being able to manage our own money, gaining property rights for women, achieving custody of our children."

"And voting."

"Oh, yes, the franchise. You wait. California will be the leader in the West getting women's suffrage. We're organizing. Maybe your next trip you can attend a meeting. There's strength in numbers." A daguerreotype of Shirley holding an infant sat on the sideboard. Shirley paused to look at it before she stepped into the galley kitchen. "Our efforts won't be taken well by the men of California, and yet we have to win them over to get our way. We're tightrope walkers balancing on a swinging rope."

"Is that . . . ?" Abigail turned to Shirley, holding the photograph.

Shirley looked at the picture in its cast-iron frame. "It's a sad story. My husband brought her here to San Francisco when he divorced me after only a year. I don't know how I chose so poorly." She sighed. "He told the court he could care for her better, and I've rarely been allowed to even see her. If he knew I was involved with women's advocacy, he'd cut off even those few visits."

"I didn't know."

"Shame has a way of silencing people."

"But why should you be ashamed? You didn't do anything wrong."

"I never should have married him. My parents warned me against him. I didn't listen. They worry over my women's meetings too, but I have to put my heartache somewhere, make a difference for my daughter's future life. The friend I told you about from Roseburg, she's divorced with a child too and has endured rebuke because of it. Fortunately her parents supported her decision, as well they should have. They married her off when she was fourteen, and the man was abusive. He's moved to San Francisco. She's hoping to gain custody of their son."

"There must be a few men who share our hopes. Ben does. I'm so grateful for that." Abigail pulled the pins from her hat, removed it. She realized how much Ben's support meant to her, his goodness and how despite letter-writing attacks on her, he never suggested she was anything more than a dutiful wife and mother. She wondered if she'd have the strength to pursue her frank letters, push to be accepted in places that barred women, if she didn't have the confidence that Ben offered.

"There's the *Pioneer*." Shirley pointed to a newspaper lying on her table. "Sit and read while I fix us tea." She heated water while Abigail scanned the single sheet. "Have you officially organized your group? Tried to vote or anything like Susan B. Anthony did back east?"

"We're starting to gather. It's so much easier with pals. The hardest is getting the word out so women know they aren't alone."

"That it is." She turned to the backside of the *Pioneer*, read the masthead. "It has a woman editor."

"Yes. One of the first on the West Coast."

"A woman editor." She thought of Harvey and his editorial against free secondary education, leaving the masses without hope of advancing themselves unless they had money. He'd influence voters with his opinions that were now able to go out across the West—if not back east. "It would take quite a bit to finance a newspaper. I've done some figuring. That's why moneymen are the ones who do it."

"The *Pioneer* has backers, I'm sure. You could meet with her on your next trip."

"I'd like that."

She might be able to submit some of her essays and articles to the *Pioneer* and gain a wider audience.

"Along with taking back fabric, I think you've given me something else to return with," she said as Shirley filled the teapot with steaming water. "A newspaper, one that speaks for women's needs and desires and encourages women and girls. That's what Oregon needs."

Yes, she would write for newspapers that advocated a better life for women and children, her children and Maggie's and all girls. Perhaps operate a publishing company. It would be her new method to achieve that most important goal of freedom for women. It could give Harvey's *Oregonian* a run for his money. But first she had to plan it out, figure out the financing, and get Ben behind it. Because it would mean a move. They'd have to live in Portland, the fastest-growing city in the region. And of course, where Harvey presided. She'd take her silent hunt right into the king's forest.

There was no move to Portland and no newspaper either. Life got in the way. Harvey's wife gave birth to a baby boy, but the family soon grieved when the child failed to thrive and died before reaching two months. Abigail sent a condolence letter, her words as tender as any she had exchanged with Harvey. No room for anything but compassion.

"Stay a little," Ben told her one February morning in 1866. Ben had been down—to use a term for horses foundering—from his having twisted strangely while lifting a leather collar over a pinto's neck. He'd done it a hundred times without issue, but this time he'd been brought home by a neighbor who had heard his shout while passing by where Ben rented land to work his teams. "Rest," the doctor had told them. This day, she'd picked up Ben's noontime food tray and what was left of the ham sandwich and the crusts of bread Chen had freshly made. Ben didn't like the crusts.

"You're always so busy." Ben patted the bed. "Come. Sit."

"If I sat down now, I'd fall asleep in seconds."

"Would that be so bad?"

"It would. I have to finish the order, among other things. Just rest as the doctor said. Or read." She heard the edge to her voice and the twinge of resentment that seeped in when he did foolish things that he knew could result in a recurrence of his back strain, forcing days in bed, leaving her to wonder if this was the incident that would seal his life as an invalid. Their lives, with him once again barely able to walk. "What I wouldn't give to have the time to reread *The Woman in White* or dig into my shelf of books I have only read once."

"You work too hard." He winced as he moved

over to make room for her. "Put the tray down. Lie beside me. Let me hold you. You do so much."

She sighed and rested her head on the pillow, facing him. He stroked her arm. In seconds she was asleep.

"Jenny? Jenny."

"How long was I out?"

"Only fifteen minutes. I knew you'd never nap beside me again if I let you sleep until you awoke on your own."

"That would have been tonight at 10:00 p.m." She yawned. "I would have harangued you when I saw the wasted time if you'd let me sleep on. There's too much to do. I've got three dresses to finish."

"You can slow down a bit. Wouldn't hurt you."

"Don't, Ben. I don't want to argue with you now about my pace or schedule."

"Me neither." He kissed her nose, started to kiss her lips but stopped. His voice lightened. "Go on. Tend to business. Maybe I'll get you tomorrow for another catnap if you see I can let you go, even when I'd rather keep you here." He flashed that smile at her, the one that had won her heart those years before.

"I hope that by tomorrow you'll feel able to get up again."

"I'm sure of it. But if not, watching my wife slumber is one of the rare pleasures to come from this . . . spine with a life of its own." He touched her elbow as though to help her sit. "Would you put my name on tomorrow's dance card?"

"Sleep card, more like it." She sat up, straightened her hair combs as he rubbed her back.

"Off with you," he said.

Maybe I should stay. The snooze had refreshed her, and he had awakened her and was letting her go, when she could tell he wanted the comfort of her presence. Maybe more. *And would it be so bad to let your husband love you?* " 'The things nearby, not the things afar,' " she quoted.

"What's that?"

"Just thinking. I hope you've no need to rest tomorrow, but if you do, I'll see if you want to have an old tired woman take a lie-down beside you."

"It's a deal, though you're far from a tired old woman."

In March of 1866 Abigail discovered she was pregnant. There was joy, yes, but angst too. She was thirty-two years old, had already given birth to four children, with only one arriving without much trouble. Months abed followed the delivery and to have both her and Ben foundering wouldn't do.

Ben was delighted. "You'll have to stay at home more."

"This is the last one now. It has to be." She'd have to read more about timing births. There were ways to do that.

"Whatever you say." He grinned.

"I imagine you can hardly wait to let your horse friends know."

"I'm back in the saddle," Ben joked while Abigail blushed.

It was probably the mood swings caused by the pregnancy, but she found herself annoyed by the children more, by Ben—even though he was up and only occasionally using his cane as the summer progressed. Even Mrs. Jackson, her partner, irritated her with her constant fluttering over the books, "questioning her judgment," rather than merely inquiring over an entry she had made. Mrs. Jackson didn't think they should branch out into dry goods, such as the wreaths Abigail had brought back from San Francisco. Such items were seasonal and no competition for the Jackson store, so Abigail didn't see the problem. Nothing irked her more than having someone question her competence or judgment. Mrs. Jackson also made noises that Abigail should pull back her letter-writing to the newspaper. But Abigail believed that in this time of government turmoil—a new president, the war ended—people were most likely to consider change. *People,* being men who had all the power over the vote. Mrs. Jackson had made noises about Abigail being a tad too strident in her letters before.

"It's time," she told Ben.

"But she's a huge help to you."

"Trying to be diplomatic is not my forte, as you well know. It takes more energy to hold my tongue than to live with a little business uncertainty."

She arranged to buy her partner out, settling the split on good terms, as she didn't want bad feelings to filter onto the customers Mrs. Jackson had brought to the millinery.

The newspaper idea would have to wait, as would the organizing of women, until after Abigail gave birth that November.

"Another voter in the cradle." Abigail smiled at Clyde, whose delivery had gone surprisingly well. He was a sweet baby who curled into her arms and gazed at her with eyes that seemed to bore right through her. As with Clara who was her first, Clyde was to be special—as their last child.

"No more babies," she told Ben.

"Of course," he'd agreed. *Why wouldn't he? He doesn't have to bear the morning sickness.*

And like her, he loved his children, whose personalities blossomed. Willis, a boy who could declaim on any number of subjects from the

Constitution to the life cycle of a butterfly and who enjoyed his lessons, always finishing first. Hubert was her outdoor child, his father's helper in the garden—except when he joined Ben in his woodshop—and who knew the name of every tree and plant on their street. Wilke loved to play games like Tiddlywinks, garnering stacks of colored winks, always urging a little competition especially with his older brother. It was a popular game. She interrupted the boys when they teased Clara Belle as she practiced scales, or pulled on cousin Annie's pigtails just because they could. The girls held a special place in her heart, and it pleased her that neither of them had blisters or backaches from the heavy work of farming or even laundry.

The work of family life had been spread out, and if it wasn't for Ben's intermittent bouts of increased pain and decreased ability to hold his own for weeks at a time, life would have gone on without major worries. Money in the teapot brought her closer to that newspaper. And she almost believed everything would turn out all right.

TWENTY

Tend and Befriend

1868

Abigail hated missing her annual trip to San Francisco in November to review spring fashions. She wired money to Shirley, who made the purchases, and Abigail paid her a commission for her work. Shirley used the money for legal fees, she told Abigail, still seeking more time with her daughter. Shirley told her one of her attorneys, Eloi Vasquez, had taken an interest in her case—and her. *"He's of Spanish descent with cocoa skin and dark eyes and I think I'm falling in love,"* Shirley had written. *"Perhaps that verse about all things coming together for good was speaking to me all the time."*

"Maybe that's so for me too," Abigail had written back.

Travel stimulated Abigail's thinking. She was challenged by dealing with new people, had no fear of disagreeing with those who saw the world differently. Their perspectives gave her ideas for her novel. She liked seeing how another state intervened in the suffrage fight. But alas, mothering kept her close to home, working in the millinery and being a seamstress. She didn't see much stimulation in that work.

Then a mother brought her fifteen-year-old daughter in for a fitting of a dress. The girl had a waist the size of an embroidery hoop, with skin as white as a baby's first tooth. *Listless* was the word Abigail used to describe her as she pinned the dress the mother had sewed. The woman hadn't been satisfied with her own efforts and so had hired Abigail to make alterations. The child's corset trussed her already ample breasts and tiny middle into an abnormally curvy shape.

"Do you like the way the dress fits you?" Abigail asked the girl, who had shrugged her shoulders.

"What does it matter if she likes it or not," the mother said. "Fix the gap between her small midriff and her bodice. The dress needs to make her look . . . inviting."

"What is she inviting?" Abigail loosened the pins and let out the material so the bodice wasn't pushing upward in such a stark fashion.

"She's of marriage age. What else?"

"Yes, she is. But many girls are waiting." Abigail kept her voice light, as though she gossiped about the latest news rather than promoting an obvious contrast to the mother's view. "Girls are going to school and finding interests, in addition to traditional roles." She fussed at the sleeves but returned to loosening the waistline. *We have to do something about the corset.* "Some of the latest fashions from San Francisco—where I've been going on buying trips—are designed to have a little fuller waistline. Just as we are all free from the war, our bodies are seeking freedoms too. Our corsets might be squeezing the life from us women. There'd be less fainting or need for smelling salts if we could take deeper breaths." She smiled, engaging the mother while she let out the dress seams.

"She does faint often. I assumed it was her weak nature—which makes her less appealing to the opposite sex, of course, and means I must do everything I can to affect that."

"Let's loosen those stays, shall we?" Abigail raised the girl's arms and did the deed before the mother could protest. "Doesn't that feel better?"

"Yes, ma'am, it does." The girl's eyes sparkled. She inhaled and let a long breath escape. *She's relieved.*

"After she's done her religious duty and married and had children, she can think about taking deeper breaths."

"The frock will fit better if it's looser," Abigail said. "And give her room to eat a bit more. Robust is invitational too." *Healthy is the finest aphrodisiac of all.* "My own Clara Belle has found less corset and more carrots give her energy, and she can sing better too."

"Really?" It was the first time the mother seemed intrigued by Abigail's words.

"Are you a singer?" Abigail asked the girl.

"She's a lead in the church choir. The young music director has shown an interest in her voice."

"You see? Let her natural talent loose and who knows what joys the Lord might bring into her life."

The mother harrumphed but gave Abigail the go-ahead to loosen the whalebone stays a bit more. The dress fit much better and made the girl look less like a wicker mannequin and more like a young woman.

"You're a fine seamstress," Abigail told the mother. "This was an easy fix. We have to pay more attention to our God-created forms and not let fashion force us into . . . unintended shapes. I'll finish this up and you can return for a final fitting next week. Will that work?"

"I hope we haven't ruined her invitational design," her mother said.

"Ah, enticements come in many forms. Natural being the best of all."

The girl smiled and her cheeks held color for the first time since she'd arrived.

That day Abigail realized she could affect a girl's future right at home. The satisfaction surprised her. Perhaps those words in the intimacy of a fitting room were part of a "still hunt." She'd make sure Clara Belle knew that her own corset fittings had influenced another young girl's future. Sway could happen any place where one paid attention, one conversion at a time.

"We have to have a specific plan for the newspaper," Abigail decided.

The entire family sat around the table. Ben ground coffee beans as Abigail urged how they might all get involved in starting a newspaper. Clara's musical talents were advanced enough that she began giving music lessons for actual pay rather than trading for beef or pork. The boys could contribute to the Duniway finances by shooting sparrows to sell to the local butcher— the ones the Duniways didn't eat themselves. Ben, back working with the horses, taking only small doses of laudanum that kept the pain from spiking, also helped.

Abigail speculated on a piece of property near the dock after a day she'd taken a brisk walk and saw the potential there. The property wasn't yet for sale but should have been. She located the owner, made an offer, and it was the Duniways'— who sold it two weeks later at double the price when a steamship operator decided it was the perfect site for his expansion. *Just as I thought.* She'd figured that out before he had.

Ben had put his name to the purchase and the sale as required. But he resisted her suggestion that they speculate on Portland property. "It'll never be as big a place as Albany," he'd said.

But off and on he bought land that she told him would be good investments in towns throughout the state. She put a portion each week of millinery income into the teapot for her newspaper.

She used old *Argus* issues to cut out dress patterns she'd seen in *Godey's Lady's Book*. She could spy a dress photograph and remake the design. She hadn't thought of it as unusual, but her sisters all brought ads to her to reproduce the patterns. She did that while she spoke with Ben. "Harvey's buying Portland property and selling like we did here in Albany. At a profit." She considered asking Harvey to make a purchase or two for her, but he'd never agree to such a thing without Ben's approval. "We'll rue the day we let land on Front Street slip by us. I could be a very rich woman if not for hesitation of the male sex."

When she wasn't working in the millinery, making patterns, dusting the plate rail in the parlor, directing the children and breaking up skirmishes between the boys, and potty training her toddler, she was imagining plot lines. If she could sell more novels, she could add to the money in the teapot and they would one day have that newspaper. *Judith Reid* consumed her days. She wrote the novel as though she were Judith, a woman who had loved an artist who disappeared. Judith, the lead character, is then taken to Oregon from Missouri, where her mother dies. Judith must care for her siblings and is forced to work in her father's sawmill. She makes the audacious decision to defy her father, resist the "invitation" of a reckless man whom her father chose for her to marry, and returns to Missouri where she rediscovers her long-lost artist, and both live happily ever after. She read her book out loud to Ben.

"I always like a happy ending," he said. "But why do the men always have to be such scoundrels. And is the first love always the best? I mean, it was for me with you, but I wonder if it was for you with me?"

He pulled his starched collar from his neck and put it in the box on the dresser top. They'd returned from church, lunched, and had the afternoon for a quiet time and so she'd read to him.

"It's not about you, Ben, or me. It's fiction. Listen to what *Putnam's Weekly* says about the novel." She picked up the popular magazine. " 'Novels are one of the features of our age. We know not what we would do without them. . . . Do you wish to instruct, to convince, to please? Write a novel! Have you a system of religion or politics or manners or social life to inculcate? Write a novel!' See, a story is the perfect way to convince women of what's possible. Readers expect to be entertained, but there has to be tension and struggle as there is in life. They wouldn't read it if it didn't have something the characters are trying to accomplish and the reader given to wonder if they'll ever achieve it."

"The women always come out smelling like roses though."

"It's the only place where we can be assured of roses. Real life promises us thorns."

"Not always." He looked at Clyde turning pages in a book as he sat on the horsehair-covered chair.

"True. But enough encounters to leave us bleeding. I write so women know there are other ways of living, especially if we stand firm and don't marry the first man who asks us. Or don't assume an early marriage is a requirement of womanhood. Just see where I'd be if I'd fallen into Mr. Bunter's trap."

"Your timing was excellent, Mrs. Duniway," Ben teased.

Except when it comes to having babies. Clyde really must be our last. "Well, you had a big part in when we got married, as did my father's poor decision."

"But everything worked out." Ben kissed her neck. "Didn't it?"

"Yes, it has. But there's so much more to do, Ben."

"There always is, with you."

＊ ＊ ＊

"I'll have to sell," Kate said.

"Probably let the help go?"

"We shouldn't have had so many children so close together."

"What's done is done, Catherine. Regrets will weigh you down. Let's think of the options you have."

There'd been an accident, an explosion on board the steamship, and Captain John was dead. It wasn't fair. So much of life wasn't. Abigail helped her sister through the funeral and the reading of the will several weeks later. Kate received the house, a small savings that would last the year perhaps, and the steamship company gave her one month of John's salary. Nothing else.

Kate's youngest slept on her breast. She stroked the child's forehead with the back of her finger. "I've been so spoiled. We could have saved the money we paid for help. I should have done my own laundry."

"Stop. Think of what you can do." Abigail put on her pragmatic hat.

Kate sighed. Even in grief, she looked coiffed and held together, her shoulders straight, not hunched over in sadness. "I guess I could teach. I know what they paid the male teacher last year, and he left for greener pastures. With that salary, I could maintain the house, maybe have enough for a nanny."

"Let's see if Sarah Maria might like to live here instead of with Fanny. She could help with the children."

"She would be of assistance. But Fanny needs her too." She sighed. "John was only thirty-eight years old. We had our whole life ahead of us." She brushed tears from her cheeks.

Abigail patted her sister's hand. "It's the way it is now. Tragedy happens. I'm not dismissing the hole in your heart." She didn't want to think of what her life would be without Ben in it. "John would want you to go on, to make the best of it. Why don't you talk to the school board? That's a good idea. You're certified and would make a fabulous teacher for Canemah's sprouts."

"It's one of the few respectable things a widow can do. Or remarry. Your old suitor has been by."

"Bunter? Oh, that man! You're not that desperate. We'll help as we can. Harvey will too, if we ask. Please don't, you know, marry just for safety. Because in the end, there is no guarantee. We women have to protect ourselves."

"I have you all," Kate said.

"Now, what will you wear to your interview? And who is on your local board? We'll see if we can politic them."

Kate smiled. "Discreetly, of course."

"That's my sister. We'll get you through."

It was what they *had* to do a week later when

Kate learned she had the job, but it would pay half the salary of the man who had left.

"Outrageous," Abigail said. "I'm going to write a letter to the editor about such unfairness."

"Can they do that?" Sarah Maria, the youngest Scott sister, had come to live with and help Kate out.

"They said it was the law."

"That doesn't surprise me. But they make the school board laws, or at least they can fudge them," Abigail said. "They could change it if they wanted to. I'll go talk with them."

"No. Don't. Please. It's a good job, one I can do. And I can sew in the evenings. Maybe Harvey needs someone at the *Oregonian* to copyedit. I'm good with details."

"Yes, you are. And a better writer than he is, if I might say so." *Better than me.* "I can use another to crochet reticules. They're popular now. At least you won't have to marry someone you don't wish to."

"Yes. Bunter has been by again. He seems to like Scott girls." They both turned to Sarah Maria.

"Don't let that man near you," Abigail said.

"I won't."

"Good. We will tend and befriend each other. That's what women can do."

Abigail's newspaper would have to wait. Family needs came first.

TWENTY-ONE

Building the Ladder

1869

In late February, in the last year of the decade, Abigail learned she was pregnant again. "Oh, Ben. I . . ."

"It's the Lord's doing," Ben said.

"No, it isn't. It's our doing." She sighed. "Six children? How will we manage? I don't mean to demean, but the matched teams—you haven't sold one all last year and you're getting older too, like me. You can't do that heavy haying or picking apples at our old place forever."

"We'll do fine."

"I've got to find something else I can do to bring in money."

"Abigail . . . what you have to do is take care of yourself now."

"At least I'll be carrying through the summer when there are fresh fruits and vegetables. Let's see if we can get more chickens. We can sell the eggs."

"We might have to dip into the teapot." He said it quietly.

"No. That's the newspaper money. We'll think of something else."

"Or God will," Ben said. "You underestimate him."

"God put us here so we'd take care of his earth and make good decisions. Tripling or quadrupling ourselves, I'm not sure that's wise at all."

" 'Be fruitful, and multiply,' " Ben said, his voice a tease.

"That would be the Scripture you'd quote."

"We men memorize certain ones." He took her in his arms. "It'll be fine, Abigail."

"It isn't always, Ben. Maggie died. John died. You were injured. Bad things do happen."

"And people overcome them. My worst worry is over your health. You've got to take fewer buying trips, let Shirley do that for you."

"I still have to pay her. Oh, Ben, I'm worried. If business falls off, what'll we do?"

"Don't wear future worries. Dress for today." He patted her back, and she let herself sink into his chest if only for a moment. "I have confidence. Something will come our way. It always has."

"Yes, but what has come has often been more misery than amusement."

Abigail wrote an essay on equal pay for women and asked Harvey to publish it. He declined, he said, because it wasn't up to the *Oregonian* standards. She fumed as she told Ben. "He said it was 'florid with female emotion' and needed better punctuation. 'Florid with female emotion,'" she sputtered. "How would he know about female emotion? That's called 'passion for a subject.' Yes, I could use a little polish with my paragraphs and exclamation points, but he's an editor, for goodness' sake. Why didn't he edit it? No, he didn't like the conclusion, and my arguments were strong. He knew if he published it, I'd change minds. One day I'll publish it in my own newspaper. And I'll write articles promoting women having the right to vote. See what Harvey says about that."

She'd forgotten in the three years since Clyde's pregnancy that the condition increased her anxiety, and she spent days in bed where she worried over fluctuations in the fashion industry and the costs of changes to her business and how they'd survive taking care of six children. Women now wanted bustles instead of crinolines. Dresses took scads more materials, and women liked the brighter synthetic dyes over those of plants. Silks and satins weighed more than linen or cotton, and women's corsets had to be reinforced to deal with the extra load. Loops of materials called panniers swooped as overskirts, emphasizing smaller waists by the many layers of fabric. Abigail lay awake at night obsessing over purchases. At least men's fashions kept to the grey, brown, and black shades, with changes in tie length the only real upgrade. Women's fashions changed so quickly that by the time she got the dresses back for fittings, the design had to be altered too. She'd sewed Sarah Maria's wedding dress, the color of cream frosting. Her sister had married a lawman. *I'll have to temper my villains now.* Sarah Kelty was the epitome of innocence and an advertisement for the latest fashion.

For Abigail, the wedding was a nostalgic time. All the Scott girls now married off to men they either loved when they began or, like Fanny, learned to love. They all thought of Maggie, wishing she could have been there. Pregnancy made Abigail teary. She'd forgotten about that too.

Since she wasn't traveling, Abigail and two other Albany women started the first suffrage association in the state in Albany. "We'll tend and befriend more women to join us," she'd declared, and her cohorts had agreed, talking with a neighbor while sweeping a back porch or sharing conversations while helping a friend peg laundry to the line. Abigail took more time with her clients, who told her stories of their trials, of a woman's "teapot" money set aside for her daughter's Easter coat, only to have her husband take it to buy himself a racehorse. Not long after that, Abigail learned that woman had died in childbirth, and the editor of the *Democrat* paper wrote condolences to the husband for being "left with the obligations of a family."

"He has a racehorse to comfort him," Abigail told Ben as she read aloud the editorial.

She wrote a letter to the local editor about 172 New Jersey women having voted for the presidency with ballots in a separate box. Of course their preferences hadn't been added to the totals, but just the idea of women making their mark like that, imagining a female with head held high, acting like the citizen she was, offered Abigail hope. Wyoming had scheduled a vote in December to grant women's suffrage. Still, the Fourteenth Amendment recently ratified had once again claimed a "citizen" and "vote" had to be male.

She put her essay rejected by Harvey in a drawer, intending one day to rewrite it. She'd ask Kate to review it before she delivered it to Harvey again. Right then, she had another kind of delivery to worry over.

The pain frightened her. It was different, more like with Willis's wretched birth when Ben had gotten lost in the fog and hadn't found the doctor. And it shouldn't have been happening yet. With the first splintering contractions, she told Ben to seek the doctor. Now. And he had. Her labor went on for hours, maybe days. She lost track of time, felt herself in and out of consciousness at times, fatigued beyond anything she'd ever experienced. Kate was there. Clara Belle's sixteen-year-old frightened eyes leaned over her with a cool rag to soothe her forehead.

Then finally—Ralph Roelofson was born. November 7, a month before he was due. Abigail was exhausted and bleeding and still in excruciating pain when they placed him on her breast while the midwife assisted in cutting the umbilical cord. But Abigail was grateful Ralph came early and was smaller than her other babies, because if he'd been full term and larger, both he and Abigail might well have died.

This child surely had to be her last. The bleeding stopped, but something was still very wrong, and she wrote to Shirley to ask if progressive San Francisco doctors might have new devices to assist women with "prolapsed uteruses" and could she find that out? *"There must be something,"* she said. *"I can't afford to be even a semi-invalid and yet that's what my body is advising me to do. The pain when I walk is almost unbearable and I leak. Ben says horses suffer from this too. Imagine. All those years before, I wrote of some women being treated as workhorses by their fathers and husbands and now, I find we can have similar ailments."*

She used Ben's cane for a time. And purchased the intimate articles that kept parts of her body in place. And she and Ben had the conversation that meant their physical relationship would need to change.

"We won't have a loveless marriage," she said. "It's never been so." They lay beside each other, she on her back and Ben on his side with his arm across her abdomen, resting on the patchwork quilt she'd tucked around her like a mummy. Ralph was asleep in his cradle beside their bed. It was early morning and the dawn seeped through the window to ease across the tin-pressed ceiling.

"I've mostly wanted the affection of your attention," Ben said. He was tearful, but he'd suffered with the delivery of Ralph, had made bargains with God, he'd told her, that if she survived, how he would never put her through such a pregnancy again. That she came to speak of it first was the way it was with them, her pragmatism preceding both his disappointment and his understanding before he could speak of either. They'd come to terms on how to proceed.

It was a new phase in the Duniway days, another adaptation they'd have to make. That too was the way of marriage and, Ben reminded her, of life.

"Just don't say 'it'll all work out.' "

"I won't," Ben said. "But it will."

"Would you look at this." Ben snapped the *Oregonian* and pointed to a short entry on the

242

front page. " 'Editor Harvey Scott has resigned his post of this fine newspaper to assume the position of Collector of Customs in Portland. This distinguished federal appointment could not be bestowed upon another with as exceptional credentials as our Harvey Scott. We regret to see him depart but wish him well.' There's an opening, Abigail."

"Phooey. Pittock wouldn't let a woman through the door to assume such a position."

"I wonder why Harvey gave up such a post."

"Collector of Customs is a lucrative job, carrying prestige and a salary no woman could ever hope to achieve. I bet he wrote that announcement himself." Harvey would have more money to invest in his Portland properties, in addition to gaining commercial connections from around the world. She guessed their friend Senator Baker had made that happen for him. "Still, it might be worth the uproar to see how the new editor would cover my effort to apply." Abigail grinned at her husband. "And my rejection as a qualified candidate—except for my gender." *I could write about it.*

"You'd make it a story, all right." Ben put the paper down, drank his coffee.

She should apply. What could it hurt? But she didn't need the disappointment. *Why torture myself?*

"I'm having a pretty good morning. I think

I'll ride out to the farm and work the team of pintos I started. Poor things need everyday adventures that I don't seem to be able to give. Maybe Harvey could get me on at the customs house."

"We'd have to live in Portland."

"I was only jesting." He backpedaled. "Our business is here. The millinery. Our boarding the working girls. The school. We're established in Albany."

"And I'm meeting with the Marthas this afternoon. Yes, Albany is home now." One Martha was a neighbor and the other a music teacher from Portland. "I've been talking with them about a newspaper. The *Revolution*, the paper Susan B. and Elizabeth Stanton operate, has increased its subscribers, I've heard. We need that Northwest newspaper." There'd been activity back east with a National Woman Suffrage Association formed and then an American Woman Suffrage Association, the former with a desire for a constitutional amendment to get women the vote, and the latter dedicated to suffrage for all, regardless of gender or race. The groups had righteous arguments covered by the *Revolution*, but campaigns for people in the Northwest would be different. Women here, as in Wyoming, worked beside their men more often than in the industrialized East. They struggled on farms and small businesses so men could see the competence of their wives and daughters, and many, like Ben, were sympathetic to women achieving more rights. They didn't like the strident "Hurrah" features of some of the promoters carrying banners, going in to men's clubs only to be asked to leave. Abigail had to watch her step in that regard. She didn't want that kind of bad publicity.

Could I become the editor of the Oregonian? No. Converting that newspaper would not be possible. It had a New England snobbishness that Harvey fit right into and advanced. Moneymen, some Democrats who wanted nothing to do with the new Republican party of Lincoln or the progressive ideas toward rights for men of color and for women. Any newspaper that didn't carry the Pittock party line would face fierce competition. But she was up to it.

Abigail's "Marthas" were not.

"It's too large of an undertaking, Abigail." The fledgling Albany association brought reality to her dreams. "We're neophytes in this."

Abigail patted baby Ralph, resting on her shoulder.

"Starting up will take hundreds of dollars. Printing presses. A place to rent. Subscribing agents, how will we pay them? And the work itself of writing and typesetting and getting the papers on the streets."

"I have children." Abigail put Ralph into his cradle. She poured tea for her friends and colleagues. "I can employ them for some of the work. As for capital to begin, I might approach Jacob Mayer for a loan. Or perhaps sell the millinery."

"But that's it. You have too many activities already. And there's your health."

"Let's see what the new year brings." Abigail tapped her hand against her cane in a nervous gesture. "We'll get through the holidays, which are always lucrative for the millinery. Meanwhile let's find new recruits. There is strength in numbers. It's a chicken-and-egg question: does the newspaper get us more recruits, or do more recruits help support the paper and broaden our cause?"

"There has to be a way," she told Ben that evening. How she would have loved to be in the position Harvey was in—able to leave behind a career she envied, step into social settings she could only hope to look at through windows of the finest hotels. Why, he'd even been given a ticket on the maiden voyage of the steamship *Oriflamme* between Portland and San Francisco. She only imagined the grandeur. If she ever booked passage on the ship, she'd be sleeping in steerage. If only she'd been given an education, she too could climb the rungs of that ladder out of the depths of a ship to the captain's table and the successful men and women who dined there. She would have to build her own ladder, find the lumber for it, and climb up. She imagined she'd be doing it herself, but Ben might have other options. He was a builder at heart.

TWENTY-TWO

The California Connection

1870

It would be my humble pleasure to serve as a delegate to the California suffrage association meeting in San Francisco in December on behalf of the Salem Equal Suffrage Association. I will be in the city for my millinery business and will, with humility and shared purpose, represent both your fine organization and the State Equal Suffrage Association of Albany in this cause that calls us all.

Sincerely yours,
Mrs. A S Duniway

Abigail finished her letter and paused, only half hoping the Salem group would allow her to add their weight to her presence at the California convention that serendipitously coincided with her buying trip. If they appointed her, they might even allow a small grant of expenses. They were a bigger chapter in the cause than Albany. She financed most of the Albany group she'd helped start, feeling ever guilty for spending family money. But then she'd advise herself that she had worked hard in the past year since Ralph's birth to get herself back on healthy feet.

She sent the letter and prepared her millinery order, always leaving herself open to discovering new items. In a previous visit she'd picked up hosiery and false hair additions, sorted through jewelry pieces, and even added a few toys she thought might sell, especially at Christmastime. And she looked forward to seeing Shirley.

"I wish you didn't have to go this time of year." Ben was having a down day, as they'd come to call the episodes of increased pain, back spasms, and debilitation from the laudanum. "The stage from Albany to Portland is unpredictable in the rainy season and neither does much for your aches." Clara Belle played the piano while Ben rested on the daybed they still kept in the parlor.

"The weather is hard on my bones if I'm at home too, and at least this way I have a little time to myself." She hung the boarders' dresses. They had three living in the attic.

"Yes, there's that. You do enjoy your time to yourself."

"And see here." She held up the mail she'd picked up on her way back from the classroom. "Here's a reply from my request to be a delegate for the Salem crowd. And look what they granted me. Not only a delegate status but a pass on the rail line from Albany to Portland and a steamship ticket to San Francisco. I won't have to take the stage. I'll be rolling in luxury. I've never been on a train."

"You should take me with you, Momma." Clara Belle stopped her playing. "Then you wouldn't be alone at Christmas."

"Oh, that would be fun, but this time I can save good money by riding on Salem's ticket. I'll bring you back something special. And what would Annie do if you weren't here for the holiday?" Maggie's daughter still lived with them.

Clara Belle returned to the piano in silence.

"What's that you're playing? 'Toll the Bell Mournfully'?"

"No. It's one I've composed. 'Bring Me Home Oh Distant Ship.' I wrote it for you."

"It's lovely."

Her seventeen-year-old daughter twisted so she could smile at her mother, and Abigail's heart clutched. She was such a help and so kind and unassuming, generous. Abigail often overlooked Clara Belle, who was especially good with her cousin and with Clyde and Ralph as he tottered around the furniture, just learning to walk. The boys brought attention to themselves, but Clara Belle was content to serve in the shadows. Maybe she should take her along to California. But the cost . . . no. She'd pay more attention to her.

"You must play that at our next meeting, would you do that?"

"I would."

Abigail vowed that in her effort to help all women rise to their potential, she not neglect the feminine presence beneath her own roof. It would be something to remind the California mothers too. The married women and mothers working in the cause bore an extra burden to make sure their own daughters weren't set aside for the larger effort. Advocacy had its price, even with occasional privileges.

The trip couldn't have gone better. She spent Christmas Day at the home of an abolitionist and her husband and met Sarah Wallis, who had been named president of the 1870 conference. She was famous in her own right, having been a part of the Stephens-Townsend-Murphy company of 1844, the first to bring wagons into California through the Sierra Nevada. Sarah was a woman who landed on her feet, as Abigail thought of her perseverance and rise. She'd been abandoned by her husband a few years after reaching California, following a harrowing winter of near starvation. Then she married a second time, only to discover that *that* husband was a bigamist from whom she got legal custody of their son, extracted a settlement for her pain that she used to start a boardinghouse and speculate in land. She later married a judge who became a state senator, and together they supported women's suffrage and were working to allow women to be admitted to the bar. At the reception for the delegates the night before, Abigail garnered up her courage to introduce herself to Mrs. Wallis.

"I've heard so many—I mean much about your—I mean about you, Mrs. Wallis." Abigail found herself stumbling over her words upon meeting the famous woman.

"And I you. I've admired reading some of your letters to the editor."

"In our little agricultural papers? You read them?"

"They're often reprinted in Emily Stevens's *Pioneer.*"

"I wasn't aware."

"You've such a way with words, Mrs. Duniway."

"Please. Call me Abigail."

"And I'm Sarah. I didn't learn to read until my journey west in 1844 and '45 as an already married woman. Educating girls is a top priority of my efforts, along with the vote, of course."

"There are so many threads to our freedom cloak," Abigail said. "Education, ratifying amendments granting Negro men the vote, temperance without prohibition—at least that's my position. I don't wish a sip of wine, but I decry anyone's right to tell me I can't have it.

And I so hope we don't bring prohibition into the suffrage cause, because men will never grant us the vote if they think we'll take away their liquor."

"California is pushing the vote by showing what kind of community goodness we can bring, beautifying cities, operating immigrant shelters for women and families, representing the arts. It's wonderful to have you able to join us. Perhaps we can meet later. I'd love to hear about what's happening in Oregon."

"That'll be a quiet conversation," Abigail said. "We Oregonians favor the still hunt, pressing prominent legislative men to bring the vote to the people, without flamboyance or efforts that might suggest we'd neglect our duties as wives and mothers."

"There's always that pressure, isn't there? Your husband is encouraging, obviously, or you wouldn't be here."

"He is." She hesitated, then, "Do you get support from the national organizations?"

"We do, but we raise most of our own funds for our activities and to publicize our efforts."

Abigail nodded. *I shouldn't advance our work at our family's expense, even though Ben approves.* "I hope to learn things from being a delegate."

The women exchanged addresses and circulated to other parts of the gathering. Abigail loved meeting these men and women. There were eastern representatives and advocates of legal reforms and women who edited regional newspapers; and there were working women, eastern-trained female physicians, one of whom advised Abigail not to let her ailments hold her back. "Our best hope of avoiding invalidism is to declare ourselves engaged in the wider world. It's a much better elixir for health than laudanum or even rest. You're fortunate you're young, Mrs. Duniway. You have much life ahead of you, now that your child-bearing years are behind you."

It surprised Abigail that she was willing to express her personal concerns to women she had only met. It was as though she'd known them her whole life, like they were sisters she didn't know she had. They were as open to her as her sisters—perhaps more. She made copious notes of other speakers and her own observations of the bustling city and formed them as articles she would submit to the *Oregonian*, not that she had any assurance they'd be printed unless she paid for it. Harvey held no sway there now with his customhouse work. News was happening here, and those righteous editors needed to cover it. There were no journalists assigned to this event. But she was here, and she'd have stories for a dozen letters to the editor. And a feature article or two—on the famous Mrs. Wallis or the editor of the *Chicago Legal News*, who'd been refused entry to the Illinois bar despite her stellar reputation as a legal journalist. Oh, yes, she had stories to tell.

This network of women mattered never more so than when Mrs. Wallis surprised her a day after Christmas with an invitation. "Will you grace us with a rhetorical presentation on New Year's Eve?"

"Speak? The way Susan B. Anthony does? Oh, I'm not sure—that wouldn't be wise." Public speaking was still considered risqué and unladylike. "Poor Susan B. Anthony had tomatoes thrown at her. I've never spoken about women's issues in public. Or any issue, really." A lecture at her schoolhouse to parents hardly counted. Abigail had addressed Fourth of July schoolhouse rallies, introducing the children before their presentations, but she had never orated to a crowd, on a subject that mattered to her deeply, from her heart. "I . . . I'm not sure my husband would approve."

"You're here over the holidays. He must trust your judgment greatly. It's safe here, Mrs. Duniway. You won't be risking your reputation among this body. We women have voices God gave us. We mustn't shy away from using them."

She's right.

Now, on New Year's Eve of 1870, Abigail's heart fluttered behind the curtains at the hotel stage. She twisted her mother's earrings. *Am I honoring her? Would Ben approve?* There was no time to send a telegram to ask. *There is time. I don't want him to say no.* Her fingers shook as she held the velvet drape and peeked out to see several hundred women and some supportive men in the audience, their feet shuffling on the polished floor, the wooden chairs creaking as they settled beneath the hum of chatter. A chandelier cast streams of speckled light over them. She'd spent the two previous evenings writing out what she wished to say but knew she did not want to be tied to reading her words, given the poor lighting.

"Are you nervous?" Shirley asked.

"Yes." She twisted her earrings again.

"Didn't you orate to your younger siblings when you were a child?"

"And to the mules and cows when they'd listen, those big eyes looking up at me while they chewed their cuds." She smiled. "Speaking is different from writing or even twisting a man's arm about a subject one-on-one." By instinct, she knew she had to be fully present at the moment to give a speech and not somehow translate words from paper to tongue. She needed to see what was happening in front of her, whether people were getting restless or whether someone had dozed off. At least she imagined she needed to see those things—and more—to make what she was saying relevant to her immediate audience. To move people, she had to give herself wholeheartedly to where she was on the stage, reaching out to the minds and hearts of those before her and not to the script on the podium with a fern set before it.

"I'll say a prayer for you," Shirley said.

The offer brought a surprising calm.

She heard her introduction, then stepped out onstage. In seconds, she would see in front of her whether she had moved people or lost them. She took a sip of water and a deep breath. Then using the voice that got the attention of her sons and their friends when they rattled through the house with swords and saunter, she began.

She was humble. Thankful to those who had invited her. She told stories. She made her audience laugh, and she brought them to tears with her own vulnerability that she saw as demonstrating strength to those before her. She spoke things she hadn't written at all, quoted Scripture she wove into the struggle of women's lives. And she appealed to them as western pioneers, people who had come from somewhere else, had chosen to live with the uncertainty of a journey with promise but without the assurance of success. She invoked Sarah's story of survival more than her own that endeared her to her California audience, most of whom were pioneers themselves, having come across a challenging landscape or survived a ship's crossing. They had lived on a frontier, made do, innovated, worked side by side with men, and come together in community to help a neighbor regardless of their race or religious or political beliefs. People applauded mid-speech, feeding her spirit. Abigail reminded them of their own pioneering moments.

And then she spoke of the American revolution. "That is the basis on which we press for women's rights. We work toward the nation's ideals rather than on what the nation might gain from women achieving the vote. It is to advance the cause of democracy, of freedom. This great nation did not intend to leave women out." Thunderous applause followed that line, as it did with her closing when she charged the audience to go forth and do great things. "Ours is a cause worth doing regardless of how long it takes or how it turns out."

She perspired as she sat down, the heavy curls wet against her neck, and at first didn't see Sarah Wallis urging her to stand back up, for the audience had done just that. The applause was music, almost as beautiful as Clara Belle's composition. By speaking, Abigail knew she'd tapped into something inside her that she had not known was waiting to escape.

> Gave public lecture. Newspapers praise. Stop. Offered salary and speaking tour of California. Stop. $800. Stop. Must extend time away. Stop. Seek your blessing. Abigail.

It was happening so fast. She'd been asked to be the Portland editor of the *Pioneer*, to go on a lecture tour of California, perhaps beyond, to inspire. *Ben has to approve!* She'd sent the telegram. Surely the money would make him say yes.

Ben's return telegram was swift and short.

Come Home Immediately. Your presence required.

"What could it be?" Shirley helped Abigail toss her clothes into her trunk, made sure the invoices for her purchases were in order and ready to ship.

"I have no idea. I've a housekeeper and manager for the store while I'm gone. Surely, he would have said if one of the children was ill, wouldn't you think?"

"It would seem so."

"I hate to see that eight-hundred-dollar salary disappear down the latrine." Abigail supposed they would have another speaker they could send, but what a joy it would have been! She couldn't think about that now. She boarded the weekly steamer to Portland and, on the way, wrote an announcement for the *Oregonian* she hoped they'd publish.

Arriving in Albany, she rushed home to find out what the crisis was. Ben wasn't there. He was at the farm with his pintos.

"Everything fine, Mrs. D. You worry things no good?" Chen seemed confused by her opening question of what was wrong.

"The children? They're all right?"

"All good. Like all time, good."

She picked Ralph up, hugged him, kissed his fingers sticky from a summer jam he'd poked into. Clara Belle put her arms around her. "You're home, Momma. I missed you. We all missed you."

"Is everything all right at the millinery?"

"Yes, fine. Why do you ask?"

Her sons came in stomping their rubber boots of the rain. "Pa's at the farm. Did he know you were coming in on the steamer today?" Willis asked.

She felt like she'd been riding in a hot air balloon and someone had turned off the fire, bringing it crashing to the ground.

Abagail telegrammed her brief article to the Portland *Oregonian*, adding a final sentence she hadn't written while on board ship.

> Mrs. A. S. Duniway of Albany arrived in this city yesterday morning to ascertain what interest can be raised here in behalf of the removal of the *Pioneer* newspaper from San Francisco to that city.

She hesitated before writing the next announcement, but she'd already made the decision weeks ago. Ben could read it in the paper as well as the next person.

In anticipation of success, she will remove shortly to this city. We have little doubt that she will find encouragement enough, unless she entrusts the canvassing business to some blockhead of a man. When women go for their own rights, they generally get them.

She considered the reference to some "blockhead of a man." *I should leave that out.* But she didn't.

"I thought you should come home," Ben said when she challenged him after supper. "The children need you. I need you. You were gone over a month."

"But it was eight hundred dollars, Ben. We could have used that money."

"We're doing fine."

"No, we aren't. We live hand to mouth, week to week. That money would have given us a breather, and we could have made gains on the newspaper fund."

"But no breather for you. You'd have worn yourself to a frazzle traveling around California on a stage. Not to mention your lecturing, in public. Who knows what sort of danger you'd be in."

"It was not your call to make, Ben Duniway."

"I guess you could have ignored me."

She glared at him. "And risk the public humiliation of your telling people not of my wonderful welcome in California but of a wife who defies her husband's orders?"

"That was your choice." He cleared his throat. "Did you bring back something special for Clara Belle? She's hopeful."

"Did you expect me to forget?" *I almost did.* "A silk scarf and a summer bonnet, so when she wears it in June, she'll know I was thinking of her in the off season as well as at Christmas, that I have her interests at heart even when she's not in front of me." She felt defensive and irritated and angry about the limitations life placed on women and Ben's restriction on hers. She took in a deep breath. "I'm back. At least the California *Pioneer* thinks I might make a go of expanding their paper to Portland. I'll never have one of my own." She lifted her carpetbag to the bed.

"Not that it's worthy of publication," Ben said, "but I thought you might want to know that I saw your brother Harvey this week."

"My wealthy, lucky, highly educated brother? Where did you run into him?" She had her back to Ben, had opened the wooden handles on her paisley bag, pulled out soiled clothes she'd need to launder. At least she had Ben's machine to make it easier.

"At the customhouse in Portland. Where I asked for a job. And got it."

Abigail twirled to face him. "You took a job? In Portland? But how—"

"How else will I get you to consider staying closer to home? I decided to follow up on my instincts of some time ago, about working in Portland and giving us a steady income so you could get the paper going. I know it's what you want. And I want to support you in it. And in life, Jenny." His face turned a shade of pink over his sparse beard. "It'll pay thirteen hundred a year."

"Oh my goodness, Ben." She sat down, the dirty laundry in her hands. "That's . . . but you'll have to give up the horse training, the thing you love? And will your back pain allow you? And we'll have to move to Portland."

"Yes, but I can work a few animals on the weekends if I'm up to it. And yes, Harvey knows I might have some difficulties, but he's prepared for that. We'll find a place to live close to where I'll work. You probably already have a house picked out, if I know you. A 'wish' house with room for a printing press." He chuckled as she nodded. "I couldn't let you take a position that would take you traveling around California when you'll be needed here to set up your own new venture. Our new venture. Duniway Publishing Company."

"Oh, Ben." It wasn't the name of the newspaper she'd had in mind. But no matter. She stood and he held her, kissed her, and she felt the warmth of his tender hands at the back of her head. He was making a huge sacrifice for her . . . for them. She had to make this paper a success. She had to use it to advance the cause of suffrage. "It'll be a wonderful thing for women, move us closer to getting the vote, I just know it. And we'll do it together, won't we?"

"Like a matched team of circus horses."

"It'll be a circus all right."

"I'll let you have the lead."

"And I'll take it. A newspaper—well, I'll be learning something new every day. But I want to call the paper the *New Northwest* because that's what we'll be advancing, the Duniway Publishing Company will be advancing it."

"Name the paper what you like," Ben said. "I signed the incorporation papers. Your task is to find us a place to live and to sell the businesses here to raise the rest of the capital we'll need. I had to get you to come home to do all that. And I wanted it to be a surprise."

"You are the surprising man," she said.

His arms squeezed her a little tighter. "You're taking me along on the ride of our lives, I suspect." His throat caught, and when she stepped back to look into his eyes, she saw tears in them. "But we're doing it together. It's all I ever wanted."

What is that little verse someone had written in Willis's schoolbook?

The things nearby, not the things afar
Not what we seem but what we are
These are the things that make or break
that give the heart its joy or ache.

She was entering a new era. She'd bring Ben along if he would come. *How unkind of me, after all he's done.* She and Ben together were beginning something special. It had been his support in the first place that told her that getting women the vote was the only thing that would change women's lives for the better. She'd remind him of that. The newspaper would be the vehicle. They'd still be a matched team if she had anything to say about it. *And I usually do.*

PART 3

Hope is an orientation of spirit, an orientation of the heart. It's the ability to begin something not just because it has a chance to succeed but because it's a good thing to do. . . . It's not the certainty that something will turn out well but the certainty that something is worth doing regardless of how it turns out.

VACLAV HAVEL, DISTURBING THE PEACE

TWENTY-THREE

Getting Ducks in Order

1871

She loved the smell of the ink that prickled the nose hairs and its viscosity, the consistency of Johnny cake batter. Willis spread the ink across the wooden tubes, preparing the presses. Abigail admired the tiny type raised in the wood that eleven-year-old Hubert's little fingers set into the box where the ink would highlight and transfer to the paper. He was an excellent speller and didn't seem fazed by the typeface being backward so it would print correctly on the stock. She loved the feel of the paper—she used good quality so people would be willing to pay money in expectation of getting something worthy that was easy to read. Even the crispness of the paper cuts, it all appealed to her. The rumble of the presses, rattling the chandelier on the first floor while the presses rolled the newspaper out on the second.

She'd rented a house on First and Washington with room for the family downstairs (along with a millinery that Clara would manage). She'd hired a foreman to help them learn the printing business, borrowed $3000 from Jacob Mayer to be paid back over time. He didn't charge her interest and she never sent him a bill for his ads.

On May 5, 1871, Abigail and Ben together turned the handle for the first edition. Like magic, the words appeared on paper, her words, the first newspaper a sort of memoir of how "we" had come to write a paper, how "we" began scribbling while as a farmer's wife, and about the business failures (she wrote that her novel had been a failure) and the successes (teaching, boarding, and dressmaking—and hopefully, newspapering). She editorialized that it was women's lack of political and consequent "pecuniary and moral responsibility" that resulted in the public being opposed to "strong-minded women," as she had once been herself. But now, she saw—and hoped her readers would see—that society kept "half the population overtaxed and underpaid, struggling, while another group of women acted frivolous, were idle and expensive." Both conditions, she contended, were "wrong," and the goal of the paper was "to elevate women, that thereby herself and son and brother man may be benefited and the world made better, purer, and happier, is the aim of this publication."

It was a lofty goal, she knew that. And they'd risked all they had and went into debt for this cause. But it was what her heart had told her, what that beam of light had illuminated about her life's mission being not only to be a good wife and mother but to advance women's God-given gifts and talents in addition to household roles. Abigail had managed so far to keep her dignity and the love of her family while being willing to be mocked and chastised for stepping out. If she could do it, she hoped other women and men would see how each would benefit by the advancing of women. Or at least not standing in a woman's way.

She watched Clara Belle speaking to a customer purchasing a reticule at the millinery. Such a gorgeous daughter, so charming and without a vitriolic bone in her body. How had Abigail raised such a gentle soul when she was such a torrent? *It's Ben's influence.* Thank goodness for Ben.

"When you've finished, come join us," Abigail told her daughter. "The first press run is finished, and I want you to be there when we lift them up and get them on the streets. I've had six months of selling subscriptions ahead of time, and today they'll be delivered." Even southern Oregon would be getting papers, as Bethenia Owens, her millinery friend from Roseburg, had been promoting the paper, readying people for this grand adventure.

"Coming, Momma." Clara Belle locked the outside millinery door to join the family upstairs.

They had to wait until the ink dried. Meanwhile, using turpentine to remove stains from their fingers, the boys gathered up the pages,

Ben spoke a prayer over the venture, and Abigail felt tears form in her eyes as she watched her family head out their Portland door to sell the *New Northwest* on the street. Even nine-year-old Wilkie could charm a dime from a grumpy man looking for someone to blame for his bad day. He held the hand of his older brother to cross the street and join the business of the Duniway Publishing Company.

Abigail found invigoration in this newspapering thing, and yes, she told herself, in the assurance of Ben's steady income that surprisingly took strain from her days. It was all in the family sphere, not unlike farming had been, but with less physical pain. Ben's sacrifice and job had made the difference in her constant chasing away the demons of foreclosure and debtor's prison. Ben had been right. Something always did come along in the end . . . she just had to trust that if she was on the right path, doing what needed to be done, they'd be all right. How ironic that it was Harvey who turned out to be a part of that answer to a prayer.

A Journal for the People
Devoted to the Interests of Humanity
Independent in Politics and Religion
Alive to all Live Issues and Thoroughly
Radical in Opposing and Exposing the
Wrongs of the Masses.

Abigail capitalized every other word, used language like "Live Issues." Kate had said it was a bit flamboyant, but it was also her style. It was the masthead, at least for now, reminding people of what the *New Northwest* was about. She showed it to Ben. "I want people to see it as a different kind of newspaper, because it is. I sent Susan B. Anthony a copy and she's pleased. And Ben, I boldly asked her to come west to do a speaking tour." They'd been in production for three months.

"Abigail—"

"Now, I would only arrange the performances, introduce her, collect the donations, et cetera. We'll split the income after expenses. I wouldn't be speaking beyond that." When Ben had called her back from California, she had assumed it was to speak of his new job, but she hadn't actually asked if he would have approved her speaking. *Maybe I don't want to know.* "I'd try to book us at the Oregon State Fair. We could all camp out together. That's very suitable. Families back east are camping all the time. The fashion industry has even introduced clothing that keeps women proper, of course, but a little freer to hike and take in the sunshine."

"You two women are not going to camp out across Oregon."

"No, no. I just meant at the fair. We'll stay in respectable hotels or at the homes of like-minded

273

women on the tour. Think of the good copy such an adventure would offer my readers and encourage women starved for entertainment in the rural areas. I think she's quite a remarkable woman. I can pluck her thoughts about newspapering as we ride in the stage or walk a few miles."

Ben sighed. "I've come this far. I guess it's not much farther to have both a newspapering wife and a public-speaking one. I'll be busy at the customhouse, so you'll have to tend the home fires. I like a good campout now and then." He stretched his back, winced. "Besides, working inside a building all day long, I'll need some nights out in a tent for my sanity."

"At least you aren't suggesting that I'm the one challenging your sanity."

"I was being diplomatic." Ben grinned. "Something I need to be in the customhouse."

"One of us should be," Abigail said, and kissed him. "Lord knows I'm a lost cause when it comes to that. Perhaps our travel from here to Victoria, British Columbia, and east to Idaho will give me lessons in discretion."

Ben smiled. "We can hope."

"Hubert, put that straw over there, against that tent side. Ben, do we have the carpet ready to roll out? Oh, isn't this grand!" Abigail fluttered about the tent at the Oregon State Fair. It was October, one of the most glorious months in the Willamette Valley, with harvested fields golden next to maples and oaks flashing their reds and greens, flirting with pure blue skies. The evenings were cool, the days hot but dry.

The family—most of it, along with sister Sarah Maria and her husband and of course the guest of honor, Susan B. Anthony—would spend the week at the fair. It was the end of the grand tour the women had made to Washington, Idaho, British Columbia, and throughout Oregon. Aunt Susan, as Abigail referred to her, had been a warrior in the wilds. For the first half of the tour, Clara Belle joined them to sing and, if a piano was present, to play music as people gathered. Then Abigail gave the introduction, which amounted to a speech of her own. She couldn't help herself. She loved the audience responses to her presentations, often saying, "I never imagined when I first declaimed to my father's grazing mules that, one day, I'd be asked to speak to legislators, which Miss Anthony and I did last week." Then she'd add: "Not such a very different audience, regardless of whether those mules in the pasture were looking toward me or away." There'd be a pause and then the crowd would laugh. Jokes at legislators' expense seemed to go over well with the masses, Abigail decided.

At the fair, they'd be competing with men hawking games that gents could play to earn trinkets for their mates. Musicians and ventriloquists along with banjo-playing farmers would perform on an outdoor stage next to them. People would wander by, heading to the tent restaurant that the Aurora Colony men and women operated, to the delight of the Duniways and others who could purchase food right on site and not have to pack for a week.

Best of all, the Duniway family enjoyed the company of the famous suffragist.

Susan B. Anthony was a tall woman, slender, who had deliberate movements, including settling down onto the straw bed in the fair-tent like a stork slowly clucking over her eggs. Abigail, on the other hand, would just plop, which she did, wincing as she sat next to her famous friend. "Clara Belle, dear, are you going to sing for us as the opening tonight? We should have a big crowd."

"Yes, Momma. In fact, I think I'll find a quiet place to practice. It is getting stuffy in here."

Abigail hesitated. "Be careful out there. There are scoundrels."

"I'll come with you. See if I can find James." Sarah Maria's husband was a law officer on duty looking for pickpockets and inebriates. "He can protect two damsels if we get in distress."

"Sing your way out into the world, now." Ben started up—a routine he'd taught his children from the time they were little. Ben sang and

Maria grabbed Clara Belle's hand and pulled her toward the opening, voices brimming with good cheer. The younger boys were all that were left of the children, and Ben said he'd take them to the restaurant if the women needed some privacy to prepare for their presentation that evening.

"Won't you remember this western trip for the rest of your life?" Abigail nudged Aunt Susan. Abigail poked her with her elbow as the girls left.

"It's my first and I suspect my last camping experience. We're stuffed in here like herrings."

"I know. Isn't it cozy? No need to shout to express thoughts or share a story."

"I confess, I prefer your Chemeketa House and the Oregon Supreme Court as audiences, though you Duniways I suspect are better to sleep with."

Abigail laughed with her. She'd grown quite fond of the eastern suffragist and her ability to adapt to the primitive conditions she'd been exposed to. They'd been heckled out of hotels with their ideas. They'd been asked to leave a home where they'd been invited when the woman's husband chastised his wife in front of them for failing to seek approval before extending the invitation. Out they went. Churches were often closed to them—pool halls and saloons, open, mostly to mock any presentations they made outside them. But in Pendleton, in a light rain, they had hesitated.

"Ben will be dismayed if it's reported that we spoke inside a saloon," Abigail said.

"No one ever made any gains without ruffling a few feathers."

"I know, but being married—"

"It's why I never did. I have enough to manage myself without the additional weight of family."

"They aren't exactly a burden. Do I make it sound that way? It's that I have to consider them in what I do, Ben especially. I never want to lose his support."

"From what I see, that wouldn't be possible. He adores you."

"Yes. He does." *But he might have his limits.* "Let's not speak in the saloon. Let's make our presentation outside it. We might gain more votes one day that way than forcing ourselves into the bar. And women on the streets can hear us. Our umbrellas and our ideas will give us something to share with our audience."

They collected money for their expenses and sometimes shared the take with those who needed it, leaving them barely able to cover their meals and hotel lodging when they couldn't secure a bed from a sympathetic suffragist in Olympia, Washington, or in a tiny frontier town like Umatilla, Oregon. In every village, Abigail sold subscriptions to her *New Northwest*, and at every rest stop, sharing beds with children or with Aunt Susan, Abigail wrote, telegramming her reports from the field for the paper to Kate, whom she'd contracted to do the layout. Sometimes they were in an actual field when she prepared her articles. She also wrote chapters for a long poem she serialized and created a rhythm for corresponding while on the road, her arthritic fingers scribbling away well into the night. She was writing with a purpose, covering their trip and experiences and advancing a cause.

She'd feel depleted by a short and interrupted night's sleep, exhausted by the stage or wagon box that took them to the next town, frustrated by changes in where they'd be allowed to speak once they arrived, at times a little frightened by the vitriol spewed by both men and women who were threatened by what they stood for: change.

But once they stood onstage, Abigail would feel something coming to her from the crowd. Her spine would tingle as she stood before a mass of mostly women who hungered for the hope Abigail and Aunt Susan's presence inspired.

Abigail was counting on this evening of the fair being a grand finale to the tour. She'd had posters printed and the boys handed them out. She hoped they'd get a couple of hundred people to attend that evening. She wanted the tour to do Oregon proud for her eastern friend. Of all the Northwest states, she hoped Oregon women would be the first to vote, and she saw this canvasing in the

Northwest and her newspaper as in service to that goal. This event at the fair was to be the crown on their royal trip.

"How many do you think were there, Ben?" Abigail shook the quilts, then placed them back over straw to freshen the beds. It had been a long but satisfying evening.

"Over a thousand, easily."

"We sold a lot of subscriptions to the paper," Willis said. At fourteen, he towered over his mother and stood nearly head to head with Ben.

"Imagine having a thousand people hear about the importance of freedom and the vote for women." Abigail placed a shawl around Susan B. Anthony's bony shoulders as the night had chilled. Musicians played in the background, and one could still hear the murmuring of fairgoers chattering as they made their way toward the exits. "Could you ever have imagined a crowd like this when I was writing my 'Farmer's Wife' letters?"

Ben nodded. "I knew you were destined for bigger things the day I met you."

"Your invitation to speak to the Oregon legislature as the first woman to do so may take the cause further than our presentation this evening," Susan said. "That's quite an accomplishment. And you quadrupled the influence by being able to write about it in your paper."

"Five hundred subscribers and climbing. My Clara and Willis and even Hubert are quite the newsboys. News-people." She ruffled eleven-year-old Hubert's curls. "Who can refuse that smile."

"Your paper probably has a wider audience, but flesh and blood coming out to hear, that word of mouth will bring you more readers than smiling sons, good hawkers that they are," Susan said.

"The anti-suffrage crowd was out too." Clara heated up tea on their little camp stove. "But I think they only had forty or so attend. I slipped in the back just to check. You and Aunt Susan are the novelty." Her sister Sarah Maria had started a suffrage group in Forest Grove where James was the sheriff and Kate taught school. And the sisters also acted as agents for subscriptions or ad sales, working from Albany or Forest Grove or wherever they lived. Even relatives back in Illinois had been conscripted to read the *New Northwest* and find new subscribers.

"Women of many persuasions are being allowed to speak in public," Susan said. "And that is an advancement as well. We cannot push the rights of some women. We must work for all, even those who resist our efforts to improve their lives."

"That is a paradox, isn't it? To have women not want more freedoms?" Sarah Maria shook her head.

"They think they'll be taken care of by their husbands and fathers, and many will. But they'll never know what they might have been able to accomplish if they had the opportunity."

"One can be both a good wife and a promoter of a worthy cause," Abigail said. "Somehow, in our writings we must make the case for issues other than the vote. It's a means to an end, not the end itself, that's the story that matters."

"Well spoken, Abigail. If we can advocate for improved property rights, for legal protections for women, the journey to those reforms will be the underpinnings of the suffrage fight and perhaps keep our organizations from tromping in the mud over issues like temperance and prohibition." Susan sounded like she was still on the platform. She stopped herself, then added, "I think you may be right, my friend, about not having our eastern groups come into Oregon with a campaign. The Northwest is unique. You can promote that singularity in your newspaper and your 'still hunt' attitude. We have to employ a number of methods to reach our goal. And we have a huge roadblock before us." She cleared her throat and this time did pontificate as though on a stage. "The Supreme Court just wrote this: 'The paramount destiny and mission of women are to fulfill the noble and benign offices of wife and mother. This is the law of the Creator.'"

"So if we operate outside that, we are defying God's laws?" Even Sarah Maria sounded aghast.

"So the court has ruled."

Abigail thought of the verse in Jeremiah about God having plans for everyone's life. Shouldn't a woman discover what her own destiny and mission were in order to be in step with Scripture, even if that meant stepping outside of her home?

"We can challenge that in the newspaper, mine and yours."

Susan blinked several times. "Did I not tell you? I had to close *Revolution*. My newspaper has, as they say in the West, 'bit the dust.' "

"I didn't know."

"It was one of the reasons I undertook the tour, to make a little money to dissolve my debt."

A bitter taste of reality made Abigail swallow. She was entering in to risk larger than what Ben had put them in by signing the notes those years before. He had done it to help a friend. *If I'm doing it for something greater than myself, will that guarantee that all will turn out well?* She didn't say those words out loud. Instead she said, "And still you gave more than half your share of the gate in Olympia for the victims of the Chicago fire."

" 'Give, and it shall be given unto you,' as Scripture says." Susan sighed. "It hasn't failed me yet. Look here what luxury has come my way since I gave away my take: friends to share tea and shelter with and a straw bed on which to lay my head."

Abigail exchanged a glance with Ben, wondering if he might be thinking what she was. If the famous Susan B. Anthony couldn't succeed with a newspaper with the large subscription base in the populous East, a newspaper that captured the action of the political capital of the country, with renewals easy to come by, however would her little paper make it in the West, where horses and cattle far outmatched readers living in sparsely settled areas. To move forward, she'd have to believe that something was worth doing no matter how it turned out.

TWENTY-FOUR

Shaping

1876

Purposefulness: Abigail hadn't realized how important having a goal was in keeping one balanced and able to pick back up after challenges and change. The first half of the seventies whizzed by, with Abigail helping found the Oregon State Women's Suffrage Association and hiring Kate full time to be the editor of her paper so she could travel, interview, investigate, and write and send back news. She missed the buying trips to see Shirley Ellis in San Francisco, but Clara Belle traveled alone for purchasing stock and also managed the millinery. Abigail sometimes took the youngest boys with her to remind everyone that she was a "strong-minded mother" and not just a "risk-taking, outspoken businesswoman," as some detractors wrote.

In 1876 she set out to visit New York City and be in Philadelphia for Centennial Day, where the national suffrage association had numerous plans to present women voter proclamations to the president. She'd said her goodbyes to her children and boarded a stage heading east. The venture cost money, yes, but she'd have ample copy for several issues of *NNW* (as she often abbreviated her newspaper now), and she was touring and speaking in Idaho, Utah, Iowa, and her home state of Illinois on the way.

"I'm hesitant to have you up on stages so far away," Ben told her as he carried her carpetbag to the carriage.

"You know there'll be like-minded men with their wives and sisters at the meeting houses. I'll be fine." She kissed him discreetly as he helped lift her up and gently settled her on the leather seat. He handed her the cane she used, a piece of bone for the head he'd attached to it, smooth in her hand. "I'll imagine you on the sideline."

"I'll be praying for you anyway."

"I know."

Public speaking invigorated, and she'd managed to convince Ben that such an activity was necessary in these times to both extend the cause of women's rights and to increase subscriptions and gain renewals. "Those poor women out there selling the paper see my speaking as both a stimulation and reward for their efforts. I can't let them down."

Her first event in Idaho challenged her position. Mid introduction to her speech, she felt a thump on her chest scarf and then another on her jaw. Audience shouts interrupted, and she realized she'd been egged by angry women who felt she was overstepping her domestic bounds.

Shouts and "Calm down" and "Shame" from both sides of the aisle rose up. She lifted her hands as though giving a benediction and said, "Let them speak. Then I will." She heard the hecklers out, then said, "My commitment as wife and mother are not strained or impaired by my presentations here. I'm the mother of six, remember, and have a daughter who has waited to marry if she ever does, choosing instead to give music lessons and to operate a millinery. I've not hurt my family one iota."

Several men began to escort the egg throwers out, but Abigail urged them to wait. She wiped her chin and neck of the scum, hoping not to ruin the hand-crocheted edging on the handkerchief she used. Clara Belle had done the fine needlework. "My husband approves and supports my efforts, for he sees that women and girls are kept in bondage by the laws preventing them from voting, from helping them define their own destinies—as well as how domestic duties can prevent men and women from moving forward. He has always helped with laundry, for example, inventing a washing machine any number of men here might purchase for their wives and mothers."

"Here! Here!" she heard a man shout out. Several applauded.

"But more, his willingness to let me be the woman I feel God created me to be is one of the greatest acts of love anyone can show another. I am first and foremost—as are each of you—a created being. 'Do not hide your light under a basket' speaks to each of us. Mister Duniway has been the reflector of that light for me, illuminating the path I believe has been chosen for me, and that having the right to vote will only make that light brighter. For each of us. Now, let me tell you about why I'm heading to Philadelphia," she said. The egg-ers sat down and the women selling papers had a bonus night after the loud applause following her speech.

She loved the countryside of Idaho and kept pictures in her mind of its scissor-sharpened mountain peaks, the artist's palette of colors as fall approached, the sounds of raging streams that cut through deep canyons. She'd regale Ben with the pictures of the Pahsimeroi River when she returned. The landscape would be perfect as the backdrop in a new novel she had brewing in her head.

As she moved east, though, flooding spread through the country. Trains she'd planned to pick up were delayed. She rode in stagecoaches around flooded tracks and had been gone four months already when she finally reached New York City where she hugged Aunt Susan.

"Your book, it's selling well here in the East,"

Susan told her. *David and Anna Matson*, her long poem, had gotten published, and the reviews continued to be good ones.

"I can learn from my mistakes," she said, still embarrassed by the negative comments that first book had brought her.

"A necessary skill for any successful woman," Susan told her. The women attended the Exposition together, applauded at the Women's Convention where she heard inspiring speeches, and then visited the Women's Pavilion, outside the exposition area, as women's inventions were not deemed worthy to be inside the main center. She picked up a self-heating iron to hold and imagined owning one. Interlocking bricks and a frame for lace curtains fascinated her. An odd traveling typewriter was featured too. She could use one of those. Each had been invented by an enterprising woman.

"These are wonderful. Oh, and there's a dish-washing machine." She would write about it and her adventures, along with her tasting something called Heinz ketchup and drinking Hires Root Beer, but those latter were offerings inside the exposition, as they'd been inspired by men.

Susan B. Anthony was scheduled to present to the vice president a proclamation on women's voting rights, but instead President Hayes was there to receive it. Abigail felt proud to be in the room where women were willing to put forth laws to advance the citizenship of women.

Her telegrams to Kate for the *New Northwest* served as teasers of stories she'd write on her return. So much she wanted to share. But her journey home was interrupted in Illinois with a terrible cough and a weakness she'd never known. For weeks she was tended by relatives and did recuperate, having lost ten pounds before she finally headed back to Oregon in the spring.

When she arrived in Portland at the stage stop—ten months after she'd left—Ben greeted her with open arms. "You will never be gone so long again," he said as he kissed her.

"I agree." *Home.* The Oregon air never felt so fine.

Ben lifted her carpetbag into the family carriage as he shared news about the paper. The boys had done a good job in her absence, and Kate was invaluable as an editor. His own health had been good, mostly, he answered when she asked. "I lost a few days of work in December. I think the cold rains get inside my back bones and twitch there until I lie on the carpet in front of the fireplace and ferret them out."

"I'm sorry I wasn't here to look after you. I've never been so sick as I was in December."

"Clara Belle was a good nurse." He hesitated, but Abigail didn't notice, chattering like a squirrel to him as he drove her back, laughing when she did, shaking his head at all the marvels she'd seen. "I'm glad you're healthy now," he said.

"Oh, I am. I can take on those prohibitionists and anti-suffrage voices with new vigor."

They pulled up to the house. And Ben put his hand on her wrist, urging her to wait. "I've been authorized to prepare you, so you can gear yourself up for the shock—"

"What shock?" She grabbed his arm. "The children, they're all right? You would have telegrammed."

"Everyone is fine. However—" He put out his hands as though to shush her. "Clara Belle is now Mrs. Donald Stearns."

"She's who?"

"The wife of Donald Stearns. They eloped in December."

"And you never told me? Why wouldn't you have told me?"

"There was nothing you could do about it. You'd have tried to come back, and you were ill in Illinois. You said so yourself. Besides, bad news is better handled in the spring than in the rage of winter."

"Aren't you the philosopher." *Don Stearns.* "He's a losing newspaperman, starting that evening rag last year. How could you let this happen, Ben?"

"She's her mother's daughter with a mind of

her own, Jenny. As we've raised her. Don's all right. Young. Allowed to make mistakes as we did when we were newlyweds. And you gave them the idea in the first place, musing about starting an evening edition. He decided to do it. And he has a wise partner who knows a little about newspapering, so she can help him."

"This is awful." Abigail had jumped out of the carriage before he could help her and had stomped up the stairs. She turned to him. "Are they in there?"

"All your children await your arrival."

"She got her brothers to defend her. Oh, Clara." She raised her voice to the sky. "Why didn't you wait? You could have gone on the stage with your voice, your musical talent."

"She still can, she'd say to you," Ben said. "She'd say you taught her how to be both a wife and mother and a businesswoman." He opened the door to the cheering of her children.

"You were gone so long, Momma."

"Working on behalf of women and girls. For you, my daughter."

"And yourself," Don Stearns said. He was tall and skinny as a split rail. *Weak.*

"Oh, dander," Willis said. "You're in for it now, Stearns."

"He's right, Momma." Clara Belle stepped closer to her husband. "You do work for girls and women, but you also do it because you love it. And no one begrudges you that—we don't, even though we miss you terribly. Ten months you've been gone, and we've carried on without you. But we have to do things that move our lives forward too. And then you got ill and I didn't want to worry you."

"But I praised you for not marrying young, for waiting for the right man."

"And I did. Momma. Mother, please, your face is getting all red and you look like you're going to faint. Please—"

Abigail growled, her fury uncontained, her face a dark cloud of rage. She knew it. Could stop it.

Clara Belle sank to the floor.

Don Stearns dropped beside her, held her head in his lap. He glared at Abigail. "See what you've done?"

"It's what *you* did, eloping with my daughter." Abigail shook as she reached for the smelling salts to revive Clara Belle.

"Stop it now," Ben said as he moved Abigail aside. "What's done is done." He and Don Stearns bent over the awakening Clara Belle, who with woozy eyes blinked.

"Am I all right?" she asked.

"Yes, you are," Ben told her. "Stearns, take your wife home. We'll have breakfast in the morning and plan the reception to invite our friends to celebrate. Won't we, Abigail?"

"You two don't live here? You have your own house?"

"They're on their own, Abigail. Let them be."

"No small feat," Ben said later. "A man who stands up for his wife against a tyrant—"

"I wasn't a tyrant." Abigail plopped on the side of their bed.

"You were. Your daughter fainted, she was so upset."

"I am sorry about that. But holy cow chips, she shocked me. And you could have told me earlier."

"They're happy, Jenny. No man would have been good enough for Clara Belle, from your point of view. They've had four months together to gird themselves before seeing you. It's too late for you to even think about an annulment, and besides, she's twenty-three years old, well able to make her own decisions."

"I hoped she wouldn't marry young like I did."

"Hey," Ben said. "Has it been so bad? Your marrying at eighteen—almost nineteen." His words choked.

I've wounded him. "No, it hasn't." She patted his arm.

"What haven't you done that you might have done if you'd waited to marry or perhaps never married at all?"

"Nothing. And more, likely because you've been there to support me—us."

294

"And haven't you said the greatest joy of your life are your children? Would you deprive your daughter of that same great joy?"

"You're right. Of course. We'll have a reception for them. I'll announce it in the paper." She unhooked her high-button shoes. "But Stearns is a competitor, Ben."

"Competitors make us better."

"I suppose they do in the end."

"By the way, while you were gone, Harvey returned as the editor of the *Oregonian*. New administration—he lost his customs post. He's bought a controlling interest in that paper, so if you want to focus on a competitor to rail against, choose him and let Don Stearns and Clara Belle make their own way. Return to your purpose— using the *New Northwest* to get women the vote."

"You're absolutely right. We'll win Harvey over and get Oregon to be the first of the Pacific coast states where women can cast their coveted ballot. There's a purpose I can work toward." One didn't have control over much—certainly not one's children—but she could control what mattered and have the courage to act on that.

TWENTY-FIVE

First Hurdle

1877

"I'm riding through quicksand with the temperance issue," Abigail told Kate as she hovered over her latest article. "I don't want to raise the ire of Portland's liquor interests who will pour money against suffrage if they think women will vote in prohibition. I support the lack of drink, but no one should advise anyone else what decisions they should make about their personal lives. I won't touch wine, but I decry anyone who will tell me that I can't. If I can only get that across."

"You do better when your articles explore those issues indirectly," Kate said. "The story when you visited the asylum or that trip with Clyde, seeing things through the eyes of a ten-year-old, people can find themselves in that kind of piece. You're pursuing something worthwhile and can still be a good mother and wife and friend to those in need. And you give legitimacy to widows trying new things, like me. Even single women who otherwise would be forced to be nannies for their nieces and nephews. Some of them can now be inventors."

"But those stories don't really advance the cause of voting. I'll keep writing about quilting bees and barn raisings, but something is missing. I've had the paper for more than five years, and we're no closer to even getting the legislature to bring up the issue."

"You had a nice response when you told of Willis leaving the nest and heading to San Francisco to make his own career as a printer elsewhere."

"I suppose all families undergo changes. I hate to see ours experiencing it this way."

Her chicks were leaving the flock and she still hadn't accomplished what she'd wanted, even with their efforts as part of the newspaper. Women still didn't control the ballot. She and two of her suffrage friends had actually attempted to vote in '72, but there'd barely been a mention of it in the *Oregonian*. Harvey gave not the slightest copy to anything that sniffed of suffrage action except to oppose it. "We have to clarify our purpose," she said. "Set a singular goal. That's how we got the paper. Now we have to use that same strategy to get the vote."

"We'll have to do it ourselves." Abigail spoke to the Portland chapter of the National Woman Suffrage Association. "We must set a specific target, a date by which we will have the legislature refer women's suffrage to the male voters of the state, and my newspaper will tout that until it happens."

A chorus of voices agreed. Abigail was the president, and her vice president added, "It will have to be 1884 for the vote. That requires that we convince both houses of the legislature to agree to refer it first in 1880 and then in 1882."

"Such a cumbersome law, making a change in the constitution go through two consecutive legislative sessions before it can be voted on by men, especially when they only meet every other year." Abigail stated what the women already knew.

"We knock down the first hurdle of 1880 and push until the next session—1882—and if it passes again, which it must, then in 1884 they will refer it to the voters. That gives us four years to make our push." The vice-chairman drew out the timeline on the blackboard. They were meeting at the neighborhood school, and it smelled of chalk dust and old books.

"They don't make it easy," someone said.

"It's the challenge that will inspire us," Abigail said. "Now let's start breaking this down. How much do we want National involved? I say very little, but I'm open to hearing your ideas."

She was open to it, but she'd already decided: they would do this the Oregon way, without visits by national suffragists—though it would be helpful if National sent them a little cash for flyers and posters and paid for ads in the *Oregonian*. Harvey might not support suffrage, but he likely wouldn't turn down ad revenue. He wouldn't run them for free as a public service the way the *New Northwest* would.

"But we might engage younger women if we had more national involvement," another member said.

"No. They don't understand us here in the West."

Another member offered, "But I've been in the East, and they'd be willing to let us do it our way. I've spoken—"

"No." Abigail said. "They'll want something for it. We have to do it the Oregon way. Now, let's move on. How will we sustain public events to educate women and their voting men?"

Abigail was aware of the silence and that she'd cut off conversation. But they didn't realize what she did. She'd given her life for this cause, and she wasn't ready to let younger, ill-informed women threaten the campaign. The real work was in the legislature, meeting with men while in session, showing them how it might be to their advantage to have women able to vote, and National could not do that. Yes, a few legislators had been impressed when Susan B. Anthony and Abigail had met with them during their tour, but Susan B. was an oddity to the men then. Now, they were wary of women talking about voting.

Abigail didn't believe that women would be somehow better voters than men, more moral or noble. Rather, she thought that the domestic lives of men and women would be better if women were seen as equal citizens and could contribute fully their talents to society at large. *I should treat my suffrage sisters as more equal by listening to them more. But we haven't time. We must persist. Without National.*

The conversation went back and forth about the role of "outsiders," with Abigail standing firm. Eventually Kate pointed out that Oregon men might resent Eastern women having a say in their activities, flashing their VOTE FOR WOMEN banners in their faces. Oregon would do it one by one. Quietly, like the moon rising, something inevitable, though at times it might seem to disappear. They would be steady, if not noisy.

"Then it's decided, at last," Abigail said. "We begin our still hunt meeting with legislators, let those eastern Hurrah women go their way—away from here. Those of you with contacts, let's make a list. And don't forget neighboring states. If one of them decides on the franchise, that'll influence Oregon men. They'll not want to be left behind. We help our sisters to the south, north, and east."

"And they'll see that good men in the West understand that women deserve the vote," another chapter member said.

"Take your husbands with you when you go to visit legislators," Abigail said. "Or fathers, to show them men support us."

"Or brothers," another woman said. "Abigail and Kate, yours is the biggest effort. To try to get Mr. *Oregonian* himself to endorse us."

"That's been a lifelong campaign, to no avail."

"Yet," Kate said.

All the Scott girls were in favor of suffrage. Making it a family affair would be the most important "still hunt" the Scott girls could pursue.

"We sisters will do our part with Harvey. If the *Oregonian* supported it statewide, that could make all the difference. Meanwhile, the *New Northwest* will begin a fresh campaign. My book is finished and published and well received, this time." Scattered applause followed. She cleared her throat. "And the newspaper debt is but one hundred six dollars." *Am I bragging? Yes.* "We can show that women are successful. And we must report back after any legislator meeting to assure ourselves that we know all of the objections and make plans to address them."

"We're aware of the argument," someone said, "that voting will bring disrepute onto women who don't belong in the dirtiness of politics. Women are to be protected from such things." She counted on her fingers. "I've heard my women friends say the same thing."

"But we do fine in the dirtiness of cleaning horse stalls," someone said, and the women laughed.

"There are other points of opposition out there. We need to address each of them. But we also need to make a list of what pushes this idea forward. Those are two different strategies," Abigail warned. "We have to manage both what pushes us forward and what holds us back."

"Do you think we can win Harvey over?" Kate asked as they walked back to the Duniway home.

"It's worth the effort. He did give Ben his job and didn't change his mind after he realized we'd be able to start the paper because of it. Of course, he wasn't at the *Oregonian* then. He may feel differently now. He also bought a steamship ticket for me when I went to San Francisco that time. Maybe he didn't realize I'd be attending the suffrage events."

"That has to be our campaign then. Both a still hunt for legislators and a family hunt for Harvey."

"You've earned a level of prominence so legislators are listening, that's certain," Ben agreed. "I'm not sure they've even noticed the formation of the Women's Christian Temperance Union."

"Oh, they've noticed." Abigail had come from a suffrage meeting where reports were worrisome about how the temperance ladies were wildly—in Abigail's opinion—entering the saloons with their umbrellas, sometimes smashing glasses and shouting at the men imbibing there, "hurrahing" their philosophy. They wanted the suffrage movement to come on board their wild ride against liquor. It saddened Abigail that even Susan B. felt the groups should join up, but doing so in the West meant women's votes would be doomed.

"Joining could affect the German vote," Ben agreed. "They like their beer, and the brewers have both financial and political influence. Republican influence. With Harvey's paper too. We won't want them against our suffrage."

She'd been more concerned about temperance supporters swilling with prohibitionists, an alliance that would put those seeking the vote in opposite camps. She'd listened to too many speeches opposing women's suffrage that began and ended with "if women get the vote, they'll bring in prohibition and men will never have another legal drop of liquor available in the streets of Portland." That was hard to imagine with a saloon on every corner. But she'd have to separate temperance and prohibition and suffrage in people's minds. That was another task of a newspaper editor—to bring clarity to busy people and help reformers see how their efforts might be received differently than intended.

Confederate-leaning newspapers had been

curtailed by Oregon's Republican legislature that convinced the postal service not to distribute "abusive and treasonous" papers. They considered those who reported with sympathy to the South and with antipathy to reconstruction efforts, like getting Negroes the right to vote, as "abusive." No one wanted the *New Northwest* to somehow end up as an illegal paper. But the tabloids would change their names or hand-distribute until discovered and be put out of business again, only to start up under another banner. That was politics and she was on the right side of it. Now. The *New Northwest* had subscribers as far north as British Columbia and as far east as New Hampshire. She'd made readers into "agents" who were free to sell subscriptions for a small commission. That expansive coverage was a feather in Abigail's newly felted hat. The *New Northwest* was still pretty small, though, which for now kept her from being the target of the *Oregonian.* And opened the door for her campaign.

Abigail had taken the steamship to San Francisco to confer with California suffragists and to spend time with Shirley Ellis. She never wanted to be too far from the daily demands on women while she worked in the loftier climes of legislative action. Shirley's struggle over child custody was yet another avenue of what drove Abigail toward more freedom for women. Her friend in

San Francisco had remarried but kept her first husband's name so it would be the same as her daughter's.

"Has marrying Eloi made your time with your daughter more difficult to negotiate?" The women walked arm in arm down the main street of San Francisco, past dry good stores and shops with dresses modeled by women standing in the window still as stone.

"I'm hoping not. I told the judge that when she's with me now, she'll have two parents to look after her, while being with her father, she only has one. Eloi suggested it as an argument. His being a lawyer helps. Truth is, I was looking for a reason to marry him beyond loving him." Shirley blushed.

"You're entitled to happiness. We women have a way of discounting that. Yet even our Lord said he came to give us an abundant life. All beings, not just men."

They spoke of the Club Women campaigns in California to push for women's rights and the growing threat of dissension between factions of temperance and prohibitionists and suffragists. It was the same in Oregon. "We've done some direct things, like putting ads on streetcars and held a few rallies, but mostly we're pushing what good things women can do for communities. We're trying to downplay temperance issues."

Back in Portland, Abigail told Shirley, the

temperance bug showed up in congregations led by "boy preachers," she called them, who sent "singers and prayers" around wherever Abigail was trying to speak about her view of temperance. She felt compelled to argue on behalf of people's rights to make their own choices about alcohol consumption or any personal decisions. Besides, she couldn't imagine how the sheriffs would enforce prohibition. She wished that Portland's religious community could see how her work was Christlike. Even her father, stern as he was, served also as a Cumberland Presbyterian elder, and he approved women's suffrage. But in Portland, only one pastor—Thomas Eliot— had welcomed the Duniways when they'd arrived. That reverend agreed with Abigail that prayer and works went hand in hand. The man's congregation worked on behalf of poor children and animals, forming a humane society. He also saw the arts—music, literature, paintings—as important to spiritual growth, spurring intellectual thought. Best of all, he supported a woman's right to vote, affirming his intelligence, according to Abigail.

"Once I stood up in the temperance meeting to speak and the reverends ordered my ejection. They knew what I was going to say, and the little choir group stood up to sing me into silence."

"Oh, Abigail," Shirley said. "You endure so many insults. I don't know how you do it."

"Kate and Ben say I invite some of those insults because of my 'acerbic tongue,' they call it."

"What did you do when they started to sing you out?"

"Well, I was hit with a thunderbolt of insight, and I shouted, 'Let us pray!' then led a half-hour prayer asking God to enlighten us all, to encourage liberty in his followers, to help us all have an abundant life by knowing him and granting freedom to all God's children, men and women, black or white. Oh, those 'boy preachers,' they were too stunned to know how to shut down the prayer."

"From the tongue of an intemperate woman." Shirley smiled and shook her head. "I could never be so bold. How is Clara Belle? Does she still sing at the meetings?"

"Sometimes. They have that new baby, and Stearns talks about moving them to the swamps of Washougal."

"You're a grandmother? How wonderful."

"Is it? A sign of my aging. I do like the little tyke, though. But there's little medical help in that Washington burg should she need it. The baby is sickly, it seems to me. And they don't have the income to bring in help. Ben and I gave her one of his washing machines, but it's still hard labor in the laundry."

"Will getting the vote mitigate those hardships, do you think? I sometimes wonder," Shirley said.

"At least it will allow women to help pass laws that let her keep the income she makes from eggs and butter and stitchery instead of having to hand it over to some man—unless, of course, she wants to do that. It's about choices." She sighed. "It has to make a difference, doesn't it? Otherwise, is this effort all for nothing?"

"Don't you get discouraged, Abigail. Or we'll all lose hope. We're working to expand women's opportunities. We all have gifts differing, isn't that what St. Paul wrote to his followers, both men and women, I might add. You do what you can do, push for legal changes, quietly but faithfully gather women to organize."

"And urge my brother to remain quiet in his opposition as he'll never support us. Then we'll have a fighting chance."

TWENTY-SIX

The Moving World

1880

The meetings were endless and not always productive, the smell of tobacco lingering on her jacket for hours after a discussion with a senator or house member. She'd come home, rub lavender on the cloth as it hung on the outside porch to air, reviewing what she'd said, how she'd managed the interview. Sometimes she thought she'd had a legislator's vote, only to learn by the grapevine that he hadn't committed at all. Other times she'd left the offices thick with memorabilia of photographs and family and the man's special interests—horses, dogs, a brewery he stood in front of—thinking she had failed to have him even entertain the idea, when a woman at a meeting would report, "He's seriously considering backing us."

She wondered.

She hated the unpredictable nature of this still hunt, but it carried more hope than the rallies and parades. Somehow eye to eye carried weight. Even Shirley had said that she thought Oregon with its pioneering ways would be the first to get passage.

Abigail found greater satisfaction in writing about the encounters. Once she told of an exchange not with a legislator but a potential voter that ended with the man saying his wife had long wanted a subscription to the *New Northwest* so she could read it at home, but she "hadn't had the money." He'd crowed that as a generous husband, he'd given the delivered paper to his wife as a gift and wasn't that grand? Abigail agreed it was, adding that "if women had the vote and control over their money, your wife might one day use *her* money to buy you a special gift. Perhaps a ticket to a pugilistic event or even a new pipe."

"You've a point there, missus," the new subscriber had said. "Something to consider."

That's all she could hope for with a new conquest: that the man would consider the possibility that suffrage might have an advantage to him. At the same time, she showed her readers how diplomacy and humor could turn a patronizing man into a subscriber, while highlighting how women were still dependent on men in order to accomplish the simplest of wishes.

It was how she had to manage legislators too. Gently, soothing their egos, always trying to find a way to show the advantage suffrage would be for them. A few listened and agreed because they believed in equality. But the women had to win over those most opposed in order to get sufficient backing. And in 1880, they did. The legislature agreed to refer to the voters the question of giving Oregon women the right to vote. The governor signed it. The first hurdle had been crossed. Now the second legislative session had to agree. "Onward to '82" became the new motto.

A spatter of rain hit the tin bucket sitting on the front porch. Otherwise Abigail wouldn't have been aware that an April freshet washed the streets of Portland, matting the leaves, turning the day to darkness. Abigail was deep in reading the latest issue of her *New Northwest.*

Kate had brought onto the paper's pages excerpts from Mark Twain and writer Bret Hart; letters from Aunt Susan and local authors too. She'd even recommended a couple of pieces written by Willis. Abigail liked seeing young writers get into print, remembering how difficult it had been for her all those years before. Frances Fuller Victor, a prominent Oregon writer, had her works appear in San Francisco's *Overland Monthly* and now Abigail's *New Northwest.* Abigail's own serialized novels appeared weekly, sometimes written in great haste. She was grateful Kate was there to give them polish, though she didn't like changes beyond improved grammar. No discussion of characterization or plot ever resulted in a pleasant sisterly conversation.

Letters to the editor often spoke of the novels and how they had moved readers, reassuring Abigail that words had power to change people. Her words could do that, both with her factual, journalistic pieces and with her fiction.

Her women readers still wanted entertainment and a chance to dream of another life they might have had, one not so burdened with hard labor. Her novels served that purpose. Sometimes, when she wrote late at night with Ben snoring softly, she understood she too dreamed of another life, when a hero would have swept her off her feet—as Ben had—but who also took care of her—as Ben had not always. She put those longings into her characters and gave them courage to take risks, seeking happiness but always "doing good" and finding ways to forgive themselves for mistakes they made. She created hopeful endings, if not always happy ones. That gave her stories realism, she felt, and she resented the preachers who described her novels as both frivolous and spiritually harmful. Her poor readers were described as sinful. There were certainly greater affronts to God they might have railed against, including real men, not fictional ones, abandoning their wives and children.

It was true, she did write of girls who became entangled with men and moralized about the tragedy of girls becoming pregnant without marriage. She could understand how such mistakes could happen—hadn't her family been involved in that through her father's wife? But such shenanigans meant a lack of discipline on the part of the woman and the man. Her novels emphasized how devastating the consequences could be when a girl didn't wait until marriage. She wanted her children to read those stories— especially her sons.

In between writing, she found herself attending more local meetings, balancing the politics between the Temperance Union's wanting to pass their reforms and Abigail's fear that the liquor industry would block suffrage efforts if the temperance ladies were successful. Abigail had good friends and supporters in the Jewish community led by Jacob Mayer, who had funded her millinery venture. She placed his ads for free, and he supported women's suffrage and said he would work on his associates in the legislature. She wrote articles defending the Chinese and how it was a Chinese man who went into his store to bring out chairs for the comfort of the women when they protested an injustice. She noted that the people she was closest to were considered outsiders, Republicans, but working folks, not moving in the circles of her brother or the wives of investors. She didn't mind being an outcast, but both Ben and Kate pointed out that she ought not to agitate those powers that be.

"How else can we take them on but through the press. We can't *only* be about the vote. Otherwise they don't even see us, and what they do see they dimish."

"It cuts into our subscriptions," Kate said.

"And gives us bad press," Wilkie had agreed.

Not a week later, someone had written in the Albany paper that when she traveled, Abigail drank and entertained men in her hotel rooms. Abigail had defended herself against one Mr. Bunter, while at the same time saying if the original accuser didn't want a slander suit, he might get the editor to retract his accusations or she'd get witnesses to some of the rumors she'd heard about him. "That should show him at last. The man has been a burr under my saddle for decades," she told Kate.

The Duniways thought all had died down, when another report appeared in the *Portland Sunday Welcome*, and Willis—back at the *New Northwest*—and Hubert decided to cane that editor, a level of force that stunned Abigail. *How I have failed them.*

"Words," she told them, tears in her eyes. "Not violence. Not ever."

The boys were arrested for assault and battery, and now letters addressed how the famous suffragist was unable to manage her own children. "See what comes of such activity," wrote Mr. Bunter.

"They're grown men," Abigail defended. "It's a sorry day when a mother's sons have to defend her."

A few of her minister friends came to her defense, and even Harvey wrote an editorial, taking to task any editor who would question the name of a "good and faithful mother." She was as shocked at his support as she'd been with the ferocity of her sons' defense of her.

"I'm not much of a mother if my children disobey or act with cruelty before I could even make a written response."

Ben whittled on a block of wood, nodded at her outrage. He put it up and set the tea kettle on to heat. "At least the jury found the boys innocent and the editor admitted it was a ficticious story."

"Bunter never apologized."

"He never will. He's a lost cause, Jenny. He'll never vote for yours. Let's hope the story winds down."

"You know it won't. It'll be a filler in the *Walla Walla Union*. Or front page of the *Statesman*." She fumed, then sighed. "Advocating for rights requires a balance between notoriety and publicity." Abigail shook her head. "A couple of the suffrage women have suggested I lower my celebrity for a time." *Could they be right?*

"We could use a little break in the financial drain your cause is taking."

"That's the very fact of things. I could be a

millionaire if I'd have invested in land instead of the paper and this important work, but what would I have in the end? I'd have money but at the expense of bettering a woman's life. A man's too, if they'd ever admit it. At least the bill to allow women to have control over their own property and money passed. Tiny gains."

"You're on target to get the '82 legislative vote."

"That we are." She had to find moments of hope in the midst of this powerless swamp of old nemeses who took her to task and sons whose methods of confrontation startled her with their vehemence. She was grateful they wished to defend her good name. What mother wouldn't be. But chastened that they thought aggression would be the proper proportion of response. *Maybe they've learned that from me?* She could get strident and perhaps "caned" with words no differently at times than the actual hickory sticks they'd used.

The Woman Suffrage Amendment was proposed in the United States Congress, a sure sign of progress nationwide. It added to the hopefulness of the individual meetings Abigail scheduled with legislators, old men sucking on their pipes and cigars. "I'm not sure why they send grown men who are not yet weaned to make laws for women," she told Ben after one visit to the Washington legislature.

"I hope you didn't say that."

"Not to their faces, but it's a good line and I'll find a time to use it."

"Not while you're trying to win them over, Jenny."

"You're right. I'm grumpy. We were making such gains and then Kate's leaving—" Her voice caught and she felt tears come. "What did I do?"

"Nothing." Ben patted her shoulder.

They'd gone to the old farm where Ben had once trained horses and saddled two calm mares. Ben had insisted that she get some sunshine and do something she once loved. She had loved the wind on her face riding a fast horse. There'd be no racing, what with her prolapsed uterus and Ben's back. But side by side with Ben, the control of the horse by the reins in her hands, the brace of breeze on this April day was invigorating. She needed that now.

Yes, they'd made good advances, first with the passage of a bill to allow women—and men—to vote in all school elections. Abigail had promoted such action in her newspaper and spoke of it at various meetings. If a woman was capable of teaching young men, she ought to be able to vote about what they should be taught. The legislature had agreed. The same year, women were granted freedom to manage their own property, own it without spousal consent.

"I need to rejoice with these new laws, but

they add to Harvey's editorials as yet another reason why suffrage *isn't* needed. 'Men are taking care of women, so women need not lower themselves to the legislative floor in order to gain rights.' " She mocked her brother with a fake voice, pontificating as he did at family gatherings. He'd gotten even more pompous with their father's death and his being the head of the Scott clan. He'd also gotten more odious in his objection to the woman's vote. Until their father's death in 1880, Abigail hadn't realized that her father had been a mitigating force on the suffrage issue between his daughters and his one surviving son.

Still, it had been Kate's leaving the *New Northwest* that had hurt her the most. She had always thought it would be Harvey who betrayed her.

"The *Daily Bee* gives her a chance to lead the team. She can write more too. And it helps Don and Clara Belle as well."

"But it's an inferior paper. He gives it away for free, Ben! No wonder those children live hand-to-mouth. How can he make any money giving a paper away?"

"They aren't children. And Kate tells me he prints invitations and posters—for a fee, of course. And he sells ads. People love free things, you know that."

Why did it seem that things could go smoothly

on a trail only for a short time but that rugged roads went on forever?

"It's time," Kate had said that morning in February when she told of her taking the new position, leaving Abigail on a boulder-strewn road just when things were looking up with the legislature. "And he offered me more money than you can afford, not that that's the best reason to do anything. You have to make cuts somewhere, and Abigail, you're a fine editor."

She was a *fine* editor, but Kate had given the paper polish and shine, freeing Abigail to travel and lecture. She'd need to do more of that, not less, with the hope to get a bill before the legislature by 1884 and continue to support the Duniway Publishing enterprise, not to mention her efforts to encourage Washington's, California's, and Idaho's voting campaigns.

"But he's a competitor," Abigail said. "And he took my Clara Belle away and now you too." She rolled her lower lip out in a pout.

"You could be pleased that your daughter married into the news business and that your sister, too, will be an editor of another paper that could promote our cause." Kate's curls cascaded down the side of her face, perfectly coiffed, and she pushed them from her cheek.

She has to get up early to have her person look so together. Abigail touched her own hair, tucked in stray strands. She planned to try the new bob look, smooth at the sides, the way Susan B. wore her hair. But Ben loved brushing her long hair for her.

"We're in the same business, Jenny, and yes, competing, but that competition keeps us sharp." Kate's eyes softened, and Abigail saw in them sympathy. And kindness. "I'll be closer to Clara Belle too. And little Earl."

"She brings the baby to work?"

"As her forward-thinking mother did."

Kate picked up her personal things, her special pen and ink set, and her teaching certificate she'd had framed and hung on the wall. "I won't stop working for the vote. You know that."

"You've cut my feathers, though."

"You can blame me for keeping you home a little more." She sneezed then, and Abigail worried for her health. "Just the dust," Kate had said.

Abigail's horse shook its head and blew through its nose and brought her back to this glorious spring day. She pulled up and turned toward Ben. "I hope she'll carry suffrage articles in the *Bee*, maybe reprint a few of my pieces." She sighed. Was there nothing she could do about this? "The world is moving and women are moving with it. That's what I told her, Ben."

"She'll use that saying as a filler."

"Just so she credits it to her older sister. Let's go back." They turned the horses on the dirt trail. Apple trees had leafed out and promised blooms. "She told me that the *Daily Bee* will be a Republican paper, so I can rest easy that we have another voice in our fight. She said she was glad I'd talked her into leaving teaching to become a newspaper editor, that I'd paid her well and treated her fairly, that we are still working together. But it doesn't feel that way. I probably took her for granted." *Do I take everyone I love for granted?*

"You're still on the same team, Jenny."

"I hope so. I don't need any more editorials complaining about my strident voice. Kate helped temper my tone." She wiped at the tears on her cheek. *Who will do that now?* The world was changing and women with it. She'd have to change too.

TWENTY-SEVEN
Drawing Closer

1882

Abigail had accepted with pleasure the invitation to speak at the Idaho statehood planning convention. It took her to a new landscape. Her stagecoaches rolled across the trails, with canvas window coverings rolled down to hold out at least a portion of the dust. But when they stopped to change horse teams, or she rose in the early morning to catch the dawn, she stood in awe at the vistas. Mountains like purple lace circled the prairies, and she was always imbued with a hopefulness, an inevitability that progress would happen for women, that such a landscape not only promised it but helped shape it. At one stage stop, she met Carrie Strahorn, another writer and wife of a railroad promoter, her husband an author as well. They laughed at the terrible coffee as they looked out across sagebrush dipped in sunrise. They spoke of women's rights. The air was crisp, and they parted as sisters in the cause, each taking a stage in a different direction.

Idaho wasn't so grand as Oregon's panoramas, Abigail didn't think. Oregon could claim the ocean's blue and the mighty Columbia as well, though Idaho had the Snake River and its massive canyons. This might be a place to live after her suffrage work was finished and women had the vote, when children were off and married and she and Ben had a quiet place for him to brush his horses and deliberate in small-town liveries about the merits of the latest leather harness or breeding stock; and for her to write.

She'd imagine that quiet life, but then she'd be in the throes of statehood or suffrage with the mix of men and women and she would see how her words inspired, celebrated the local heroes while singing the praises of Thomas Jefferson and reciting the preamble to the constitution, something she'd required every student to know when she taught school. The words refreshed, and who could deny their call that "all men are created equal"? She merely had to get the legislative men to think loftier, more expansively, that man in this instance meant human. She wrote out her speech for the paper, infused with the goodness of the Idaho landscape and her men and women. But once written down, Abigail never looked at the paper on the podium when she gave her speeches. Instead, she let the words from her heart inspire the efforts of the suffrage men and women. Then she'd be back in Oregon, pushing her still hunt, the landscape in the background— legislative corridors at the front.

• • •

Clara Belle's husband had sold his *Bee*, and Kate, instead of returning to the *New Northwest* as Abigail encouraged, took instead a position editing the *Evening Telegram*.

"It's Pittock's paper. He owns Harvey's press. Why—"

"Abigail, it isn't personal," Kate said. "You're still on a hummingbird's budget in an eagle's flight path. You can't afford me. And Pittock asked me to stay on. He's changed the name. Don will manage and sell subscriptions, but he has other interests. I'll have total editorial control. I rather like that idea."

"What are Stearns's other interests?" She got most of her news about Clara Belle through Kate. She hoped that wouldn't stop. She wanted to visit Clara Belle, but . . . she still couldn't forgive her, that was the truth. And then there was Abigail's schedule, always pulling at her.

"He's hoping for his land speculation to be productive. The prune orchard."

"In Washougal? He's finally moved them there to the middle of nowhere." She remembered the hardscrabble farm and the terrible loneliness. "We'll be fortunate if Clara Belle and Earl can get through the winter without pneumonia."

Kate sat across a large desk, tidy as always. "Clara Belle seems excited about the move. She is so optimistic, that girl. She loves little things. Her music. Stitching. She always looks so fashionable too. She's an attentive mother."

"So was I."

"It wasn't a criticism, Jenny. Merely an observation."

Abigail stepped over her defensiveness. "What does she know about pioneering in remote places? She has no idea how much work it's going to be in that undeveloped land." Abigail remembered how the little girl had hung on to her skirts in their log home, sometimes standing on her mother's toes, the two pretending to be an elephant thumping around the wide room, bonded together as one. Abigail had made it fun despite her own pain and debilitation, especially after Willis's delivery. Maybe she should have made it harder—as her own childhood had been—to better prepare her daughter for the realities of life. Then Clara Belle might not have married for love but for pragmatics.

"Perhaps she likes the idea of pioneering the way her parents did it." Kate left the desk and sat in the chair next to Abigail. "You advance that spirit in your speeches. We're going to reprint the one you have in the Idaho Territory."

"We can all relate to pioneering. It's a romantic period in people's lives. And it calls up our forefathers, so it brings into their minds and hearts, I hope, the idea of liberty and the inevitability of it, if we pursue the goal. The world keeps moving—"

"And women are moving with it. I know. I'm glad your trip went well."

"And now the road takes us to the legislative session. Cross your fingers."

"I'll do that."

They spoke of Kate's children, talked of her daughter's engagement to a doctor in town, but conversation came back to Clara Belle. "She is helping to support him. I do know that," Kate said.

"And who will she give music lessons to in that swamp?"

"The paper will pay her for some correspondence. The area is growing. They have a new dock, and a farm produce boat leaves at seven in the morning and returns by 2:00 p.m., so Clara and Earl could visit. Or you could go and spend the night."

"Not with that man. No. I'll send my prayers for her. Are they taking her piano? I hope so."

"Try to see her before they move completely."

"I will. Ben will make sure we do."

"He already has. While you were off in Idaho."

"I enjoy that territory. I even thought Ben might like it too. When we get old. We could live in a lodge in the wilderness." She made her voice light.

"It's always good to have a place to think of final settling, but I thought you had left log cabins behind."

"I said a lodge, not a log cabin. I'll want a little

luxury in my old age. If I can keep the paper going and get a little money for my speaking. Once we get suffrage, we can sell the paper. Until then, I have much to do until all the West's women have the vote."

"You'll always be a reformer. I just wish for your sake you'd take more time for being a grandmother and a wife. I get wistful sometimes, seeing you leave Ben as you go off. Makes me miss John so much." Kate cleared her throat. "And I'm sad for you that you're passing up moments you'll never have again, experiences I so wish I still could have."

Kate was right, of course. But Abigail couldn't see her way to memorialize the pleasures, let alone permit them to take precedence over the cause that drove her life, even if that cause kept her from enjoying it.

"Give Clara Belle my regards. And tell her I'll come see her. I will."

And she fully intended to do so.

She was invited to speak to the Oregon senate on behalf of Resolution 2. The associations had been working toward making this happen for ten years. Abigail had been given twenty minutes to speak to SR2, and Ben and Willis sat in the gallery. Abigail hoped her son was proud of her. He was quite an orator himself, and she hoped he'd speak well of whatever she had to say.

The resolution giving Oregon women the vote would have to pass the senate. Then be introduced in the house and passed there. Another resolution, related to prohibition, had also been proposed, and she clearly wanted the two separated so didn't speak to it at all. She spoke to what united men and women with this proposed law, but more, using her most ceremonial speech, she appealed to the men as husbands and fathers, reminding them that the Negro had been given the right this resolution called for now for Oregon's women. "Ought not your mothers and sisters and daughters have the same freedom?" Wasn't this the very end those who died in the Revolutionary War had given their lives for? She used a term, "aristocracy of sex," that had resonated when she'd spoken to the Illinois Legislature.

Abigail had to appeal to these senators, not through the mundane of referring the resolution to the men of Oregon for a vote two years in the future, but to the larger issue of liberty. And she'd loved it that she was introduced by Senator Hirsch, whom she'd known since the days when his partner, Jacob Mayer, had loaned her money for her millinery. And Willis saw it all.

The next day, the women in the gallery watched as the SR2 passed 21–9. Applause broke out but quickly turned to the flashing of white handkerchiefs the way Chautauqua audiences expressed their glee. The women were pleased beyond words and wanted the senate to know it but didn't want their noise to get them removed for lack of decorum. The following day, Abigail was asked to speak to the same resolution in the Oregon house where there'd been a more lively and disunifying debate. She held her tongue and said only that she felt the resolution spoke for itself but that passage would put them all on a winning track for women and for themselves. It passed 29–25. White handkerchiefs fluttered the air.

A grand celebration at the Salem Opera House followed. Men and women of the cause sang the praises of the supporting legislators, and Willis gave a rousing speech. She was so grateful Ben and her sons were behind her. She wished Clara Belle had been there.

"You've done your part, Ma," Willis said as they rode in the coach back to Portland. "You birthed five votes and Pa's is the sixth from the Duniway house. The beginning of a precinct."

"Not the recommended way to achieve votes. Better to win them over from another mother's womb." She patted his hand. "But I'm glad you've taken up the cause."

Harvey's *Oregonian* published her senate address the day after the house passage; *New Northwest* carried the senate speech the day before the *Oregonian*. Harvey had made no editorial comment against the passage, for which

Abigail was pleased, though she wished he'd find a way to support her life's effort.

"Harriet, we've one battle left." Abigail spoke to the vice president of the Oregon State Women's Suffrage Association after the vote. Abigail called Harriet Loughary the "Patrick Henry of the new dispensation" and knew this mother of nine could have made as strong a case as Abigail had. Harriet was a fine speaker with a teacher-husband who, like Ben, was a partner who supported the cause. "I should let her present more," Abigail told Ben. But she hated letting loose of the limelight.

The first two steps were climbed. The resolution had passed in two consecutive sessions. It would now go to the vote in 1884.

"We must work even harder to educate the public, praise the legislature, and try to hold the arguments about prohibition as far from suffrage as brew masters are from coffee grinders." Abigail expounded to the association gathering.

"We might take a moment to applaud our efforts," her vice-chair said. "And some of us take a well-deserved rest."

"If you're speaking about me," Abigail countered, "never you mind. This effort is my lifeblood. If I stopped now, well, I'm not sure but that my blood would stop flowing."

"Perhaps you Scott sisters could focus on your dear brother and silence his opposition."

"We'll do better than that," Abigail said. "We'll get him to support us."

Kate gasped. "Jenny," she whispered when Abigail sat back down. "That's so unlikely."

"Nothing is impossible. Who but us could make this happen? I'll schedule an appointment with Harvey next week."

But later, lying awake with sleep escaping her like the wayward sheep of Sunny Hillside Farm, she wondered if she hadn't pushed too far, promised too much in response to the vice-chair's assertion that Abigail rest a bit. *Am I so strident to the cause? No. I'm the very reason we have come this far.* They could push Harvey to their side. After all, the legislature—his colleagues and friends—had seen the light and voted for the referral. His sisters would bring a little sunshine to his countenance. They just had to find the correct lamp.

Abigail saw her opening with her brother and how the *New Northwest* could assist. It had to do with Harvey's alma mater, Pacific University in Forest Grove. She named the woman in her article, Bridget Gallagher, and told of her story, of how as a young girl, she'd been taken advantage of by a married man. She'd given birth to a child out of wedlock. Few means of support were available to this young woman tending her child as best she could. She became a woman of "negotiable affections," Abigail called it. Eventually, the woman became a madam of an ill-reputed house. She made donations to the community, gave loans to young girls so they didn't have to resort to her "profession" which men kept possible. She wanted more for her son and had sent him to live in Forest Grove, a town founded by Congregationalists, Abigail made sure to note, where she attempted to enroll him in Harvey's alma mater.

> She was coolly informed by a professor that the child of such a mother could not be received in their ranks! And yet this school is a noted asylum for Alaskan, Japanese, and Chinese pupils, and is just now preparing to receive in its Christian fold a reinforcement of fifty young Indians of both sexes. Who checks to see if their mothers are all chaste and of the highest reputation? No wonder there are infidels in the land. No wonder they are multiplying in Forest Grove. Ah me! A.S.D.

Harvey sent her a note suggesting that she did her woman's cause no good deed by consorting with prostitutes. She replied that since the men of the state had relegated all women to the class of idiots and prostitutes in their inability to vote that she saw no harm in attempting to aid the *son* of such a woman in gaining an education. Kate had wondered if she might have gone too far in bringing up their brother's educational institution.

"I'm going to appeal to his Christian nature in this. He asked me to publish a series he'd written on religion and I agreed. It's fitting for us to have this discussion."

"But it doesn't help us get him behind the vote."

"It can't hurt."

"Yes, it can, Jenny."

But she'd gone to visit him anyway, praying she could hold her intemperate tongue.

"It's your alma mater, Harvey. You ought to stand for its motto to educate and to perform its Christian duty to the same." His office walls were covered in wood so polished she could almost see her reflection in them. Tall, narrow windows brought in summer light. It was the office of a legislator-in-waiting and it reeked of power. She inhaled. She would not be intimidated. "And I hope you can see that this is one of the very reasons women should be allowed the vote. So they'd have a say about fair treatment, be able to make their own way when men destroy their reputation, without resorting to prostitution."

"The woman is a prostitute."

"Yet even our Lord consorted with such women, seeing into their souls and past a tarnished reputation. As a full citizen, with rights to vote, she might well have made different decisions. Perhaps she could have taken the child's father to court, gotten him to provide for *their* child. Perhaps she could have gotten a loan and started a boardinghouse? She'd surely have had more options. For now, she wants the best for her son." Abigail looked at a portrait on the wall. Of Harvey. *That would have cost a fortune.* "How can your school deprive him of that when it's said to be a Christian academy? Are we not charged to look after widows and orphans?"

"This child you speak of is neither."

"He might well be with his mother a nonentity in the public eye or, worse, the lowest of women. That did not stop our Lord."

He was quiet, so she knew she'd hit a nerve. He sat, fingers made into tents, his forehead wrinkles deep and familiar in their groves.

"One day you might run for public office," Abigail said. "Might it not be wise to be able to show that you have compassion for all your constituents? In this instance, you'd be educating a voter."

"I can see the value in educating the lad."

She remained silent.

"I'll write to the professors."

"And urge them to allow him into school? Not just be tutored privately somewhere?"

"Yes. I'll urge that."

"Good, because I've had a fair number of letters from supporters, including other professors. You'll want to be on the winning side of this one, Mister Scott. Editor Scott. And am I assuming too much, perhaps one day, Senator Scott?"

Harvey's face turned tomato-red above his dark beard.

And with his revealing countenance, she saw her suffrage argument, the one her sisters could make with their brother.

"He'll want to be with winners. We simply have to convince him that the referral will pass. Because it will, I know it." Abigail reported to her sisters taking tea at the Duniway house. "And that women will vote for reasonable, good men."

"I don't know," Fanny said. "I think if we can keep him from writing editorials against the vote, we'll be doing good. To get him to write one in favor? That's an enormous task."

"But one we have before us."

"*You* put it before us, Jenny." Sarah Maria crocheted as she spoke. "You might have gone too far."

"Nonsense. We have less than two years, but we'll canvass the state, get a show of hands at every meeting, monitor the numbers coming out for the presentations, count our *yes* legislators, and spend time in their districts."

"We can give out little premiums when people come to the events."

"All right. But no parades," Abigail said. "No flashing banners or taking over saloons."

"I wasn't proposing that. Small reminders, pins to wear, that show they are supporters. Quietly, but that might open up discussions for them while they shop or get a dress fitted. We'll give them things to say." Sarah Maria held up the baby bib she'd been working on. "I could perhaps stitch in *Votes for Women*."

Her sisters laughed, but Abigail tapped her finger to her lower lip. "You might have something there, but an opposing man will surely say that babies spit up on the very idea of a woman voting. No, our biggest task is to give supporters words to counter negative conversations. And to convince Harvey that it will pass and that those same women who get the vote will want to vote for a man like Harvey—educated, wise, and a supporter of women's rights—when he runs for Senate."

"Do you think he wants to do that?"

"I'd bet my life on it."

TWENTY-EIGHT

Thirty Years and Counting

June 1883

They returned home from the Annual Pioneer
Association gathering on a beautiful June day.
Ben had come with her, and she'd planned to
simply mingle with old friends and mention face-
to-face the constitutional amendment that was
the referral for the 1884 vote. She wore a green
ribbon with words "Votes for Women" written
in black over a white backing. She would speak
one-on-one and listen to any new arguments in
opposition so she could address them. But the
main speaker—a man—had gotten ill and she'd
been asked to read his presentation. Which she
did, joking that here was an example of a "woman
representing a man" and soon women would have
the vote and a woman might represent a man
in the legislature. People had chuckled. Abigail
never lost a chance to mention the vote. There
was nothing controversial in her saying so.

When she finished reading the missing
speaker's manuscript, she spoke for thirty
minutes more, quoting words of a revered pioneer
named Jesse Applegate, who had said how he

wished his wife—now deceased—had shared liberty with him in her lifetime. Everyone in the Pioneer Association loved Cynthia Applegate, and Abigail built on that shared regard to remind the men that Cynthia Applegate was the example of the kind of wise women Oregon cherished and it was only right that such women be permitted to share liberty with men. "Next year, you men have a chance to make that happen for your wives and daughters." Polite applause followed.

"I think that went well, don't you, Ben?" Abigail removed her hat, lifted her thick curls from her neck, and fanned herself, then went into the kitchen to slice the loaf of bread she'd brought back from the picnic. Both Ralph and Clyde had joined them. She wasn't sure where the older boys had spent the afternoon.

Ben followed her into the kitchen, chewing on his pipe stem. "I didn't know you were going to lecture today."

"I wasn't scheduled to. It was because their speaker became ill. I told you, remember?"

"Oh. Yes. I do now. I always like it when you mention this Oregon country, all its beauty and that line about there being 'lessons of liberty in the rock-rimmed mountains that pierce our blue horizons with their snow-crowned heads' and on like that."

"Do you? I'm impressed you remember that line, word for word."

"You've said it before, and I always have an image of the view from our Sunny Hillside farm." Ben pulled a chair out from the table and sat. The family still congregated in the kitchen area, despite their having turned the old millinery into a large-gathering living room where suffrage meetings were often held.

"Oregon pioneers relate to the expansiveness of this country, at least most men do. I try to equate our land with the effort of the men and women drawn to it and help make them take that leap that, in such a country with its wide expanse, men must open their arms to women's spirit too, to our capabilities to make right decisions. I mean, the law allows drunkards and wife-beaters to vote, why not wonderful women like Cynthia Applegate or widows like Kate who have no man to represent them?"

"You don't need to convince me, Jenny."

She smiled. "I do go on, don't I?" She patted his shoulder as she moved behind him to open the larder. *Is he getting thinner?* "I know I ruffle feathers. Often." *I'd like to be revered like Cynthia Applegate is.*

"It's your way. But you also give us good pictures in our heads of how liberty and rimrock ridges join hands."

Back at the table, she sliced ham and cut chunks of cheese. The younger boys waited patiently. "And that's my calling. Our calling, to make waves for liberty." She held the knife up as though it was a torch.

"Momma." Fourteen-year-old Ralph stepped back out of her way.

"Ma's pontificating," Clyde said. He sat at the table, having gotten the mayonnaise from the icebox. He had whipped it up himself with eggs and oil and spread it on the sliced bread.

"She does that a lot," Ben said. "But seldom with a knife." The men in her life laughed.

"My words are my weapons." She smiled and finished cutting the bread for their light supper. Chen, the Chinese cook, had taken the day off.

They ate and chattered, and the boys told of overhearing suffrage conversations that spoke well of passage in the vote the following year. But Ben's forgetting that her presentation hadn't been planned concerned her. She was sure she'd told him that. Lately, he had been surprised at things she'd told him of—where she was going, when she'd be back. She made sure Willis and Wilke knew, so that if she needed to be reached, she could be. They were so close to achieving this goal, together. She didn't want to think about Ben's not being able to remember how important it all was and his part in it.

The associations, national and local, had been doing their educating, writing, speaking, forming new local suffrage groups, attempting to force the liquor industry from going against the franchise. Abigail traveled too, but she also stayed a little closer to home, paying attention to Ben. She didn't want to ask how his work was going. Maybe it was routine enough that his memory lapses wouldn't be obvious. Tuition for the youngest boys meant they could use every dime that came in.

On one of those days at home, Clara Belle visited, bringing four-year-old Earl with her. He seemed listless, but Clara was in high spirits, exclaiming about their log home. "I've found work in Washington Territory sewing for a new hotel in Washougal. The Columbia River is so majestic, Momma. And you can see Mount Hood from our cabin. It's beautiful country. And growing. I made all the window curtains for the hotel, crocheting each edge. Come visit us and we'll take supper there."

"You're having to sew? What's that Don doing that you're compelled to work?"

"Momma, you still stitch in the evenings. You even talk about it in your speeches, how you have to sew and pay your own expenses half the time."

"I do it because I like to."

"You do not like to sew." Clara Belle laughed. She had the most engaging giggle, Abigail thought. "You grumble all the time you're threading the needle. We children just learned to overlook it."

Abigail harrumphed. "How are things with the battle for the ballot in the Washington Territory?"

"You know as well as any of us, Momma. There are good rumblings that this year we'll see passage. A year before Oregon."

"That's all right. It'll push Oregon legislators to see their neighboring men make a sound decision."

"They almost passed women's suffrage in 1854, but it lost by one vote. I hope we don't miss that close this time," Clara Belle said.

"Surely those legislators have learned their lesson. Oh, this law-promoting is worse than sausage-making."

Clara Belle laughed again. "Remember that time we had to catch up the hog to butcher? Papa was away and Uncle John helped out."

"You were so young. I'm surprised you remember that."

"You hooted after you got cleaned up from the muck. I don't see you laugh much, so I guess it stayed in my memory as special."

Abigail hadn't thought she didn't snigger and chortle all that often, but perhaps Clara Belle was right. "Are you laughing much yourself these days?"

Clara Belle looked away. "Don's working a lot." Her daughter nodded at the scraps of cloth Abigail had cut out and were spread across the table. "Are you making something for the fair?"

"I had to. I wrote about how dreadful I thought it was that women were relegated to spending precious time on stitchery at the end of their hardworking days, only to earn a few coins as fair premiums. They could be taking needed rests or promoting the vote. I suggested we women were meant for bigger things, bigger inventions like those I saw at the exhibition in '76. Well, I got some letters about that."

Clara Belle picked up the cloth pieces, rubbed them between her fingers. "It's very soothing, quilt-making and stitching. And I end up with something beautiful and warm for my family. Some items I sell but that feels good too. I've met other women that way, made friends and been inspired. Maybe you ought not to disparage the domestic arts, Momma. Artists need a community."

"I don't think my quilting will ever be considered art. A couple of letter-writers challenged me to make a quilt. I wrote—foolishly perhaps—that any fool can make a quilt. After making so many through the years, only a fool would spend so much time cutting and stitching back together those little pieces. I started this one after Ralph was born. Anyway, I've been charged with making a patchwork quilt out of silk and satin. Terrible material to work with. Not unlike suffrage having to take scraps of ideas, shape them to fit the men who will vote, and somehow come up with a glorious result we want. After the fair, we'll sell it to raise money for suffrage."

"You see, stitching does have a higher purpose."

"I suppose. Where's Don traveling to? Has he gotten you help?" Abigail gave Earl a book she'd gotten, filled with sketches of horses and simple words he might recognize if Clara Belle had been teaching him.

"I miss my husband, the way you missed Papa when he was in the mines."

"I hope you're not having to work *that* hard, so hard as I did then."

"I can do it. Earl takes long naps." She leaned over as he pointed to a word. "Dressage. It's a special kind of riding people do back east." Then to her mother she continued. "I thought I had enough wood chopped for the whole year, but it's cool near the river and it looks like I'll have to store up a few more cords." She flexed her muscles. "Now my arms are as strong as my piano-playing fingers."

"At least you have the piano." Later Abigail would remember that Clara had not confirmed this statement. Abigail went on to express a warning instead. "Chopping wood by yourself is not a good idea. What if you drop the ax or cut yourself, all alone out there? I'll send your brothers up to ready you for the winter. Your father will want to go too."

"Women have been chopping wood and building fires for generations, Momma. It's work that makes us stronger, helps define who we are. You did it yourself. And when we left the farm, you brought that old broom along, as a symbol, remember?"

"Humph." *Can it be that the years on the Illinois farm, the years on Hardscrabble have shaped me more than I realize?*

"We can make a party of it," Clara continued. "I'd like to show you my home, Momma. You'll come, won't you, if you send the men out to rescue me?" She grinned.

"I'll see what my schedule allows."

She saw the frown across her daughter's face. *There it is again, this avoidance of a happy potential.* "A family gathering would be a good get-together. We'll see what we can arrange." Maybe Kate was right about her aversion to things that could touch the tenderness of her own heart, that gaining the vote had robbed her of the very things that might bring her joy in a battle that had already taken thirty years of her time. She could not let it matter. This suffrage work was worth doing, no matter how long it took or whom it took from.

"You take that businessman." Abigail pointed to the list of men they'd need to nurture through this final phase. "I'll take these. You know the routine. Curry and comb, pamper and praise. I will personally be on my best behavior."

The members of the association chuckled. Abigail on her "best behavior" could still bring a stinging rebuke if she thought it necessary.

When she was invited to speak to the Washington Territorial Legislature and celebrated with them the passage of women's suffrage, she traveled to Olympia at nearly her own expense. The organizations had been unable to secure stable financing, and Abigail had reported in her role as president of the Oregon association that she'd neglected this year to prepare or tabulate a statement of receipts and expenditures. "I tried it for two months, and the balance on the wrong side of the ledger became so large that I feared to keep it up, lest the unpleasant reflection over statistics would so discourage me that I would not have the heart to carry the work to completion." That confession, or perhaps chastisement, had resulted in a small reimbursement for her expenses, but her vice-chair had also told her that the treasurer would want an accounting. She'd have to ask Ben to help—if he could.

On her way back from her speech-making, she had taken the steamship to Washougal. With directions at the landing—people had heard of the Stearns place—Abigail tromped along the path into the thickness of trees and brambles, blackberries, and bushes that someone had cut back from the roadway for the main path. But the side path she'd been told to take to Clara Belle's house wasn't so neatly cleared.

Ben, Willis, and Wilkie had chopped wood for the Stearnses. Ben had supervised, he assured Abigail, had not strained his spine. He'd reported back on the conditions. "Pretty primitive," he'd said. She had not joined them. Too many duties. "But our Clara Belle has turned that hut into a home. The way you did at Hardscrabble. You two have more in common than you might want to admit."

"Is she eating all right? Is Earl well? He looked so thin when they were here last."

Ben shrugged. "I didn't go through their cupboard. Earl is growing, though he is a skinny boy, but then Don is tall and lanky. And Clara Belle is willowy too. He sings like an angel. I wouldn't worry over their food supply."

"I'm glad you took some hams with you, anyway."

"She seemed grateful." He paused. "She asked after you, said she knew from her suffrage group that you'd be visiting the Territorial Legislature and hoped you might stop by. She read your association report saying you'd given 296 speeches last year and figured one of them should have brought you near Washougal and that your invitation to Olympia would."

"That swamp is a far pace from Olympia."

347

Why do I still hold an affront to their long-ago elopement? It was the reason she had not joined the men for the work party. She felt a failure that, after all this effort on behalf of women, she had not protected her daughter from the very hardships she'd had to endure as a young wife. Ben told her that letting go of past pains wasn't hard. He'd had lots of practice and could show her how it was done. Abigail wondered if he was being sarcastic, but that wasn't like him.

Now, here she was, at her daughter's home. She saw the stack of cordwood first, nearly as tall as the roofline. Her brothers had done well by Clara Belle. Their grandfather would have been proud to see his sons stand up for their only sister. She missed her father.

A dog barked, noticing her arrival, and she took in a deep breath as she put her hand out to its nose, let it sniff, then scurry back beneath the porch where Abigail heard the sound of squealing puppies. A dog would be a good companion if she ever stayed home long enough to make a friend of it.

Abigail stepped up onto the porch. A single rocking chair with a colorful patched pillow was tucked into the side. *Only one chair.* She lifted her gloved knuckles, prepared to knock on the door, when she saw a knothole not filled in. She could look right into the house. Clara Belle lay on a cot, Earl beside her on the floor stacking blocks. Clara

Belle lay so still. *Is she dead? Did that man kill her?* Abigail didn't knock but lifted the latch and stepped right in. Earl looked up at her, startled.

"Hi, Earl. I'm your grandmomma. Do you remember me?" He shook his head no. "I'm going to wake your momma."

"She sleeps quiet," he said. A splatter of freckles crossed his nose.

Abigail squatted down, patted his shoulder, then touched Clara Belle's, expecting her body to be cold, swallowing back the tears, then brushing them away with anger directed toward the child's father. "Clara Belle?"

The girl opened her eyes.

Abigail leaned back. "Wake up, baby. It's your momma."

"Oh, Momma." She sat up, looked frantic. "You've caught me napping. I didn't know you were coming." She brushed at her hair, smoothed her sleep-wrinkled dress.

"I was afraid it was worse than napping in the day. Are you well?"

"Just tired. I'm fine. I really am."

"You scared me half to death, lying like that."

"I'm sorry. I . . . I was . . . weary. We dried apples."

Abigail scanned the room and saw the strings of apples hanging from the rafters. She also saw a sparsely furnished house. Except for Clara Belle's stitchery on the windows, a crocheted doily on the back of a narrow couch, the room didn't have much to say for itself. It looked stripped of any grandeur.

"Where's the piano?"

Clara Belle kept her voice light, forced, in Abigail's mind. "It wouldn't stay tuned in all this moisture. Don . . . we sold it. Another child will have the chance to play it with parents who can afford to bring the tuner in from Vancouver."

"He sold your piano. Your pride and joy."

"Earl is my pride and joy. I can still sing."

"Now will you admit your marriage was a mistake?"

"Momma. I have a son. I eat regularly. I have a fine roof over my head and friends not far away. There's even a church here now where I can sing. What more could I need?"

"A husband who looks after you in the style you deserve."

"He's doing the best he can."

"Where is he, by the way? I saw no evidence of prune orchards or whatever it is he said he'd cleared land for."

"It's further away from here." She stood up. "He's sold it anyway. Let's get you a little bite to eat. Earl, I bet you're hungry too."

"I'm always hungry," he said.

"Me too." Abigail brushed the boy's curls with her gloved hand. *But it's for more than. I'm hungry for a better life for my daughter and her son.*

TWENTY-NINE

Victory or Defeat?

November 1883

Autumn foilage had splattered the roadways, colored the grass beneath like a patchwork quilt. November arrived, with a few maple and elm leaves holding tight to their branches. Abigail sometimes thought of herself as like those tenacious fronds, clinging, refusing to let go. The campaign was seven months away from the momentous vote. With her sisters, she'd proposed a plan to bring Harvey to their side.

Abigail had sent letters to her brother thanking him for remaining quiet about the suffrage question, for allowing the "good citizens of Oregon to make up their own minds." And the *Oregonian* had not spoken about the referral at all as yet. They'd kept him neutral. Now they needed to turn him to their way.

"The *Oregonian* will have to take a position before long," Abigail said. All the living Scott sisters met at the Duniway house, preparing the final stage of their plan. "Kate has gotten us a meeting with him, at his home, so he'll see this as a family issue." They agreed to let Fanny and

Kate do most of the talking in his ornate parlor.

Something burned between Abigail and Harvey. She was the older sister and he the fair-haired baby boy, and perhaps it happened with all siblings that way, between older sisters and loving younger brothers, both longing for the same approval to witness in their parents' eyes—and each other's. Her parents never knew of their arguments out in the field, the anger they could arouse in each other. Once, Harvey was so infuriated with her that he took a stick to Abigail, beating her back. Barely able to walk back to the house, she withheld her tears, wouldn't give him the satisfaction. She couldn't even remember what it had been about now, but sometimes, with the raise of an eyebrow or the grimace on his mustached face, she felt her stomach clench. It was the visage he'd chosen just before he struck. It became a warning sign, like the rattle of a snake. She didn't want to provoke him.

The sad thing was that she did love him, had rescued him from a laundry fire, admired his accomplishments while still being envious. He had everything she'd ever hoped for. So why he was so oppositional to her still escaped her. But then, she was oppositional to him as well.

She would keep her words to herself. He knew where she stood and the arguments in favor of suffrage. She would let her sisters make the case with him.

"So that's our hope, that before the actual election in June, you might see yourself writing an editorial promoting the referral." Kate had concluded her presentation.

Harvey adjusted his glasses. "You know my concern about women getting the vote and then ushering in prohibition, something I oppose."

"We know," Fanny said. "We oppose prohibition too, not because we think control of liquor would be a bad thing, especially on the streets of Portland, but because, like you, we believe in individual freedom. People ought to make their own choices of whether to sip wine or not."

"You'll have to work hard to assure the powers that be that enfranchised women are not of that persuasion. The liquor industry has already placed ads opposed to your referral based on that assumption."

"Which is why your opinion is so crucial, dear Brother." Abigail kept her voice calm. She sank back in her chair with Fanny's grimace at her.

"My own wife does not share your views. I'll be inviting dissension in my household, to do what you ask."

"Ah, but a man is still the master of his castle, is that not so?" Abigail leaned forward. She wondered if they ought to be courting Mary rather than Harvey. It surprised her that he would even acknowledge his second wife's opposition.

He'd been widowed eleven years when he met his wealthy second wife. Not only had he landed wonderful jobs, but he had wooed an intelligent (though misguided when it came to suffrage) partner as well. *He wants to show us how generous he is in going against his wife in order to satisfy his sisters.*

"Master, indeed." Harvey tapped his finger on the blotting pad.

"The most important thing, Harvey," Sarah Maria said, "is that in our canvassing, we believe the resolution will pass. You wouldn't want to be on the wrong side."

"Your electoral instincts will be up for scrutiny," Abigail said. "There are rumors of your interest in a Senate run."

He jerked his head toward her. "No decision has been made." He tapped again. "It's your judgment that there is support for the referral?"

"Yes," Harriet said. "Southern Oregon, Eastern Oregon, we hear nothing but positive words. When Abigail speaks, men come to her events and applaud."

"Do they now?"

"The legislature is simply following their constituents, as good lawmakers should. That's why the referral passed last session and why men are going to the polls to vote for the very first time on this momentous occasion," Kate said.

"The *Oregonian* needs to be on the winning

side." Abigail said the last with a fist punch to the air.

"I'll think about it. I have to maintain my integrity. And I do have an editorial board I need to respond to. I can't do this simply because you ask."

"You could do it for Papa," Sarah Maria said. She had a childlike voice. "He supported the cause."

"He did. Well, he had a house full of smart women." A small grin leaked beneath his bushy mustache. "But I have to think of the man who lives with a shrew or a scold or an idiot. Who will speak for him if I don't?"

"Let him speak for himself," Abigail said. "He already has the right to vote."

She watched to see that raised eyebrow. It did not come. But the frown returned, and she vowed to keep her distance from Harvey until the vote.

Six weeks after the sisters met with him, Harvey posted his editorial. It was written in response to an *Oregonian* reader who had objected to Washington's passage of women's suffrage.

Harvey started by saying the reader noted objections raised by those who hadn't really thought through the issue. He didn't say that ignorance was the cause of opposition, but he implied it. "And listen to this, Ben." Abigail read from the paper, her hands shaking. " 'And is any man really prepared to claim that his wife, mother and sisters'—he said sisters, Ben—'are inferior to his own judgment, in patriotism, in love of good government.' " He went on to note that they weren't disqualified from getting the vote as people who might not perform certain citizen functions like building roads or serving on a jury or fighting in wars, because "half the citizen men avoid doing these things too."

Harvey concluded with words Abigail breathed in. He had heard them. He was behind them. " 'A woman is capable of exerting an influence in public affairs which the state needs, and this influence can be made effective only through suffrage. Prejudice may for a while prevent it, but no argument can stand for a moment in its way."

"Holy cow chips, he's done it! He's supporting us! The referral is ours!"

She sent a note to Harvey expressing her thanks, valuing his influence, calling on their father's memory to say how he would be so pleased, "looking down upon us and using his influence from that sphere—along with our mother's—to bring about this outcome that the Scott women had so long proffered." It was the culmination of a lifetime of work. She just knew the referral would pass.

A certain giddiness prevailed in the Duniway household. Abigail sang with Ben as she packed her carpetbag for travels to speak and support the effort. She found herself smiling on the stagecoach for no reason at all. *Harvey has come through.* Back in Oregon, suffrage women and their groups spent hours at small gatherings in agreeable churches, courting women whom they urged to convert their husbands toward the cause or support the men who already furthered their campaign. Letters went to newspapers throughout the state. Abigail wrote editorials quoting her brother and serialized novels that sang the praises of women who had to be capable because of the poor decisions by their men. She celebrated the legislators who had the referral voted in, and she wrote of how a woman could govern herself and her family, so why wouldn't one expect her to govern her fellow citizens with wisdom and grace. The women hung posters and they wrote songs of suffrage—Abigail wrote one that she wished Clara Belle was available to sing—and their meetings rallied the faithful with the hope that they won a few converts to their cause.

Around April, with barely a lamppost free of a "Votes for Women" poster, Abigail swallowed hard when she saw that the *Oregonian* had published letters both in support of suffrage and in opposition. The paper itself had not repeated Harvey's earlier stand.

"I'm surprised Harvey hasn't come out in favor as he did last November," Abigail said. She and

Kate stood in the dappled sunlight beneath an elm tree after worship one May Sunday. "Other papers have made their opinions known. You'd think the mighty *Oregonian* would have too."

"I haven't wanted to ask Harvey," Kate said. "He's built a moat around his newspaper castle where family isn't supposed to cross."

"So, no inside information about when they'll take their stand. It's getting close to the election." Abigail turned slightly to avoid the bright sunshine streaking through the trees.

"I haven't wanted to say, but he's scheduled to be back east on election day. He leaves a week before."

"Will he post an editorial? Has he done that in the past?"

Kate shrugged her shoulders.

"But he does support us, right? We are so close. His November editorial sang the highest suffrage note."

The night before the vote, Abigail lay awake. She thought of how her life's work had been shaped by her mother's words, wishing she'd had sons because a girl's life was so hard. She considered the decision to marry Ben, which had been hers and came from love, but with a tinge of resentment that it had to be so rushed because of her father's own wish to marry again. And the losses—of Sunny Hillside, but more, of her sister's death from following her husband to the

358

wilds of the Oregon coast where she'd died of tuberculosis, having no other choice but to do his bidding. And Clara Belle's decision. At least she now lived in a territory where she had the vote. Abigail had put so much of her life into this effort. And tomorrow would be the culmination.

She woke Ben. "What if it fails?"

"Not likely. And if it does, you'll begin again. You won't have to wonder what you'll do with your time." He punched the pillow and went back to sleep.

It has to pass or all our work—all my efforts— will have been for naught. "It must pass," she said to her sleeping husband. "It was divinely inspired. How could it not?"

She read every issue of the *Oregonian*, looking for encouraging words, supportive editorials, a repeat of Harvey's fine deliberations. Nothing. Not a single word in favor—and none against. He chose a neutral stand. *The coward.* He kept his light under a bushel. She'd have thought better of him if he had openly changed his mind. *Maybe not.* But the euphoria of that November editorial had sunk like a rock in the river.

The vote was held June 2, 1884, but it took three weeks to tally the ballots that had to come from hither and yon over the mountains and through the canyons of this massive state. Still, Abigail could see from the first reports in the Portland precincts that it was going down. *"It does not look well,"* she wrote in her June 5th editorial. The sisters stayed on pins and needles, planning the celebration yet fearful of jinxing it by assuming too much. Abigail could hardly write her articles for the paper. She sketched out another novel, a shorter story. She tried to pay attention to Hubert's wedding plans. It would be such a year of merriment, and yet the foreboding of that spring night crept over her like a heavy fog rolling in from the river, holding her hostage.

Then the tally was counted and reported. They were defeated: 28,176 opposed to 11,223 in favor.

It was as though she'd lost a child. She didn't say that out loud at the suffrage meeting, for with her sat her niece and her sister Fanny, who had lost children, but the depth of Abigail's grief took her to that tearful trail. When at last the vote was complete and the numbers available for posting at the capital for publication in the newspapers across the country, it was Abigail who had to tell her sisters and then the state and nation that the referral had failed. Her *New Northwest* carried the story. She added in the announcement *"We are not defeated,"* even though she felt they were.

THIRTY

Postmortem

How could the vote have been so strongly opposed when their face-to-face discussions had nearly always ended with words of support? How could such a worthy cause, an inevitable hope, something so worth doing, have lost? Negroes had the vote, a race many men thought inferior in every way but who now began to be seen as equals, as citizens at least. Equal in their ability to vote, though she had read of poll taxes and other encumberments local jurisdictions flaunted against those people. Still, they had the right. It had to happen for women, too, and even Harvey had supported it. What had gone wrong?

"We'll have to analyze what precincts we won and where we lost," Kate noted. They had gathered at what Abigail called the "postmortem" to take apart the body politic.

"It appears we won in the countryside." Sarah Maria looked at the tiny marks recorded on the clerk's report. "Those farmers and ranchers know we women are no threat but rather helpmates. It's in the cities where we lost. Actually, it was Portland who voted against us." She turned to her youngest child, a four-year-old daughter, who leaned into her side. "We'll get you the vote yet."

"It was the liquor industry." Harriet crocheted while they sorted through the embers of defeat. "Washington Territory's women voters have been blamed for stricter liquor laws, and Portlanders likely saw empty glasses in their future."

Abigail had written that Washington women were at risk to lose the vote because of the heavy spending by San Francisco and Portland liquor interests funding a repeal of the women's suffrage there.

"We Washington voters have passed prohibition kinds of legislation," Clara Belle said. She had taken the produce boat to offer solace to her mother. "And they don't like it that women are on juries, and we might find for plaintiffs against corrupt liquor industries. Did you know they pay three dollars for jury duty? One woman told me it was better than a trip to San Francisco, that she got a day of rest, her family was still there when she returned home, and she had money to put aside for a rainy day."

"I'll write about that," Abigail said. *But how will I write about this defeat?*

Earl played with a cousin in the yard. Children's chatter was a wind chime sounding through the open windows, lightening the timbre in the room.

"Even the brewers turned against us." Fanny sighed.

"And they said as much in those German newspapers that reach most of Portland, despite your newspaper's efforts to counter them, Abigail." The vice-chair of the association shook her head. "We worked so hard. Maybe we should have brought National in."

"No. Oregon's men would have their backs up if we had brought in eastern women," Abigail said. She had to defend their tactics and yet, her strategy had not won them the vote. "Though we could have used more of their money returned from our dues, that's certain."

"They weren't keen on being asked to stay out while we requested funds," Kate said. "But I agree, Oregon flies with her own wings, as our state motto reads. When Aunt Susan's group said they should 'leave Oregon severely alone,' she was right."

At least she'd helped those Washington women get the vote. But here in this blessed state, she'd failed. Perhaps she should have come out for prohibition, but people ought to make their own decisions about the morality of drinking. And supporting it, she knew, would bring the liquor industry down upon them.

"What a waste of our effort." Another young reformer spoke up. "All those posters and meetings and—"

"We had nearly twelve thousand men who understood and voted for us," Fanny said. "Next time, we'll double that. We must refocus our efforts in Portland before the next referral."

"The next referral." Abigail's despair dropped into the room like a horse stepping on a woman's toes. "With biennial legislative sessions, that means getting passage again in the '86 session, '88 session, too, with a hope for a referral vote in 1890. Or later. It's another long walk toward uncertainty."

"There's a move to permit citizen initiatives, where with a certain number of signatures, ordinary people can make proposals for a general vote. We can move faster if that passes." This from a younger member.

"Maybe the men are right. Do they know something we don't know?" said another member.

Still another acolyte to the cause raised her voice. "Perhaps we should go back to our kitchens and parlors and bring up our sons so when they are men, they will grant their mothers the vote, if not their sisters and wives."

The young woman's comments held merit for Abigail. She was tired. Maybe staying home, spoiling Earl, and waiting on other grandchildren, writing her novels, tending to Ben, perhaps that is what she should be doing with the rest of her life. She'd be fifty years old this October and her bones felt it. She could lay down the sword of truth and righteousness, having witnessed her daughter be able to vote in Washington. They could sell the paper, the Portland home, and move to Idaho, where Ben had fallen in love with land near Hailey. *Why not?* That beam of light that had led her to spend her days promoting this cause, maybe it was only sunshine coming through the window. If it had truly been God's work, wouldn't the referral have passed? They'd misunderstood, she and Ben. And she'd led her brother down the primrose path, telling him they would win. And he'd supported them—safely, months before the vote. He probably wouldn't ever talk with her again. But then, she wasn't sure she ever wanted to speak with him again either.

"You told me it would pass. I believed you." Harvey paced his office where Abigail had gone to lament that they'd both lost something that mattered.

"I . . . I had reason, strong reason, to believe it would pass. In the rural areas, it did."

Harvey harrumphed. "What do they know out there. Do they even read the newspapers, find out what's happening around the world?"

"Perhaps if they had free high school education, more would be better informed."

"Don't go there, Abigail." Harvey pointed his finger at her. Rage filled his eyes.

He's frightening me. "I'm more distressed than you are. To spend my whole life on something and have it defeated? You can still run for the Senate whenever you want. But our work means slogging through two more sessions if we are to continue the fight. Maybe I'll move to Washington. It's a big territory. Did I tell you they invited me to run for governor?"

He guffawed. "That'll be retracted when they realize how inept you are in understanding the electorate. They'll likely repeal the woman vote anyway."

"Why didn't you repeat your support? Your November editorial made my heart sing, made all suffragists celebrate. You have so much influence."

He glared at her. "Do you have any idea how many letters the paper received after that . . . that . . . lapse on my part?"

"Lapse? But the argument was well written, wise. When women do get the vote, and we will one day, they'd vote for you when you run." She saw a flash of pain cross his eyes, his own political career careening out of his control. "We Scotts don't like to lose, do we?"

"This vote was not *my* loss."

"No. It's mine. I'm devastated. But I am grateful that your *Oregonian*—you—supported it, once. I just didn't understand why you stayed neutral at the eve of the election, printing as many negative letters as those in support. Yes, I counted. The greatest newspaper in the Northwest stayed neutral." She sighed. "I came to thank you for that early support and ask for it again as we move forward."

"It will never happen again, dear Sister. Never. Ever. Ever. From here on in, I stand with the majority of men in this state and never, do you hear me, will I write an editorial in support of the woman vote. In fact, I will confess my error and write editorials to defeat any future attempt. If you continue this fight, you will do so without my backing, and I will do everything I can do to defeat it." He spoke to the window, then turned to face her. "I had to convince my board. And now, I have to wear my shame. Now go. I don't want to see your face here again begging for my support for anything. Ever."

Her steps from Harvey's office were heavy. She was grateful for a cab close by to take her home. Old confetti from the anti-suffrage crowd scattered in the streets. Her life's work, ended. Her relationship, such as it was with her brother, broken like a cane. She thought she could go no lower.

"We can't sell the paper," Ben said. "It's our livelihood. We have children employed by it." Their three oldest sons were engaged in some aspect of the business and the younger boys hoping for professions that would require they attend eastern schools. The paper was needed to support them. And Ben's job was here in

Portland. The cause that defined her life, it was here. No, there was no rest ahead in Idaho.

She thought of other times of despair. When her mother had died. When her brother had passed. When her father had the crisis of marriage. She had gotten up from those days realizing that when fatigue settled in, the worst thing one could do was to take a nap. Better was to increase her curiosity, expand her effort, multiply the time she spent in educating both men and women to the importance of the climb toward the peak of justice. It was what she'd done when Ben signed the notes and they'd lost the farm. It was that disaster that had spurred them on to new things: she'd begun the school, the millinery, and found suffrage as a life's mission.

"The only thing to displace the bitterness of defeat is the taste of victory." Abigail heard herself say those words even though she wasn't sure she believed them anymore. "We begin again. Grief cannot hold us back. We are wiser but not worn down. Let us ponder what we know, and come next week with new strategies that might very well mean putting a wolf in sheep's clothing into Harvey Scott's shed."

"Rather than a wolf," Kate said, "we need a shepherd."

"With a shepherd's staff to gently, diplomatically, bring in the fold," Fanny added. She winked at her sister.

"That leaves me out," Abigail said to the knowing laughter of her siblings.

But she was also out of this campaign. She was tired. She would use her words to inspire, to further the cause in her newspaper, but perhaps it was time for her to step aside. Her heart wasn't in it anymore.

The women began again with letter campaigns and meetings, speeches and sparring, without Abigail's enthusiasm. She worked on her novel, meddled a little in her sons' lives—Hubert had fallen for one of the boardinghouse girls but had proposed to another. She hovered over Ben, who suggested when she was asked, that she make the trip back east through the snows of the spring of '85. "It'll do you good. You'll come back ready to take up the mantle."

"I'm still carrying it."

"You are. But you're not meeting with legislators, pressing your still hunt. Maybe you should be."

She made the trip meant to negotiate a truce between warring factions of associations working toward suffrage passage and seeing—with horror—the growing influence of prohibitionists attaching themselves to suffrage. It pleased her that she was asked to be the diplomat. Even Susan B. Anthony felt the causes must join hands, the position causing the two old friends to disagree.

But in Abigail's fifteen hundred miles of travel and forty-nine speeches given nationally, she could see that linking these two great causes would doom them both.

What she also found was that she came alive with the challenge; doing something worthy beyond her own life and family invigorated. She loved the travel. Oh, the coaches were uncomfortable and the trains cold as winter through the mountains at night. And the porters weren't always quick to pick up her bags, even when they saw she used her cane. The Washington, DC, hotel she stayed in often had mice, and the different foods in Philadelphia made her stomach queasy. But in both places, she felt the stirrings of liberty, of what must have driven the Founding Fathers to risk everything for a new nation. Her writing was better from these places, and her words soared when she spoke in the churches and halls, bringing news of the forward-thinking West—Washington Territory's advancement especially—to the burdened East. She never doubted on those days that she was doing the Lord's work, lifting the downtrodden, visiting women in jails, freeing the spirits of all beings of God's creation. She gained fuel for the fight when she traveled. Returning, she felt the old stirring. Things didn't always turn out well, as Ben proposed, but some things were worth doing, regardless. There was another campaign to wage.

THIRTY-ONE

The Things That Sustain

1885

"A little old age, Ma," Willis had said.

"How old is he?" Hubert's wife asked.

"Barely fifty-five," Abigail said. "He worries me."

"He seems to know details of the past." Wilke bit a radish, crunched it.

"Yes, but what he did yesterday or even a moment ago escapes him." Abigail sighed. "The other day, he stood right next to me when Clara Belle was here telling us that she and Don and Earl were considering moving back to Oregon."

"I wonder why they'd do that?" Hubert said.

"We chatted about it. Little Earl didn't look well, if you ask me, but she said it had to do with Don's work, whatever that is. The man is so elusive. Ben was there, heard it all. Clara Belle walked away, and I said to him, 'Won't that be lovely if Clara Belle and Earl come back home?' and he said, 'Clara Belle's moving home? Why didn't I know about that?' I mean, he had been listening to the conversation. Not thirty seconds had passed."

Into the silence that followed, Hubert said, "That is concerning. But he's no trouble, really, is he, Ma? He takes care of his needs. And it's only temporary. It's just a quirk, maybe. Of old age."

"He's tidy about his person, as always. Dignified in that." She felt torn between a growing interest in getting back into the arena while watching Ben wane. "I worry that he might get lost if he goes out alone. And there's his job. How long will he be able to keep it? And he asks me repeated questions. I'm not much for patience, you know."

"You might have to stay home a little more, Ma."

A leaf falling from a tree to the forest floor would have been louder than the silence that followed Willis's observation.

"You might have to sell a few more subscriptions," she snapped back. Inside, Abigail felt her throat close. *How can I be so unloving as to fear more time with Ben? And why does suffrage work offer more sustenance than caring for a loving man?* She used the travel to escape; she could see that now. Ben had recognized it before she had. And he'd encouraged it. He knew her better than she knew herself.

He had treated it with hot lemon. For months. Don Stearns had seen the symptoms, he told

Ben and Abigail, and thought that it was a deep cold from the vapors off Lake Camus where he'd moved his little family.

"But you're still living in that swamp. If you had but told me, we would have gotten a doctor there or brought you all here. Sooner. How could you not see it was consumption?"

She had to find someone to blame. Had to. Her daughter was dying and there was nothing she could do about it.

She picked up doilies from the back of the horsehair couch, smoothed them, moved them, her fingers hopelessly busy over nothing. This inability to make things happen—to improve Ben's memory, protect her daughter, gain the vote for women after all her effort, sacrifice, and yes, time away from family—her life was as useless as these doilies.

"Maybe I'll recover, Momma." Clara Belle hacked out the words, the act of talking bringing on a wracking cough that brought pain to Clara's face and to Abigail's heart.

"Of course you will. You must. If only we'd known. We could have found a mountain place with pure air to bring you healing. Why didn't you write, Clara?" She turned to her son-in-law. "Why didn't you?" She ignored the tears he brushed from his cheeks, didn't give him a chance to defend. "You . . . you need to go, Don. I can barely stand the sight of you. Earl will stay here. He needs to be close to his mother now, emotionally, if not able to touch and hold her."

"It would be better if he came home with me. He's my son."

"No. We need to watch for symptoms for him. It's clear your diagnostic abilities are lacking."

"As are your mothering aptitudes," he choked out.

Abigail gasped. "How dare—"

"Jenny . . ." Ben reached for her hand.

"I brought Clara here at her insistence, but I'll not give up Earl."

"Please." Clara Belle coughed. She turned her eyes toward her father. "Don't let them argue." Her lips tinted blue with the effort to stay her shallow breath.

Ben was having one of his good days. "Jenny, Clara Belle doesn't need any more troubling." He sat on a chair beside the daybed she lay on, the very one he'd rested on after the horse accident while they all listened to her playing the piano. *No more.* "What would please you, Daughter? To have Earl here?" She nodded yes. "And Don?" She hesitated but nodded yes to that as well. "Son, you are welcome to stay."

"Ben."

He raised his hand to silence Abigail. To the Stearns family members, he said, "Jenny's grieving. She has a sharp tongue sometimes, but it's how she plugs the hole of pain. If you want

374

to be here with Clara Belle, you're welcome. No need to separate the family."

Abigail snorted, but she saw the pleading look upon her daughter's face, and she inhaled. "You can remain. Of course. All of you."

Don's eyes were on Clara Belle. "I fear our feuding would bring you stress. I'll come often. I promise."

Abigail couldn't let Don be the better person. "Ben's right. What matters now is Clara's peace and healing. We can pray and hope," she said. "You're welcome here, Don."

"Then we'll stay for you, Clara Belle."

A feeble smile crossed her daughter's face. She pressed her hands in prayer and nodded to him, her mother, and then to her father. Speaking was simply too tiring. Abigail could see that, and she'd need to remember it, not upset her daughter. It only made her weaker.

And yet her outrage at Don for not calling a doctor, for waiting so long, for taking her away from them those years before and the piercing sorrow of such an imminent loss as a child's death would not be enough to caution her every time. She would rail at this man who, like Maggie's husband, had ignored the signs of illness until too late. The very sight of him would bring out the worst in her.

"I've got to make that meeting back east," Abigail told Ben that evening.

"You can't leave. Not now."

"You're a greater comfort to her than I am. You and the boys. She said to me, 'You have a mission, Ma.' She understands."

"Not just for her sake, Abigail. But for yours, you should be here. You could read your latest novels to her. She'll enjoy hearing Hubert's wife giving piano lessons, just as she once did, and you can enjoy the music too."

"I feel helpless here, and frankly, the very sight of Don . . ."

Ben patted her back, then took her into his arms. "My Jenny. How you miss the things nearby. Can't you see there is no real joy in the things afar?"

"You're remembering that little autograph book poem. The second line though is 'Not what we seem, but what we are.' I'm not the loving parent that you are, Ben. I'm a demanding, domineering, controlling—"

"Stop. Don't punish yourself that way. Who you are is a devoted, benevolent, and loving mother who pushes grief away. Didn't you read to me what Shakespeare wrote, that one should give sorrow words?"

She nodded, tears dampening his shirt.

"It was something about if you don't speak what your heart feels, it will break. Silence isn't always a good thing, if I recall it."

"Yes. *Macbeth.* But when I speak, it comes out

376

stinging. I'm better to be away, Ben. You're here. You'll comfort her. The things afar will bring me consolation in the end."

"No. They won't."

Abigail packed her bags while Ben sang old songs to Clara Belle. Earl watched as Abigail folded her dresses, put her curling iron, powders, and perfume into the burgundy bag she had carried with her through the years. "You look after your grandpa now, you hear? Make sure he doesn't go outside without his coat. Evenings can get cold. Will you remember that?"

Earl nodded. She hugged him, his thin little shoulders like a bird's frame. She would fatten him up when she came back. She knew when she returned, all would be different, but she would do all she could to keep Earl with them. She had to. His father lacked the proper judgment to raise a child. Anyone could see that. It would comfort Clara Belle in the hereafter to know that her son was safe. She had already begun that campaign by letting Don and Earl remain and removing herself as a point of contention so her daughter wasn't disturbed in the last days of her life. One had to begin a campaign for change long before one thought one should.

Abigail found little peace in this latest trip back east. The division between temperance and suffrage and prohibition swirled around the eastern cities and in the halls of women gathering. When asked to speak, she sounded defensive, she knew, but she'd been accused of taking money from the liquor industry—she hadn't. Her having championed the plight of a brewer's widow in Walla Walla, Washington, a story she'd told in her speech, had gotten her labeled as a traitor to the cause of controlling the blight of alcohol, betraying the temperance movement. Her colleagues couldn't seem to understand that she cared about the property rights of women too, not only their right to vote. She supported even widows of brewers who'd been left with debt by a brewer husband. Abigail advocated helping the woman turn the brewery into a cannery or develop another kind of business that would help the community and this woman. But no, because she was associated with hops and foam, Abigail was labeled as a traitor.

She penned a letter to Shirley.

> The hardest thing is that I'm supposed to be a communicator, someone who, with written and spoken word, can express difficult perspectives facing us. But I am failing at this. I can't seem to find the handle of this pot so that I can remove it from the heat. I fear Washington Territory will repeal the vote for women because our fair sex are indeed voting for prohibition.

I am lonely here in this eastern city of government, sitting on a park bench beneath a canopy of trees. I am misunderstood and I begin to see that it is my own fault. But I lack the wisdom, my dear friend, to know what to do about it. And my usual rebirth is clouded with grief for Clara Belle's impending death, for all I didn't do and might have and now it's too late. I can only pray that one day I will find a way to be understood, by myself, if not by those around me.

It happened that Abigail was home when Clara Belle breathed her last; Don wasn't there. He'd gone back to Washougal to tend to business, and so on that late January day in 1886, Abigail sat stern-faced as Ben sang "Rock of Ages" to his daughter. Clara Belle's eyes were closed with the smallest flutter of her eyelids now and then to suggest that she heard. And then the certainty of it caught Abigail by the throat, her sob swallowed so as not to have Clara hear it. She held her daughter's hand, rubbed her palm, and prayed, oh she prayed! Her brothers sat around the bed, heads bowed, hands clasped between their knees. Hubert's wife accompanied Ben's singing, and he looked strong beside Clara and her labored breathing, and Abigail prayed that her daughter's suffering would end soon, as the pain of watching, listening, of powerlessness wore upon them as the coming of a heavy storm.

She had thought once that losing the vote had been like losing a child. It was nothing like it. Outliving the flesh of one's flesh was a grief like no other. There was no map to follow, no way to get over the pain, only try to find a way through. She and Ben and the mothers and fathers of deceased children walked in a wilderness, far away from any promised land.

"I'm going to visit Shirley," she told Ben. "The air in San Francisco will perk me up. Should I take Earl with me?"

"Leave him be. He's getting into a routine here. And he's a good help to me. Reminds me of things."

She felt a tinge of guilt but slipped over it. Clara Belle had been buried, and Don had returned to Washougal, reluctantly leaving Earl behind.

"It's nothing out of the ordinary, Don." Abigail had tugged at her black neck scarf. "We've had nieces and nephews and the sons of friends stay with us for a time. You'd have to hire a nanny or someone to look after him. Visit anytime."

Defeated, Don had left his son behind.

"I asked Earl to remind you to put your coat on in the evening." Abigail washed an ink stain from her fingers as she spoke to Ben. A dove cooed in the elm tree.

"Oh, yes, he does that. But he also notices if I've already eaten a bowl of mush when I ask Chen why he hasn't gotten breakfast out for us yet." Ben chuckled. "Craziest thing." He shook his head. "I guess food doesn't taste all that good if I can't remember that I just ate it."

Shirley welcomed her, and Abigail felt the greatest comfort in the arms of an old friend who had lived a lifetime with another kind of lost child. She and her husband Eloi had children together, but her eldest daughter—now grown with children of her own—was still the heart-child. That girl, taken from her by the legal system, had given Shirley direction toward helping women seek their rights in divorces they had not wanted and been unjustly granted. Eloi, with his dark hair and gentle eyes, would put his arm around Shirley as they talked, a gesture of protection.

"Clara Belle's last words were that I needed to get back into the fight. She said she was going on ahead and that I had work to do here. But I'm not sure how to do it now."

"It'll come to you, Jenny. You're in an understandable slump. Such a disappointment to you—Clara Belle's death, losing that vote."

"It was. But I snapped back, or so I thought. And then encountered the tension back east that doesn't appear to be going away. I seem to be the crux of the contention. My outspoken views at the conventions about us not lining up with prohibitionists. And then my writings."

"Maybe you should do what you always wanted to do and just write your poems and novels."

"I can't support myself on that."

"You could sell the *New Northwest*."

She stood thoughtful, the waning sun sending glittering reddish light across the bay. "But how would I carry on the mission that Clara Belle wanted for me?"

"Edit someone else's newspaper. Kate's doing that. Write for someone else, earn a salary."

"Oh my, who would hire this outspoken old woman?" The friends laughed.

"You're not old."

"But I am outspoken."

"It's who you are. You're a reformer, Jenny. An activist. You see injustice and must act on that. The way you do it can change through the years. With less stress from the newspaper, you could give more time to your speaking and even publish a collection of your speeches, to inspire others to keep the faith. What is it you always say—'the world is moving and women are moving with it'? We just move differently, to adapt to the times."

Shirley's words formed a knot at the end of a thread that Abigail could imagine pulling through a new cloth.

"I'd have to talk to the boys. And Ben, of

course. He talks about Idaho and the Lost Valley. It is beautiful country, and with water, we might grow crops. I convinced him that if I could write in a dusty stagecoach stop, I could surely write in a cabin shadowed by mountains while streams rushed nearby." She'd even thought it might become a gathering place for campaigns. Perhaps offer refuge for women and children in need, but she didn't think Ben would go for that. *Is that the way my mission to elevate women will take now? I'll advance the place of women in public life by retreating into a wilderness?* Her prayers asked for guidance.

She called a family gathering as soon as she returned to Portland.

"What would you do, Ma?"

"Why, find a ranch in Idaho, as you boys and Ben have been touting for some time now. We could all move there. I'd find my little 'lodge in the wilderness' and write. I could be a correspondent to the new buyer, and Idaho still doesn't have the vote. Yet. They could use me. And of course, I can travel back here, stay with Kate or Harriet or Fanny or Sarah Maria. Goodness, what's the benefit of all those sisters if one can't impose upon them from time to time— not to mention nieces and nephews."

"Earl would like it, though I doubt Stearns would," Hubert said.

"Should we tell her, Pa?" Clyde asked. Her second youngest son was sixteen already. He had a beard. How had her boys grown up without her noticing?

"Tell me what?"

"We've already found a place that Pa likes. I like it too," Ralph told her. "Hubert took him last week."

So that's why the Idaho images were so readily available to Ben.

"We were trying to figure out how to buy it, but now, if we sell the paper, we could do that." Hubert added, "We boys made a down payment on it."

"You bought something without my even agreeing to it? Not knowing if you could pay for it?" *Encumbering me?* "Ben?" *What has happened to our partnership?* "When were you going to let me know?"

"I quit the customhouse, Jenny. It was time. I couldn't . . . well, I forgot important things."

Like telling me you'd resigned.

"Earl and Hubert and me, we went to Idaho. You were traveling like you do." He grinned. "I didn't take your teapot money, Jenny."

Shame washed over her. She hadn't been aware that Ben's problems had become severe enough that he had recognized his need to quit work. They hadn't even discussed it. As usual, she had been so involved in her own world afar that she hadn't seen what was happening nearby.

Yes, Clara Belle's death had come during that time, and travel had been a way of her grieving. But Ben grieved too.

"Oh, Ben. I . . . you could have telegraphed me at Shirley's. I would have come home."

"You needed your time there. You always come back with new ideas. And it happened." He looked around the room at their sons and Earl. "Where's Cora? She always fixes my evening cocoa."

"It's not night yet, Grandpa." Earl eased up beside Ben.

They've moved on without me.

The swirl of getting the books in order filled her time: deciding whether to sell the presses separately or give a credit knowing new ones might be warranted. Deciding whether to put the house on the market too, how to let subscribers know about the changes. When she'd had any second thoughts about the sale of her work for the past sixteen years, the enthusiasm with which her sons were willing to divest of it kept her from being tearful. Even changes that resulted in things one wished for could carry heartbreak, she decided. At least Clara Belle didn't have to see that her beloved Washington had repealed the woman's vote when the Territorial Legislature found it unconstitutional. What had Shirley said when she pierced Abigail's ears? "Pain comes before the glory." She'd felt that when they left Hardscrabble Farm and when she sold the school and millinery. As with her other losses, she would grieve in time. And maybe these back-to-back devastations with Clara's passing and the voting loss, perhaps in order to move forward, one needed things so upending.

With Ben, Wilke, Earl, and Hubert, they traveled to the Wood River district, east to Idaho. The land the boys had found for Ben had a large log cabin on it, with several bedrooms and a wide porch that wrapped around the house, offering a vista of green and snowcapped mountains they called the Lost River Range. It was in the Pashimeroi Valley. They'd made a good purchase. The expanse caused her to take in deep breaths. This would be a healing place; she could feel it.

"What would you say about using the bunk-house to house women and children in need? We could perhaps start a utopian community like the Aurora colony, where all are equal and—"

"Ma. No," Wilke said. He put his hand up to stop her. "This is our place, not the whole world's."

Yes, this would be a space to get away from the world, to stop rehashing the arguments at National, put away the sting of the charges made against her as being in the hands of the liquor industry. Breaking with Aunt Susan had been painful. She hated being misunderstood. Here, she could be heard again, write with more clarity. She had written a letter to Shirley about the planned move but also pouring out the anguish of Clara's loss and her trouble with National. *"I will die as I have lived, misunderstood by those I love best and serve most."*

She sat on the porch steps while Ben smoked his pipe from a rocking chair downwind of her. *Can I really give it all up to come here?* Her stomach tightened at the uncertainty that clutched at her. She felt most in control when she drew her own map, and this move had only vapors of that. She remembered asking her students once to define *powerful,* giving her definition first. "I think it's a word that means one can set a goal and then figure out how to make it happen." That was being powerful.

But her students had told her no, it was wealth. Another boy said, "No, when you're big and strong like Mr. Duniway, that's powerful." But it had been the smallest child, the quiet one, who had taken her breath away.

"I think powerful is when you want to quit but you keep going."

Maybe there'd be enough with the sale to pay for the ranch and still have a small house in Portland, permit her to "keep going." The winters might be brutal in this valley, and having a refuge among the association women of Portland could be her escape—if she found she needed it.

A meadowlark flitted from a shrub. She'd have to learn the name of the plants and trees, and she'd become familiar with the sound of their dry leaves crinkling in the fall and discover how the Pashimeroi Valley got its name and what were the weather and the ways of this place. A neighboring rancher stopped by to explain a sound that was like horses crossing a creek. "Salmon spawning," he'd told her. "Slapping the water as they splash over each other."

"Imagine," Abigail had said.

She rose and found her foolscap paper. They'd brought personal things with them on this trip. The "lodge in the wilderness," as she began to call it, had come furnished with beds and linens and dishes and even a dog. They'd have to hire a cook and a housekeeper. She'd want time to write.

September 2, 1886. Blanche Le Clerq, a Tale of the Mountain Mines. It would be a novel about a wealthy mineowner who falls in love with Blanche, who refuses to marry him unless he accepts her passion for the stage and realizes that women can be public and wise and chaste and willing to rule *with* him and not *over* him.

"I've started another novel, Ben," she called out to him after a time.

"I thought you owned a newspaper."

"We did." *How many things will I need to repeat?* "And I have another story to serialize for it. I'll mail it from Ellis, Idaho, so Willis can get the first chapter into the next edition. He's staying to help the new owner."

Ben nodded and smiled at her. "This is good, Jenny. We'll get horses once we move. We can do that, can't we?"

We are moved. "Of course."

He sighed. "I'll have my two loves back again: you and my pintos."

At least he put me first in the lineup of his loves. That was what she needed to do for him now too. Put him first. The vote for women would follow, surely, as inevitably as the mountains that rose before them. She'd spent her life doing something worth doing. She'd continue but in a new way from a new place. It was how the world moved and women with it.

THIRTY-TWO

No Worry in the World

1893–96

Abigail adjusted her hat. At least the fashion now allowed for the brim to be flattened at the back so a woman could lean against the stagecoach leather without worrying about smashing the brim or removing her hat to hold in her lap—if alone in the carriage. Dusty as it was, the trip was the balm she needed. She'd been spending summers at the lodge, looking after Ben. At least helping the boys look after him. Clyde was home from Cornell for the summer, and Ralph helped as well, so she was free to take the call. She lowered the canvas window to prevent the dust from rolling in. She'd be in Boise by evening, geared up, as they said about harnessed horses, to work.

> Come at once. The Women's Christian Temperance Union is spoiling everything. They've arranged for a hearing before the convention, in advance of ours, asking for a clause in the new Constitution to prohibit liquor traffic. They won't get it,

of course, but they will prohibit us from getting a Woman's Suffrage plank, if you don't come.

Eighty miles she'd traveled by train after nearly two hundred miles by stage. She'd been in remote Blackfoot when the letter reached her. Still, she'd arrived on time.

"Oh, thank goodness you're here." The head of the local suffrage association met her. They hoped they could insert women's right to vote into the proposed statehood constitution.

"It's the prohibitionists that'll kill us," Abigail said. She felt a kinship with those women fighting the opposition to suffrage, making the cause her own no matter what state or territory she might be in. "And the women who support temperance, they'll be our death too if we let them."

Abigail brushed dust from her skirt, grateful once again that hoops had gone out of style. Her added weight wasn't complemented by the new hourglass jackets over skirts, but seeing her reflection in the full-length mirror as she entered the hotel made her decide she looked "formidable." Just what a woman needed these days to take on the politicians. "I'm beginning to think that the hops growers are the ones promoting temperance and prohibition, in the background of course. They know the very idea that women will vote to take away the average man's access to liquor will keep them from voting yes with their pens."

"You never tire," her colleague said. She set Abigail's dusty carpetbag on the floor in front of the desk at the Boise hotel. "I thought you might like the quiet time in your room before tomorrow's speech at the legislature. Otherwise I'd be so pleased to have you stay at my home."

"Very thoughtful," Abigail told the younger woman, though she wondered if her reputation for late-night talks of a woman's plight—and sometimes a bit too much of her own—might have influenced where she stayed. She actually would have liked the give-and-take of civic conversation. It fed her, got her dander up so she was fiery in her presentations. Her sons tired of her constant talk of suffrage, and Ben . . . well, Ben didn't talk much at all anymore, occasionally of simple things: how the dog loved to jump into the stock tank on hot days, or the smell of sagebrush wafted by a gentle breeze. He was aware of what was right in front of him, the present moment, but carried little interest in politics or even how well the boys were doing or how well Earl, Clara Belle's son and their only grandson, had taken to ranching.

At least that was one good thing that had happened from their land purchase—Earl had found an interest. The boy was also the one to write long letters to her when she was in Portland

and had become a stable caretaker to Ben. She found him to be a better letter-writer than talker when she was with him, though.

The invitation came on behalf of women getting the vote. She could promote her cause and add a side dish of comradery she now missed inside her own home.

"I'll see you in the morning. Thank you for welcoming me."

"This is the great Abigail Scott Duniway," the woman told the hotel agent. "We've reserved the best room for her."

Outwardly, Abigail brushed away the compliment, but she took it inside, let it fill her up.

The presentation went so well that Abigail found herself beaming as she boarded the stage to return home, savoring her own words. The July heat brought out her fan, and she wasn't looking forward to the journey, but she could bask in the accolades of how creatively she'd organized her presentation. She had pointed out—the legislators having just heard from a temperance promoter—that they were witness to how women were able to hold different views and weren't all of one mix. The observation served her argument that this was what the framers wanted when they created this American idea, that moving toward freedom and the vote for all would simply bring out stronger discourse, more rational ideas for discussion from all citizens.

They'd applauded politely as they had for the temperance folk. But she'd felt hopeful that they'd include a separate plank in their state constitution. She'd travel back to support it if needed. It was what she did.

"I have become a magnet for opposition, it seems," she told Ben. They rode side by side on the path that followed the stream running through their Lost River property. Ben's mind was clearer after their rides, she'd noticed, though she didn't know why. She could hear the stream. Water, too, had become a point of contention, with their neighbors disagreeing about a diversion dam they'd placed to irrigate their fields being seen as interrupting the water needs of downstream neighbors. *Is there nothing in my life that doesn't carry controversy?*

The dog they'd inherited, Champ was his name, followed along behind. No one had any idea how old the mutt was, but she guessed he was ten or more. He didn't bound about like a puppy. His long hair easily matted if she or Ben or Earl forgot to brush him. As with her, middle age had set in to Champ.

"The magnet is in the barn," Ben said. "What did you need it for?"

"Nothing. Sorry I mentioned it." She wished

she had someone to talk over her frustrations with, someone to bounce her ideas off. Earl chattered of cattle raising. She wrote to Clyde, who responded, but he was busy at class—he had transferred to Harvard. It would be as good as or better than Harvey's legal degree. The other boys, minus Hubert, lived at the Clay house in Portland and did not write often. Ralph was a full-fledged lawyer now, and Wilkie worked as a proofreader for the *Evening Telegram*. Willis stayed in the printing business too as a proofreader for Harvey's dreaded *Oregonian*. Hubert and Cora had gone to New York to make their mark brokering lumber from the West. Children, scattered to the winds like maple leaves. Their lodge-in-the-wilderness ranch had simply not been enough to support them all, with wheat and cattle prices plummeting. Abigail would rather be in Portland herself, but Ben did so much better here, especially in the summer months. And right now, suffrage action was in Idaho. She hoped she'd be invited to give a rousing speech and find someone to talk politics with afterward.

"The magnet's right where I put it," Ben said. "I haven't misplaced it."

She patted his arm. "I know, Ben. It's fine. Let's head back to the house. Earl's coming later."

"Earl? Where did he go?"

"He's working some of his own cattle now, Ben. And he's teamed up with another rancher.

We've had to sell our cows, remember?" Ben didn't. What people were calling "the panic" had hit them too. She'd wanted to sell the ranch when the market was still good, but the property wasn't even in her name! How Ben had managed that and how there was still $4000 owing stung her. The boys must have known but had not invited her into the decision when they'd expanded the boundaries, buying new property just as the economy was toppling.

"I remember now," Ben said. "He's a good cowboy. Did you see the way he lobbed that rope around the calf? Wouldn't be without him for the branding."

We won't be branding here again.

She turned him toward the ranch house. Geraniums bloomed in large pots on either side of the porch steps. The one plant she could keep from dying, it seemed. They were cheery, and their presence lifted her spirits, though not high enough. She sighed.

"What's the matter, Jenny? Are you sad?"

"Weary. Nothing for you to worry over."

"I don't have a worry in the world, Jen." Ben took her hand, kissed the palm. "Everything always turns out all right."

As they watched the sun set, she repeated her hoped-for words of a wonderful outcome. She hadn't gotten everything she wanted—most importantly the woman's vote. But oh, didn't she have an amazing story to leave behind? Daughter, wife, mother, grandmother, teacher, milliner, businesswoman, writer, poet, newspaper owner, public speaker, activist—a new word people were using for those who sought change for worthy causes. And now rancher. And all along, friend. Ben had been right. Things had turned out all right. They had weathered great disappointments and great loss. The world was changing and women were changing with it. She'd be so grateful for that. As she thought of her ever-hopeful and adventurous life, a shiver ran up her spine.

The letter asking her to speak to the Columbian Exposition in Chicago brought a welcome change. Here was a prime opportunity to once again be on the national stage. And they would pay her and cover her expenses. It was to celebrate the quadricentennial of Columbus's discovery of the Americas, and she would use that idea of discovery to frame her entire speech. She wrote on the porch table at the lodge, Ben rocking in the chair beside her.

"Ben, I've come up with a doozy of a speech." The dog thumped his tail on the boards at the sound of her voice. Ben said nothing so she spoke to Champ. "I'm going to invite them to think what exploration would have looked like if Columbus had landed on the West Coast instead of the East. We'd have an entirely different country. We'd all have pioneering spirits pushing us east, creating not only geographic explorations but economic, social, moral, and intellectual discoveries with a different cast. I'll show them that men and women would have been seen as equal, discovering 'with' each other. Don't you think that sounds like a good approach?"

Champ lifted his head, his tongue hanging out, responding to the enthusiasm in her voice.

"The dog gets it." She spoke to Ben's silence.

Her speech was innovative, and she could encourage the idea that there were new opportunities in the West. Women could homestead and become property owners. There were new possibilities in this rugged mountain landscape, just as there'd been for her. The energy of her having thought of such an inventive approach kept her mind spinning with new metaphors and imagery that she thought the largely eastern audience would find compelling. This was the fervor she'd been missing. Even when she'd written *The Coming Century—Journal of Progress and Reform* and gotten it published through '91 and '92, she hadn't felt the zest and zeal of knowing she'd be speaking to a large crowd with an inventive presentation. Spoken words had power too. They could help people look at things in different ways, and that was worthy work, even if how people chose to act because of those words weren't her ways.

She took Ben back to Portland and headed east for the speech. It was a marvel of a time for her, despite her need of the cane and her female parts causing pain.

"Such a wonderful speech, Mrs. Duniway." "Thank you for coming so far and at such a physical cost to you."

Abigail soaked in the praise, even though she knew accolades shouldn't fall on her but for the cause. Still, she wrote to Shirley and her sisters about the excitement of the exposition. *"Maybe Oregon will do something like it for the 100th anniversary of the exploration of Lewis and Clark in 1905."* Of course, Harvey had been selected to chair that event. Maybe by then they'd be successful with the vote and he'd have to recognize the reality of women's suffrage whether he liked it or not. There was a new campaign set for 1900. She would be involved. She'd already designed the banner.

She had lost the Ben she'd known and loved years before. The boys said the same thing, that the Pa they'd adored and tended wasn't the man they said their final goodbyes to in October of '96.

Ben had witnessed the three weddings of '94 when Clyde, Willis, and Wilke all found their life mates and married. And while he likely didn't realize it, Idaho passed women's suffrage in a statewide election with every county except Custer—the one they lived in—voting yes. It was good Ben didn't know about that. Abigail was sure it was over that water argument they'd waged with neighbors.

They'd sold the ranch, not getting nearly enough for it, but back in Portland, she and Ben had found a quiet life. She wrote her novels. More than nineteen, the last one in two parts, completed before Ben's death. She noted that she'd been most productive during the years she had the newspaper, as though having a dozen brands in the flames gave her impetus and order. She wasn't writing articles much, except copies of her speeches. The buyer of the *New Northwest* had gone under less than two years after the purchase. She learned later that it was a friend of Harvey's who had bought it, and she wondered if perhaps he deliberately ran it into the ground. But her sons assured her that without major investors like the *Oregonian* attracted, a newspaper's success depended on a commitment like hers that carried the charge ever forward as she had. The boys had withdrawn their shares of the business and moved on to new lives, first the ranch in Idaho and then later, when it was sold, on to legal work, university presidencies, and becoming the state's printer. It was as it should have been.

But she missed Ben. Missed his calm and wisdom and shared understandings, especially about Mr. Bunter, who continued until his own death the following year, still a bachelor, complaining about strong-minded women.

Most importantly, Ben was now in a place where he truly didn't have a worry in the world. Her worries were pecuniary ones. She badgered the boys into setting up a trust they paid into, giving her a small monthly income. Not enough to hobnob with the women's club members in Portland, though she had founded that club, but someone had paid her dues. She thought it might have been her daughters-in-law. She liked the work they were doing for Portland's beautification, but she yearned for the fight for the vote. For all the confidence she exuded when on the stage or in the fight, it was Ben's assurance she was doing something worthwhile that had sustained her. She had resented him at times during the marriage—the notes he'd signed, leaving her off the ranch title, his need for care when they had so little funds and she needed care herself—but when he told her not to worry and to do what she knew well, she'd carried on. It was what women did.

THIRTY-THREE
Abigail Scott Duniway Day

1905

Shirley came to the Clay Street house to retrieve Abigail. A spring rain served as prelude to a warming sun, both bringing out the smells of pine trees and lifting Abigail's spirits. Kate settled the pins in Abigail's hat, held the mirror for her to assess the look. It was the week of the big 1905 Lewis and Clark Exposition, and the National American Woman Suffrage Association convention had been meeting for several days now in Portland, their activities wrapped into the exhibits. Her brother Harvey, chairing the exposition, had surprised her by inviting the association to meet as part of the events in Portland. She'd been wary but hoped perhaps he had come to his senses and would support the suffrage amendment on the ballot for 1906. Abigail had read an opening speech, "Centennial Ode," her voice a bit shaky as she still struggled with her rheumatism and the aftereffects of having two toes amputated when the infections wouldn't heal.

"I hope I'm up to the day's events," Abigail

said. "I've wanted my eastern colleagues to enjoy Oregon hospitality, but I haven't been up to much of it myself."

"Your minions have taken care of things." Kate tied the hat bow beneath Abigail's chin. A banner reading "Votes for Women" flapped from the porch railing.

"Don't get the strings caught in my double chins." *I've put on so much weight just sitting around.* "I need to leave those morning donuts alone."

"If Maria was still here, she'd have rustled up precious knitted gifts or made sure everyone went out to see Multnomah Falls," Kate said.

Abigail lamented not being able to organize everything as she had in the old days.

"Your youngest sister, Maria, right?" Shirley clarified.

Abigail nodded. "Died in '01. The year after we failed yet another vote. I think it broke her heart. At least she wasn't alive to see the '03 defeat too. That was another tough loss. Miss that girl. Miss dear Ben too."

Abigail held the mirror. Gone were the long curls. Her hair was smoothed beneath her hat, a bun snuggled in at the back of her neck.

Shirley nodded approval. "California still doesn't have suffrage either, so don't be too hard on yourselves."

"That's two of our dear sisters who made the

Oregon Trail journey, gone to be with Momma and Papa." Kate sighed.

"Not sure what good I'll do you or the cause today," Abigail said. "I haven't yet, it seems." They walked out toward the landau Harvey had sent Shirley in to retrieve Abigail. Another surprising generosity of her brother. *After all these years does he feel guilty?*

"I wouldn't be here today without you, Abigail," Shirley said.

"Me? What did I have to do with it?"

"You've been a kaleidoscope of goodness in my life—and that of hundreds of women. Specifically, don't you remember what you said when Clara died? That it was the nearby, not the faraway, that mattered in life, that you wished you'd have moved right next door to her when her husband took her to the wilds of Washougal."

"I did wish I'd done that."

"I did do that when our Mary and Walter bought their land in Idaho."

"I don't think I realized that was why you and Eloi left San Francisco."

"Well, it was. And you were a part of that."

"Not my ranch. Ben's gone and so is that land with a river named Pahsimeroi running through it. *Pa-simmer-eye.* I love the sound of that Shoshone word."

"You've always loved words," Shirley said. "It was what drew me to you on the trail, when you read from the journal you kept. You were a map for me."

"Isn't that strange. I remember dreaming of maps after Momma died. Life doesn't give us one, does it?"

"We do what we see to do and trust there'll be a light to guide our way in the dark times." Abigail hoisted herself into the carriage, and Kate slipped in beside her. Shirley did the same from the other side.

She could hear the *clop-clop* of the horses' hooves on the cobblestones. "Now whatever good I can do, I'll do right here in Oregon," Abigail said. "But I'm afraid some of the NAWSA members would say I've done more harm than good, Harvey and I have. He wrote the most scathing editorial opposed to us before the 1900 and 1903 vote, and I suspect he'll do the same in '06. Look at this noggin." She patted the hat on her head. "Bumps everywhere from this suffrage work. What do you suppose Harvey's up to, being so nice to the association? Such work we have to do."

"But pleasure too, Sister," Kate said.

Shirley laughed, then turned to face her friend, hands over Abigail's gloved ones resting in her lap. "You never really knew your influence, Jenny. It wasn't in the big campaigning or even the novels and newspapers. It was in the everyday living that you did, writing your own map for how to proceed from tragedy and trials, disappointment and defeat. You cared for and about others and learned lessons in your still hunt."

"Some took me awhile. Like holding my tongue."

"Oh, you're still working on that one," Kate said.

"You did all that without even knowing it, I suspect, how you brought hope to our lives." Shirley had tears in her eyes.

Kate said, "A fierce love for justice and liberty for all of us. That's your legacy."

"A passion, I'd say, for anything you put your heart toward. Even when things didn't pan out," Shirley said. "When no gold sank to the bottom, you never begrudged the effort of looking for it and helping others swirl the waters in their seeking." Shirley put her arm through Abigail's.

"If you only knew," Abigail said. She thought of Ben, Clara, her other children too. There were regrets. But Ben would be the first to tell her not to worry over the past. "I didn't know I needed to hear such good words. Thank you, Shirley, Kate."

"I am so excited about this day," Shirley said. "Your children are already at the pavilion, along with Eloi and Fanny and all the nieces and nephews."

"My children? Aren't we just having a little tea to encourage campaigners?"

"We are doing that, too, with you, dear Abigail, as the sweetener," Shirley said.

Abigail guffawed and the horse's ears twitched to the sound. "Sweet has never been a moniker given to me."

"It only takes a pinch to stir up a little joy," Kate said.

The driver chirped at the team and the horses pulled forward a little faster. The breeze cooled her face.

"Today," Kate said, "we're also celebrating the Abigail Scott Duniway Day."

"We are?"

"Your brother Harvey arranged for it. The entire day is about you, Abigail." Shirley blinked back tears.

"Harvey organized it?"

"He'll be there for the photograph taking, with you and Susan B. in the front row."

"I'm . . . speechless."

Both Shirley and Kate laughed. "That's something for the woman who gave more than, what, fifteen hundred speeches? I can hardly wait to hear what you don't say today," Kate said. "The woman who spoke up for liberty. That's you. The woman who stays the course, even when there are boulders in the road."

Epilogue

1912

Abigail

Well, it finally happened. Oregon women finally earned the right to vote. I lived to see it! My brother Harvey did not. He was far away in Maryland when he passed three years ago, unexpectedly, but then is death ever expected? Even with an illness it comes as a shock. He needed emergency surgery, and it ended badly. He left his family well-off, his wife a millionaire, but she earned it having to live with him all those years. Oh, I should let it go now. I've had my life as rich as his, and we found a truce before the end, despite his editorials at each campaign urging defeat. And he had his own defeat when he ran for the Senate.

Oregon went through six suffrage campaigns before the vote arrived. Washington women got their say—again—in 1910. California beat us too, voting it in last fall. I suspect Harvey's opposition had something to do with Oregon's delay, and perhaps my own fractious ways contributed as well. Kate notes that. I can take criticism from her.

I have time now to write my autobiography. I've already begun, and the title will be *Path Breaking: An Autobiographical History of the Equal Suffrage Movement in Oregon.* I'll write of the struggles but also the triumphs. We had them both, but that is what passion is about, is it not? The ups and downs, being in the thick of things and then wasting away at times in the thin of them. Women were appointed to public posts even before they could vote. Oregon had a female public health officer, and Lola Baldwin became the first woman detective in the entire nation. She served right here in Portland. Even a female market inspector happened before we had the vote, and why not? Who better than a woman to know about pork and health and, yes, enforcing the laws that we had no say in making but can recognize justice when it's needed?

I'll write too of my greatest achievement and greatest assets—my children. I love them so, and they are coming here for this big occasion. I wish Sarah Maria and Maggie had lived to see this day and Little Toot. And Ben. And Clara Belle, who sang at those suffrage meetings and gave me permission to continue on even while she breathed her last. Both she and Ben had those glorious voices. Ben thought I didn't notice and perhaps I might not have said so as often as I should have, but I heard them and take comfort in those little things remembered, the things nearby.

There are photographers arriving soon to take my picture with Governor Oswald West while I sign the proclamation affirming Oregon's women have the right to vote. He's coming right here to my Clay Street home, and I'll sign it on the library table where I've written so many of my books and speeches. I've a finely tanned hide from our Idaho ranch (Earl, my grandson, tanned it) to spread across the tabletop. Shirley and her precious Eloi are here too. And other suffrage leaders. Now I hope to live to actually vote in 1914, the first elections when we'll be allowed. But even if I don't, it will be a life well lived—for all my mistakes.

Our past president, Mr. Roosevelt, gave a speech about citizenship while we here in Oregon were fighting our fifth campaign for the vote, and I remember feeling the most defeated after that 1910 disaster. But I read the president's speech, and he said something I cling to still. That the men to be celebrated are those in the arena, fighting the big battles even if they end in defeat. Well, he said "the man in the arena" is the one to be praised for being there, but I'm sure he would see the merit in putting women in that arena too. We too can fail deeply, but we fail by daring greatly. And that is how I hope to be remembered, that I dared greatly and so shall never be known as "those cold and timid souls who neither know victory nor defeat."

Oh, the governor's here. The world is moving and women are moving with it. Isn't that grand! Now where's my best hat? I must look festive for the occasion that celebrates something truly worth doing.

Author's Notes
and Acknowledgments

Abigail Scott Duniway is one of only six women whose names are written in the halls of Oregon's government chambers, but she is perhaps the most known for her forty decades of working for women's suffrage and for the famous rivalry with her younger brother, Harvey Scott, editor of the *Oregonian* newspaper. Until I began research about her, I didn't know that Abigail also owned and edited a newspaper, quite a feat for a woman in any century. Her suffrage work through so many years without success speaks to the continued efforts today in seeking justice and liberty for women. We remember the one hundredth anniversary of the ratification of the Nineteenth Amendment to the Constitution passed in 1919 that granted women the right to vote. Abigail's hard-fought victory epitomizes the need for a vision and the persistence to bring it to fruition. As was said generations ago, "Women's work is never done."

Dozens of scholars and historians, sociologists, and genealogists found Abigail's life and work of utmost importance. I am deeply indebted to them and to descendants whom I was able to confer with. The intricacies of the suffrage fight between

National and American suffrage organizations, the vitriol of temperance and prohibition workers, and Oregon's own path toward the vote are not detailed in this novel. But references will direct those who want more about those battles. The Library of Congress hosts a website of the National American Woman Suffrage Association collection. It includes a timeline *One Hundred Years toward Suffrage: An Overview* compiled by E. Susan Barber.

My interest was in Abigail the woman, wife, mother, sister, friend, novelist, newspaperwoman, overcomer, in addition to her decades as a champion of women's rights.

She was a complex woman. Despite the laws working against women, Abigail became one of those rare beings, a woman who was the editor/owner of the *New Northwest*. Her brother Harvey Scott edited and was later co-owner of the *Oregonian*, a competitive paper with the potential to support or denigrate suffrage. While their feud is legendary and written about, I was interested in other relationships, too, including parents and other siblings including sister Kate, who also worked as an editor for both papers and the Duniways' son-in-law's paper. Abigail's husband, Ben, has been portrayed through letters Abigail wrote in later life to her sons, as being less involved in his wife's advocacy. But he did go to the mines with Harvey, had the terrible accident, cosigned the notes. He held the customs job for fifteen years following his injury, and that provided financial security. They did move from Albany and later to Portland and began the paper about the same time. He invented the washing machine and trained horses, and their six children suggest they were a team until Ben's later years with his deteriorating health condition. Abigail's superior intellect; her unceasing drive on behalf of women; her extraordinary production of twenty-two novels, poems, song lyrics, and essays; her giving over fifteen hundred speeches at a time when women were not encouraged to be public; and her being one of the elite women who owned and operated a newspaper in America who still kept her dignity and national reputation—those were avenues I wanted to explore in this novel.

This novel is based on facts. There were so many facts to sort! Abigail did teach in little Cincinnati, Oregon, and Needy, near the communal society of Aurora; she ran Hope School and the Union School, named so all would know that the Duniways supported the North in the Civil War. They sold Hardscrabble after the disasters, bought and lost Sunny Hillside Farm, moved to Lafayette and later to Albany. Abigail opened her millinery and successfully negotiated with Jacob Mayer to help her advance her business. She took in boarders to help finance her efforts and contribute to the family's support. In 1870, Abigail went to California to give a speech at the women's suffrage meeting there and likely would have met the California president at the time, Sarah Montgomery Wallis of my *One More River to Cross*. She was offered the *Pioneer* editing role and $800 for her tour, and Ben sent the telegram ordering her to come home when, like a good wife of the time, she had asked his permission. I speculated that he had news of his own job at the customhouse to share with her, but he may well have told her no for other reasons. Nevertheless, it was after that that the family moved to Portland and Abigail borrowed $3000—we don't know from where. And she did indeed start a newspaper, the first edition being May 5, 1871. Copies of the *New Northwest* are available online. The entire family was involved in the Duniway Publishing Company for sixteen years. The sale came the year after their only daughter's death.

Clara Belle's elopement and move to what Abigail called "the swamps of Washougal" did happen. Today, it's a very fine community where my granddaughter and her family live.

Schools are named for Abigail, parks and other public entities honor her passion and persistence, despite the fact that Oregon had six campaigns to win women the right to vote—more than any other state. Perhaps it was Abigail's clarity of purpose and her ability to overcome the setbacks during forty years that makes her so remarkable. Her powerful brother opposed all her public efforts, though the occasional support he gave her by buying steamship tickets or sponsoring Abigail Scott Duniway Day is documented and adds to the complexity of their relationship. He did indeed write an editorial of support in late 1883. But before the 1884 vote, he left town and was neutral in that election. The 1883 editorial was the only time he supported women's suffrage, and he wrote scathing opposing editorials ever after. The fact is that Oregon did not pass women's suffrage until after the death of Harvey Scott. Oregon was the seventh state in the nation to approve the woman's vote, eight years before the national amendment. Surrounding states passed suffrage before Oregon. Washington in 1883, repealed in 1887 and renewed in 1888 and also repealed. It was finally passed in 1910. Idaho in 1896. California in 1910. Abigail wasn't able to travel much to support the 1912 effort that did pass. Her health had continued to deteriorate, but she hung banners proclaiming "Votes for Women" and dispatched messages of encouragement to suffrage supporters.

In 2016, an Oregon commission met to choose possible new statues for the National Statuary Hall in Washington, DC. Abigail was chosen as the first woman for such an honor, which has not yet been carried out. She was also the first woman nominated from Oregon for the National Women's Hall of Fame.

Most of the incidents in this story are based on actual events. The status of women—having no say in business dealings but being responsible for a father's or husband's bad debts; lack of control over their own earnings; the inability to offer opinions at public discussion without scandal; the agony of unwanted divorces and custody battles favoring the father regardless of his capacity to care for the children; and more—these were all part of the struggle women faced in pioneering territories of the West that often left women destitute and without influence over much of their lives.

Abigail's father's scandal in the early chapter did occur and strained the siblings. Ben and his injury and his affable character are all documented. The tornado and fires; Ben's fine singing voice and being a househusband, going to the Idaho mines, receiving the customs job from Harvey; Abigail's millinery success; the boarders; Abigail's property speculations; the 1861–62 flood's impact on the Duniways; the deaths; and even some of the strains recorded in letters kept are a part of the true aspects of this story.

Susan B. Anthony did come to Oregon, and the two women toured the Northwest, camped out at the Oregon State Fair along with several of the

Duniways including Ben. Abigail was present at the Centennial celebration in Pennsylvania when Susan B. (whom she sometimes referred to as Aunt Susan) presented the women's proclamation to President Ulysses S. Grant. (The vice president had been scheduled to receive it, but that office was vacant the entire year of 1876. That's another story!) The Nineteenth Amendment to the US Constitution used the same wording proclaiming women nationally now had the right to vote. Oregon was the twenty-fifth state to ratify this amendment in January of 1920, but by then, Oregon women had been voting for six years.

Abigail did live to register to vote in Multnomah County, Oregon. She also served on a jury and wrote her autobiography before dying a few weeks before her eighty-first birthday. An infection in her toe that would not heal ended this extraordinary woman's life, a woman who traveled far and wide on behalf of raising the quality of life for all women and, she believed, for men as well.

But fiction is the realm of emotion in addition to history, and exploring how Abigail felt about her life and effort is what intrigued me.

I did not dwell on the intense debates between the suffrage groups and the temperance and prohibition forces, nor Abigail's arguments with certain religious forces (because she did not support prohibition, believing people needed freedom to make their own choices in all things). I was interested more in the personal relationships and how Abigail's family dealt with her national persona at a time when women were not public beings and risked scorn for using their voices. An 1829 trial of another outspoken woman/writer/newspaper editor, Anne Royall, in Washington, DC, for being a "common scold," might well have been Abigail's fate but for her image as a faithful wife and mother (*The Trials of a Scold, The Incredible True Story of Writer Anne Royall*, by Jeff Biggers [Thomas Dunne Books]). What did Abigail's passion for women's liberty cost her?

Only three characters are "fully imagined": one is Mr. Bunter (though there was a rejected suitor who found ways to complain about strong-minded women through the local press, and that person may have been the sender of the valentine that upset Abigail so); Shirley Ellis and Eloi Vasquez are also imagined characters. Shirley became a composite for the many friends Abigail would have had. As part of an auction in a First Presbyterian Church Bend fundraiser, Jan Tetzlaff bought the right to name a character in one of my books. Shirley Ellis was Jan's dear friend who died too young, and a part of her compassion and care for others I hope lives on in my Shirley. Eloi Vasquez is another character honoring a friend of Rory Johnston who bought the right to name a character by helping an Oregon literacy program called SMART (Start Making a Reader Today). Mr. Johnston chose his deceased friend Eloi Vasquez, a good, kind Californian, whose name and memory fit perfectly as a wise attorney and second husband of Shirley.

It could take an entire book to acknowledge those many souls who assisted me in sharing this story—some do not even know. I was heavily dependent on *Rebel for Rights: Abigail Scott Duniway*, a premier biography of Abigail written by Ruth Barnes Moynihan. The book's pages are thumbed and marked, and I am grateful for her scholarly and engaging work. A second book, equally marked up, is *Yours for Liberty: Selections from Abigail Scott Duniway's Suffrage Newspaper*, edited by Jean M. Ward and Elaine A. Maveety. This research, in addition to online access to copies of the *New Northwest*, proved invaluable. Another significant online source, "She Flies with Her Own Wings" (http://asduniway.org/) is a site of many of Abigail's speeches (including the Columbia Exposition speech) with introductions to each by USC professor Randall A. Lake. Dr. Lake graciously corresponded with me about her public speaking life and directed me to his chapter about her in *Women Public Speakers in the United States, 1800–1925: A Bio-Critical Sourcebook*, edited by Karlyn Kohrs Campbell (Greenwood Press). Librarians at the Knight Library at the University of Oregon and at the Oregon Historical Society offered exceptional help, and I'm grateful. An article by Judge Susan P. Graber, United States Circuit Judge for the Ninth Circuit Court of Appeals, titled "The Long Oregon Trail to Women's Suffrage," proved invaluable. In 2019, I was honored to be a part of a panel celebrating Pioneer Courthouse in Portland, where Judge Graber and professor and historian Tracy J. Prince and I spoke about the passage of the Nineteenth Amendment. The courthouse was the site of the customs office, though it was built after Harvey Scott would have served in that role.

When publisher, writer, and editor Steve Forrester of EO Media invited me to write a chapter for a book he is publishing called *Eminent Oregonians* (forthcoming), he couldn't have known that I had already considered Abigail for my next novel. His interest as I worked on that chapter helped frame questions to answer for this novel, and I'm grateful. He also provided me with a book by Debra Shein, *Abigail Scott Duniway*, Western Writers Series #151, whose survey, analysis, and insights of Abigail's novel writing gave support for characterizing her fictional efforts. I am also grateful to Marianne Keddington-Lang, whose editorial queries for that chapter expanded my understanding of

Abigail's journey. Abigail's own writings were also accessed. She was prolific and active into her eighties. A writer friend once told me that writing was a good profession because one could do it into one's old age, as Abigail showed.

Once again, my research friend CarolAnne Tsai located resources I might never have discovered. I am deeply indebted to her for reading early drafts as well. Robert and Kate Speckham, descendants of Abigail's youngest sister, Sarah Maria Kelty, spent a morning sharing their extensive collection of photographs, ephemera, and documents, including a copy of John Tucker Scott's tear-stained letter sending Sarah Maria to live with her older sister Fanny because of the consternation with his second-marriage circumstances. Bob's contributions to Find a Grave websites introduced me to him, and his willingness to share family documents and stories tenderly kept is deeply appreciated. He also had an extra copy of the 1997 *Oregon Historical Quarterly* special issue about the famed rivalry between Abigail and Harvey, written by Lee Nash, then a professor of history at George Fox University in Oregon. It referenced the one editorial written by Harvey in support of suffrage that he later retracted—to Abigail's great disappointment. Janet Meranda again lent her copyediting expertise to assist me. I am grateful for that and for her information about the DAR chapter named for Abigail.

I'm grateful to two special endorsers, Francine Rivers and Susan Butruille, both writers and students of suffrage history. Susan pointed out important corrections in the manuscript for which I'm very grateful and clarified the importance of referring to these hardworking women as *suffragists* and not the dismissive term *suffragette*. Abigail was definitely a suffragist.

I lifted the phrase "holy cow chips" from a writer colleague Randi Samuelson-Brown, who used the exclamation while we sat around a table in San Antonio talking about stories. I told her if I ever used that cheerful phrase, I'd mention her name with gratitude. I gave it to Abigail to use, and it seems fitting.

The Bend chapter of the American Association of University Women introduced me to *Reflecting Freedom: How Fashion Mirrored the Struggle for Women's Rights* by Eileen Gose and Kathy DeHerrera (self-published) that posed ways Abigail and her millinery work might have both informed and advanced her interest in women's liberty. Other authors' works that assisted me were Oregonian Sheri King, *Oregon's Abigail and Her Lafayette Debut*; *Covered Wagon Women Diaries & Letters from the Western Trails, 1852* (edited and compiled by Kenneth L. Holmes & David C. Duniway) and an edition with an introduction by professor Glenda Riley. Abigail's own *Path Breaking: An*

Autobiographical History of the Equal Suffrage Movement in Pacific Coast States (Shocken Paper Back Series); *Abigail Scott Duniway and Susan B. Anthony in Oregon: Hesitate No Longer* by Jennifer Chambers (History Press); Elinor Richey, author of "Abigail Scott Duniway: Up from Hardscrabble," in *Eminent Women of the West* (Howell-North).

To my Revell team, a humble thank-you. Editors Andrea Doering and Barb Barnes, their cadre of copyeditors extraordinaire, terrific publicist Karen Steele, marketing guru Michele Misiak and her team of cover designers, and the sales staff . . . every one of you. It couldn't be a book without you.

My agent of nearly thirty years, Joyce Hart of Hartline Literary Agency has been a gift beyond description. I am grateful for her prayers, wisdom, and good humor. Thank you is hardly enough.

Friends and family both near and far gave sustenance and encouragement. My brother and sister-in-law; Jerry's children Matt and Melissa Kirkpatrick and Kathleen and Joe Larsen sustained us through Jerry's ongoing treatment so I could concentrate on Abigail. Webmaster Paul Schumacher (I've spelled his name correctly this time!) and my prayer team of Judy Schumacher, Gabby Sprenger, Carol Tedder, Susan Parrish, Loris Webb, Judy Card, and significant others who held us in their prayers and hearts, including Mike and Marea Stone, Sue Kopp, Sandy Maynard, Kay and Don Krall, Dennis and Sherrie Gant, Laurie Vanderbeek, Karen and Tim Zacharias, Ken and Nancy Tedder, Jack and Carol Tedder, Maggie Hanson, Deb and Jim Barnes, Sarah Douglas, and other family and friends who brought special love during the writing of this book while we faced the death of a dear nephew and Jerry's diagnosis and treatments. You know who you are. I thank God for you. Thank you as well to the prayer team at First Presbyterian Bend and the ministerial staff.

Champion of support is my husband of forty-four years, Jerry, who at ninety (when this book is released) and with thirteen compressed vertebrae, and beating three cancers, and now fighting another, nevertheless in this book helped me understand what Ben might have endured physically as well as the challenge of living with what Mr. Bunter would call a "strong-minded woman." He offers what every writer seeks: kindness, no matter the place in the writing process, where failure seems inevitable; encouragement to get up and write again. That is what love looks like. I'm humbled and grateful.

And to readers: Madeleine L'Engle once wrote that when we create, we co-create. We co-create with Spirit and with readers. Thank you all for your co-creation, taking these stories and making them your own. You have made my literary life. Thank you.

Jane at jkbooks.com

Discussion Questions

1. What influence did the journey on the Oregon Trail have on the life work of Abigail "Jenny" Scott Duniway? Have you made a long journey to arrive where you are? What has influenced you as you travel without a map?

2. Early on, Jenny worried about not bringing disrepute onto Ben or her family. Was she successful in her life? What changed her attitude to make her more outspoken? What role did writing play in how she changed?

3. How did the landscapes of the Northwest inspire and challenge Abigail's view of the role of women in public life? Are there landscapes that you turn to for inspiration, respite, or escape?

4. Biographies of Abigail paint a picture of a single-minded woman who traveled far and wide, was a prolific writer, outspoken and often acerbic in her interactions with others as she fought for justice for women and ran her businesses. This author focused on the vulnerable side of Abigail; her need for support from her family, especially from Ben, and her uncertainty at times. Which Abigail rings true, or are both reasonable

explorations of a complicated woman? How are our own complexities mirrored in this activist's story?

5. What part did the loneliness and isolation of Hardscrabble Farm have on Abigail's future endeavors? Have there been times when you've felt alone in a struggle? What helped you through it?

6. Abigail was the descendant of Cumberland Presbyterian ministers from Illinois. Her father was an elder in Oregon. How did Abigail's nurturing in the faith affect her efforts on behalf of women? Why did religious communities oppose women's right to vote? Were Abigail's strategies to address their worries successful?

7. How did fashion affect the women's movement? How did it influence Abigail's activist life?

8. Abigail grieved her daughter's illness by traveling, going somewhere not so close to the pain, giving herself to work. How might her absence have been seen during that time? How does grief affect a life's mission? What, if anything, did Abigail learn from grieving so many deaths in her life?

9. Was Abigail the most successful suffragist in the West even though Oregon did not get the vote until 1912? After the defeat of 1884, how did Abigail keep going? Are there lessons for

us in this century when we face uncertainty and defeat?

10. Has your perspective on suffrage changed as a result of reading this woman's story? If so, how?

11. The author was once denied (in 1968) a public library card unless her husband signed for her to have it. Have you experienced the impact of a woman not having equal rights? How did it make you feel and what did you do about it?

Sign up for Jane's *Story Sparks* newsletter at jkbooks.com and follow her on Facebook and BookBub.

Jane Kirkpatrick is the *New York Times* and CBA bestselling and award-winning author of more than thirty books, including *One More River to Cross, Everything She Didn't Say, All She Left Behind, A Light in the Wilderness, The Memory Weaver, This Road We Traveled,* and *A Sweetness to the Soul,* which won the prestigious Wrangler Award from the Western Heritage Center. Her works have won the WILLA Literary Award, the Carol Award for Historical Fiction, and the 2016 Will Rogers Gold Medallion Award. Jane and her husband, Jerry, divide their time between Bend, Oregon, and Rancho Mirage, California, with their Cavalier King Charles Spaniel, Caesar. Learn more and sign up for her monthly *Story Sparks* newsletter at www.jkbooks.com.

| Books are produced in the United States using U.S.-based materials | Books are printed using a revolutionary new process called THINKtech™ that lowers energy usage by 70% and increases overall quality | Books are durable and flexible because of Smyth-sewing | Paper is sourced using environmentally responsible foresting methods and the paper is acid-free |

Center Point Large Print
600 Brooks Road / PO Box 1
Thorndike, ME 04986-0001 USA

(207) 568-3717

US & Canada:
1 800 929-9108
www.centerpointlargeprint.com